THE
HAPPIEST
PEOPLE
IN THE
WORLD

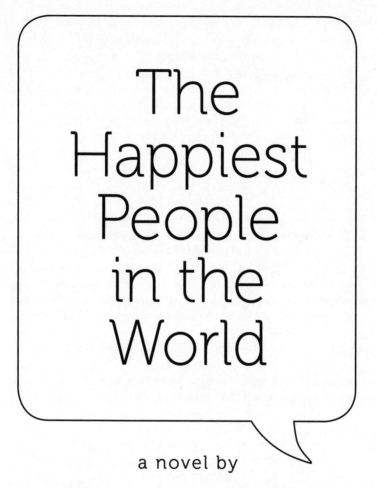

The Happiest People in the World

a novel by

Brock Clarke

ALGONQUIN BOOKS OF CHAPEL HILL   2014

Published by
ALGONQUIN BOOKS OF CHAPEL HILL
Post Office Box 2225
Chapel Hill, North Carolina 27515-2225

a division of
WORKMAN PUBLISHING
225 Varick Street
New York, New York 10014

This is a work of fiction. While, as in all fiction, the literary perceptions and in-sights are based on experience, all names, characters, places, and incidents either are products of the author's imagination or are used fictitiously.

Library of Congress Cataloging-in-Publication Data
Clarke, Brock.
The happiest people in the world : a novel /
by Brock Clarke.—First edition.
pages cm
ISBN 978-1-61620-111-1
1. Cartoonists—Fiction. 2. Refugees—Fiction. 3. Danes—
United States—Fiction. 4. Satire. I. Title.
PS3603.L37H37 2014
813'.6—dc23   2014024021

10 9 8 7 6 5 4 3 2 1
First Edition

For Lane

He is the quintessential Dane, with his fear, his iron resolve to repress what's happening around him. And his indomitable optimism.

—PETER HOEG, *Smilla's Sense of Snow*

The game could continue, and now she could fight with her own weapons. Which she believed were pure.

—TOVE JANSSON, *The True Deceiver*

"I could kill him. . . . But would that be enough?"

—MURIEL SPARK, *The Finishing School*

THE
HAPPIEST
PEOPLE
IN THE
WORLD

PART ONE

. . .

1

. . .

The moose head was fixed to the wall, the microphone in its mouth was broken, but the camera in its left eye was working just fine, and as far as the moose head could see, this was just another Friday night in the Lumber Lodge! Perhaps even more Friday night than most Friday nights. In fact, it was barely evening at all—the camera had just begun recording, as it did every night, at 5 p.m.—but it looked a lot like closing time. The smoke, for instance! New York State law had been insisting for years now that no one was allowed to smoke in this bar or in any other bar, but this law, like most laws—including the United States' laws preventing un-authorized surveillance of its citizens—was often ignored, and wow, was it being ignored tonight. The smoke was so thick the moose head was barely able to see the people it was intended to spy on. Finally, at 5:04 p.m., the smoke had thinned enough for the moose head to tell how very drunk all the people were. They were so very drunk that they were sprawled out on the floor, all of them—the boy who was clearly too young to be in the bar in the first place (another law broken, ignored); the blond woman who spent more time in the bar than anyone; the

man who was wearing a red hat with a white letter C on it; the
man who, along with the blond woman, the moose head had
watched put up streamers all around the Lumber Lodge the
day before; the woman and the man and the other man who
had put the microphone and the camera in the moose head in
the first place; the man with the ruined hand; the man with the
garish shirt; the woman with the black hair who was clutching
another red baseball hat with the white letter C on it; the man
with the new haircut; the dark-skinned man the moose head
had never seen before—all of them lying on the floor, obviously
drunk, obviously completely *plastered,* grabbing at each other,
reaching out for each other, yelling at each other (the moose
head could not hear them but could see the O shapes their
yelling mouths made), wrestling with each other, hugging each
other, crawling away from and toward each other across the
beer-and-booze-stained wooden floor. The stains were dark—
darker than the usual stains—but then again these people were
clearly drunker than the usual drunks, so they must have con-
sumed alcohol darker and stronger than their usual alcohol.
The moose head was not capable of judging these people; the
moose head simply watched them the way the moose head had
watched so many other drunks on so many other Friday nights.
By 5:11 p.m. all but four of them had passed out. Among the
still-conscious was one of the men who had put the microphone in the moose head's mouth and the camera in its left
eye. He pushed himself up on his elbows, looked confusedly
around the room, as though not sure to which person, which
people, he should attempt to crawl, and whether he wanted
to help or hurt them. Finally the man shouted something at

the moose head—which, of course, the moose head could not hear, because the man had not fixed or replaced the broken microphone—and then fell off his elbows and to the floor again. The man wearing the hat was also awake, and with his free hand he had taken the other red hat out of the black-haired woman's hand and was attempting to place it on her head. He finally managed to do that. Then he, too, passed out. Across the room, the boy was on his knees, saying something to the blond woman. The moose head could not see the boy's face now, but the boy's shoulders were shaking, clearly with laughter. By 5:16 the boy had collapsed onto the blond woman's chest. That left the man who had helped the blond woman put up the streamers the day before. The moose head could not think, but had it been able to, the streamers would have explained the extreme early drunkenness: it was a party! But anyway, the man was on his feet now. The moose head could see that on the floor, next to the man's right foot, was a gun, and that there were several other guns scattered among the passed-out bodies. The moose head could not worry, any more than it could think or judge, but had the moose head been able to worry, the guns might have worried it. But maybe not. Because the man kicked the nearest gun as if the gun didn't worry him even a little bit, kicked it away from the passed-out drunks and in the direction of the moose head, then kicked the rest of the guns in the direction of the moose head, as though this were a game, a game called kick the guns in the direction of the moose head. Then, when he was done with the game, he started running around the room, periodically bending over, shaking people, clearly having a good time fuckin' with them (before the moose head's microphone stopped working, the phrase it had most often heard coming out of the drunks in the Lumber Lodge was the phrase "Oh, I'm just fuckin' with you"—"fuckin' with you" apparently being the thing that the less drunk had a good time doing to the more drunk). Finally the man reached the blond woman and the boy. He knelt down next to them, his back facing the moose head. As with the boy, the moose head could not see the man's face, but the moose head could see the man put his arms around the woman and the boy. The moose head watched the man hug them for a long time, watched his shoulders shaking harder even than the boy's shoulders had, obviously laughing, just laughing and laughing as though he were the happiest person in the world, as though he knew that nothing bad would ever happen to him, or to any of them.

PART TWO

· · ·

2

. . .

In September 2005 the Danish newspaper *Jyllands-Posten* published twelve editorial cartoons, many of them depicting the Islamic prophet Muhammad. The newspaper had solicited the cartoons, and published them along with an explanation: "Modern, secular society is rejected by some Muslims. They demand a special position, insisting on special consideration of their own religious feelings. It is incompatible with contemporary democracy and freedom of speech, where one must be ready to put up with insults, mockery, and ridicule. It is certainly not always attractive and nice to look at, and it does not mean that religious feelings should be made fun of at any price, but that is of minor importance in the present context . . . We are on our way to a slippery slope where no-one can tell how the self-censorship will end. That is why *Morgenavisen Jyllands-Posten* has invited members of the Danish editorial cartoonists union to draw Muhammad as they see him."

They did that. One cartoon—depicting Muhammad with a bomb in his turban—was particularly controversial. Once the cartoons became known outside Denmark—it took some time for them to become known—they caused several Middle

Eastern countries to boycott Danish products and goods, and also caused protests and riots in several of those same countries and in Denmark as well. More than one hundred people were killed in these protests and riots. The Danish Embassy in Pakistan was bombed, and Denmark's embassies in Syria, Lebanon, and Iran were set on fire. There have been several attempts and plots to kill the creator of the most controversial of the cartoons, and in 2010 the Danish police arrested five men who were suspected of planning an attack on the offices of *Jyllands-Posten,* the newspaper that first published the cartoons.

That much is pretty well known.

What is only slightly less well known is that soon after the first Danish Embassy was torched, soon after the first death threat, soon after the first attempted murder of the cartoonist, the editor of a newspaper (the *Optimist*) in Skagen, Denmark, asked his staff cartoonist (he had only one; it was a weekly newspaper with a small circulation) to draw a cartoon depicting in some way or other the controversy over the by now infamous cartoons of Muhammad.

"Me?" the cartoonist asked. His name was Jens Baedrup. He'd worked at the paper for nine years. Mostly he drew cartoons of local interest: tourists eating hot dogs while walking too slowly on the pedestrian mall; grizzled fishermen acting surprised at seeing fish they'd just caught on display at the market, as though to say, What are *you* doing here?; Skagenians caught in bad weather and making the best of it. In fact, his most recent cartoon had been of a man and a woman standing under a roof and the man saying, "At least we have a roof over

our heads!" and the woman not saying anything, just looking
miserable, because she was drenched, and so was he, because
the rain was blowing sideways and the roofed structure they
were standing under had no walls.

"Yes. You."

"Why?" the cartoonist asked. Of course, he'd been following the whole thing on television, on the radio, in the newspaper. It made him anxious, angry, annoyed, the way things do
when you don't know whom to blame. But then again, those
cartoons had been published in a Copenhagen newspaper, and
Skagen was as far away from Copenhagen as you could get
and still be in Denmark. In fact, it was common for people in
Skagen, after learning of some outrageous news coming out of
the nation's capital five hours to the south, to shrug it off by
saying, "But that's Copenhagen."

"Because this is important," the editor said. "I think you'll
do a good job. I can't think of anyone I'd rather have do this
than you."

The cartoonist recognized that this was tainted praise, or at
least praise with an ulterior motive, but that did not mean he
was immune to it. He thought for a minute. He would have
asked his wife her opinion, but she had gone to visit her parents
in Aarhus and wasn't due back in Skagen for another week. He
could have called her on the phone, of course. But things had
not been going too well with them. Lately, every little disagree-
ment threatened to turn into a large argument, which then
threatened to turn into a referendum on the marriage itself.
And one of the things they most often argued about was the
cartoonist's unshakable optimism, his belief that everything

was going to be just fine. He knew, if he called and asked her whether he should draw the cartoon, she would question his mental health. I don't know what you're so worried about, he would then say. I think everything is going to be just fine. And then she would mockingly call him "the Skagen Optimist," which, in addition to being the name of the newspaper, was also the name of his weekly cartoon. In fact, the cartoon of the man and his wife getting wet from the sideways rain had been based on something that had happened to them. Twice. The cartoonist thought that by having the wife in the cartoon remain silent (in real life she had not remained silent), his wife would not recognize herself in the cartoon. But this turned out to be yet another example of his overoptimism.

So instead of calling his wife, the cartoonist let his mind argue with itself, the way it does when it's about to let you do something that you'll later regret.

You really shouldn't do this (his mind said).

But I'll do a good job; the editor said so himself.

The editor is a liar.

Yes, but no one is a liar all the time.

But you don't even have a strong opinion about all this.

Who better to draw a cartoon like this than someone who doesn't have a strong opinion?

Tell that to the people who have strong opinions.

This is the *Skagen Optimist;* no one is ever going to see the cartoon anyway.

Then why do it?

Because it's my job.

And with that sentence, a good many arguments that should go on for much longer are brought to a close.

"Fine," the cartoonist said to his editor. "I'll do it."

"Good," the editor said. "I'll need it before you go home tonight."

After receiving his assignment, the cartoonist took a long walk through Skagen, his heart narrating his journey: Skagen, the town between two seas; the town with the pretty yellow houses with the red tile roofs and the neat yards; the town with the wet wind and the cold sand; the town that painters in the nineteenth century made famous for its light; the town where the eastward-moving waves from the North Sea crash into the westward-moving waves from the Baltic Sea, and the spectacle is so great that even the skeptical end up taking too many pictures; the town so orderly and good that even the hulking tankers from Sweden and Norway and England and Germany patiently wait in lines that stretch from one sea to another before easing into the docks at Skagen Havn. The town where my parents were born and where they died. The town where I was married in the big white church with the little white clipper ships dangling from the ceiling in between the chandeliers. The town I have lived in for forty-two years. The town I love.

It is said that the Danes are the happiest people in the world, and if that's true, then the people from Skagen are happier even than that. That was what the cartoonist was feeling. And he was also feeling that some of the cartoons in *Jyllands-Posten* had made him unhappy, and so had the violent reactions to them, and now so had his assignment. That's when he got his idea.

He went back to the newspaper's office, drew a cartoon featuring a group of unhappy Danes (one knew they were Danes because they were frowning inexpertly, as if unhappiness had come to them only recently and they didn't quite know how to show it, and one also knew they were Danes because they were white), and hovering over them, like an ominous cloud, was the cartoonist's rendering of the now infamous cartoon of Muhammad with a bomb in his turban. Once he was finished, Jens handed the cartoon to his editor, saying, "I think this is pretty good."

The editor looked at the cartoon. He had been the newspaper's editor for three years, and he hated the job: the constant deadlines, the ink everywhere, the reporters' bad-tempered arguments about what constituted good grammar, the general sense of everything having been much better yesterday. He could have just quit, but the newspaper's publisher was his father. The paper had been owned and run by his family for almost two centuries. Quitting the paper would be like quitting his family: something that seemed less possible the more he wanted it. The editor just hadn't been able to figure a way out of the whole mess, until now.

"I do think it is pretty good," he said to the cartoonist. Then he published it the next day.

Less than a week later, the *Skagen Optimist* decided, after someone had thrown Molotov cocktails through its windows, to shut down after nearly two hundred years of continuous publication. Meanwhile the cartoonist, accompanied by agents from the Danish Security and Intelligence Service, had gone to his in-laws' house in Aarhus. His wife met him at the door.

She knew by now about the cartoon: it, and the cartoonist, had made the television news. She also knew about the death threats: they'd made the news, too. "Everything is going to be just fine," Jens had told her repeatedly on the phone over the previous week.

"Oh, Jens," she'd replied. "What were you thinking?"

"I was thinking everything was going to be just fine," he'd said.

But she didn't know yet about their house: someone had set fire to it six hours earlier. He told her about it.

"Gone?" she said.

"I'm sorry, Ilsa," he said.

"Gone," she repeated. Her eyes were far away: he could see her seeing their house, their marriage. Gone, gone. Skagen would be gone for her, too. Jens would always want to go back to Skagen, but the agents told him he wouldn't be able to, because of their plan for him. Ilsa would be able to go back there if she wanted. But she wouldn't want to. She was from Aarhus. That was her home. For her, Skagen would always be the small town with the burned-down house and the ruined marriage. And that, to Jens, felt like the worst thing that had ever happened to him.

"Where will you go?" she asked him.

He cocked his head toward the car idling in the street behind him. "They're figuring that out right now," he said. And then he told her the plan. The plan was for the agents to announce that Jens had been killed in the fire. The agents had recommended this. They'd told Jens that whoever had set the fire wouldn't stop trying to kill him until he was dead. So they were, with his permission, going to declare him dead. "It's the best way," Jens told Ilsa, repeating what the agents had told him. He looked to see whether Ilsa understood all of this. She looked back at him with big, solemn eyes.

"What do I have to do?" she asked.

"You have to act like I'm dead," he said.

She nodded. "I can do that," she said.

After that, neither Jens nor Ilsa seemed to know what to say. Jens fought off the urge to tell her again that everything would be just fine, even though he really did believe that was true. He also fought off the urge to tell her he was scared, although that was true, too. Because what do you say when a marriage ends like this? Jens pictured a cartoon in which a man and a woman, the woman standing in front of a burning house and the man in front of an open grave, handed oversize wedding rings back to each other, the woman saying, "Well, *that* was a mistake."

And then Jens turned, walked to the agents' car, got into the backseat, and closed the door. The car drove off. There were two agents in the front seat; Jens was by himself in the back. After a moment he said, "That was horrible. But I do think I got through it fairly well." But the agents didn't respond. Possibly they didn't hear Jens, because he was crying so hard as he spoke, or because they were busy figuring out where they were going to take him next, where he was going to run.

3

...

B ut where?" Tarik asked Søren. It was eight o'clock, the morning after the fires. They had just read about the cartoonist in the newspaper. Not the newspaper whose offices Tarik had burned down, of course; a different newspaper, a daily out of Aalborg. *Murderers*, the Aalborg newspaper had said. *Religious extremists. Terrorists.* "Run," Søren said. Neither of them thought of themselves as terrorists or religious extremists. And strictly speaking, it was Søren, not Tarik, who was the murderer. Because Søren was the one who'd burned down the cartoonist's house. "Should we run?" Søren had said.

"But where?" Tarik wanted to know. They were out in Grenen, reading the paper, sitting next to the dunes that were next to the parking lot. Søren and Tarik were eighteen years old. Their jobs were to answer any questions people might have about the machines that dispensed the parking passes you were to put on your dashboard before you went out to the point to watch the waves. But nobody ever had any questions, not even the really old people who didn't know how anything worked. The machines were pretty much self-explanatory. It was a crummy job, no less crummy for being so easy. Basically the two of them just slouched around the parking lot all day like bored teenagers everywhere. Sometimes, when the parking lot was especially empty, they got on their *cykler* and played *følg leder*. Sometimes they read the newspapers people left behind on benches. That was where they'd seen Jens Baedrup's cartoon: in someone's abandoned copy of the *Skagen Optimist*. Yet another cartoon featuring Muhammad with a bomb in his turban! It was unbelievable, they agreed. They couldn't believe it. They felt insulted by the absolute stupidity of this guy. The terrible, lame newspaper that'd printed the cartoons, too. Did they really think they were saying something new and profound about the other cartoons, etc.? Or were they just hateful people stirring up more trouble? Either way, they were stupid. Please stop drawing and printing these stupid cartoons, Søren and Tarik wanted to say, or would have, if these cartoonists and newspapers weren't too stupid to listen, and if Søren and Tarik weren't too angry. Angry, it was clear exactly what they were going to do, what other people did in other similar situations: they would burn down the newspaper building, the cartoonist's house. But they'd never meant to kill anyone. That was clear to them, even though their anger hadn't made it clear to them that when burning down occupied buildings, killing someone was always a possibility. But the newspaper out of Aalborg had made this obvious enough. Now, they were trying to figure out what to do about it.

"Turkey?" Søren said. He and Tarik had been born in Denmark, but all four of their parents had been born in Turkey. Søren and Tarik knew nothing about the place. They'd have to ask their parents for help. Their parents would have to ask them why in the world they wanted to go to Turkey. Tarik would have to tell his parents he burned down the newspaper building. That was bad enough. But Søren would have to tell his father (his mother had died a few years earlier), Dad, I killed that cartoonist. "I can't do it," he thought and also said.

"We're not going anywhere," Tarik agreed. He crumpled up the newspaper, was about to throw it into the dune, then changed his mind and tossed it into the nearby trash can. Soon the cars began to pull into the parking lot. Tarik stood up to take his helpful position near the parking-ticket dispensing machine. But Søren sat on the ground, eye level with some dune grass.

"I killed that man," Søren said.

"Stand up," Tarik said. Søren did that. "And keep it to yourself." And for four years that was what he managed to do.

PART THREE
. . .

4

...

Two years later, as Jens Baedrup was in one city (it was Berlin) to which he'd already run preparing to run to somewhere else, Jens asked the agent guarding him where she would run if she were him. The agent was standing at the window, looking at the street, her right hand on her holstered gun, her left hand holding the radio to her ear. With her free ear she must have been listening for the sound of Jens's suitcase shutting and latching, and when she didn't hear it, she turned around and said, "*Hurry.*" Long before this, Jens had been handed off by the Danish Security and Intelligence Service to a series of agents who spoke to Jens and each other in an accent that could have meant they were Americans or could have meant that they'd learned to speak English from watching American TV. As for Jens, his English was both unaccented and perfect, as it was, of course, required to be by the Danish educational system.

He shut his suitcase and asked her, "Where are we going now?"

The agent looked back out the window and sighed in a way that seemed intended to let Jens know how peeved she was that he and his little cartoon had put her into a position where she was forced to actually do her incredibly boring and dangerous job. "You know about as much as I do," she said. This, of course, was completely untrue. As with everyone who'd kept him safe, she knew exactly why he had to leave and where he was going next. As with every one of his safe-keepers, she never told him what she knew, including why he had to keep running if everyone thought that he was already dead. ("Credible threat," was all she would say when he asked. "There's a credible threat.") As with every one of his safe-keepers, this made Jens totally dependent on her, and it also made him fall in love with her a little bit, and it also made him want to go somewhere remote where he would never see her again.

"If you were me, and you wanted to go somewhere so remote that no one would ever find you," Jens asked her, "where would you run?"

Without hesitation she said, "Broomeville."

"Where?" he said.

"Exactly," she said.

5
. . .

Matty was in his office, even though it was Friday night. Outside, it was dark, dark; inside, the overhead lights were flickering like there were small animals up there, chewing on something important, or just running back and forth, enjoying their Friday night, having a good time messing around with the long fluorescent tubes.

"I'm not even supposed to be *thinking* about you," he said into his cell phone, "let alone *talking* to you."

"So don't talk," she said. "Just listen."

So Matty did that. She talked for a long time, long enough for him to understand that after he'd ended their affair seven years earlier, she'd been so angry at him and at Broomeville and at the fucking *world* that she'd decided to go to work for the CIA, long enough for him to understand that—in her capacity as a CIA agent and his capacity as an American citizen—she wanted him to do her a favor, long enough for him to get up out of his chair, walk out of his office, out of the building, out into the parking lot. He kept turning in circles while he listened to her talk. Way off to the west was the big dark nothing of the lake; to the east was the big dark nothing of the mountains; a half mile to the north was the town, the little square that was actually more like a trapezoid, the gazebo, the monument, the diner, the bar, the other bar, his house, which—before they died—had been his parents' house, the river that eventually ran into the lake; right in front of him, to the south, was the Broomeville (New York) Junior-Senior High School. But from where was she calling? In what direction was she?

Anyway, when she was done talking, Matty said, "You have got to be kidding me."

"You sound different," she said. "Are you outside now or something?"

"The CIA?" he said.

"I bet you're standing in the parking lot."

"How does someone just end up in the CIA?"

"The old Broomeville Junior-Senior High parking lot."

"The sky is full of stars here," he said.

"The sky is full of stars here, too," she said.

"Are you outside?"

"No, but I'm just guessing."

"What exactly did this guy do anyway?"

"I can't tell you that."

"Why not?"

She didn't say anything right away. The only thing he could hear was breathing, and he wondered, Why is it that when someone breathes in your ear on the phone it's either sexy or sinister, but when someone does it in person it's mostly just annoying? "Because I don't want to," she finally said.

"Fair enough," Matty said, and immediately he wished he hadn't. She had once accused him of saying that—"fair enough"—way too often and in response to things that weren't fair enough at all, and then they'd gotten into a fight about it, his gist being, did she have to be such a bitch, and her gist being, she wouldn't have to be such a bitch if he didn't say "fair enough" all the time.

"There are no jobs," he said.

"Then fire someone. There has to be at least one person there who deserves to be fired."

"There's no one," he said. But too late: he was already thinking of someone. "I'm not giving your buddy a job," he said anyway.

"Any old job will do," she said. "And he's not my buddy."

"No," Matty said.

"Let me just make two points."

"He's an internationally wanted criminal."

"He's not a criminal, Matthew," she said, "unless being clueless is a crime."

"But he is internationally wanted," Matty said. "People are trying to assassinate him. And you want me to give him a job in a school. A school full of children."

"But that's one of my points," she said. "People are trying to assassinate him *here*. People get assassinated *here* all the time. But no one ever gets assassinated in America."

"What about Martin Luther King Junior?" he said. "What about Abraham Lincoln?"

"Well, there are obviously exceptions," she admitted.

"What about the Kennedys?"

"Fair enough," she said, and then they both laughed.

"I have missed you," Matty said.

"That's my other point," she said.

6

· · ·

After Matty got off the phone, he thought about the last time he'd seen her, a Saturday, early morning, seven years earlier. They had been sitting in her car, which was parked outside Doc's Diner, in downtown Broomeville.

"You said you were going to tell Ellen about us," she'd said.

"I did," he'd said.

"And that you were going to leave her," she'd said.

"I can't," he'd said.

"Do you love me?"

"I really do."

"Then why can't you leave her?"

He'd thought of all his reasons why: his guilt, his fear, his son, his teachers, his students, his job, his town, his wife, his life. "I just can't," he'd said.

"You're so *gutless*," she'd said.

"I'm what?"

"Gutless," she'd said. "Without guts."

"Fair enough," he'd said.

"Wow," she'd said. "I really want to hurt you right now." And Matty could tell she meant it, and so he got out of the car, missing her before he'd even shut the door behind him, but still feeling like maybe he'd avoided some trouble that was much bigger than the huge trouble he'd already gotten himself into.

Now it was seven years later, and he was in his office, thinking about the last time he'd seen her. "Am I really going to do this?" he said out loud. Then he went down to the Lumber Lodge.

As usual the bar seemed smoky, even though state law had been insisting for years now that no one was allowed to smoke there. Also as usual, it seemed to Matty, the place was populated by devils, tired, overfamiliar devils whose every action, every word, was totally predictable but who would probably still be able to ruin your life without trying very hard or maybe without even meaning to. He'd gone to high school with almost all of them.

"It's Friday night!" Sheilah Crimmins was screaming into her cell phone. She had been pretty in high school. No, she hadn't. But she'd been prettier. Now her clothes were always too tight, even the clothes that were supposed to be loose clothes, and she always looked red and damp, except for her red hair, which now looked dry and rusty and obviously the casualty of too much product, and she always seemed like she was on the verge of falling down, which was probably why she spent most of her days at school sitting in her chair. She was like a lot of people Matty knew in Broomeville: she would have been an essentially OK person if she weren't so lonely. Matty would have felt even sorrier for her if she weren't so loud.

"It's Friday night!" she screamed into her phone. "And you're in the DR, but I'm in the Lodge. You lose, motherfucker, you lose!" Then she saw Matty and said to him, without moving her mouth away from the receiver, "Bossman!" And then she said to whoever was on the other end of her phone call, "That was Bossman."

Sheilah Crimmins was the person he was looking for. But just for now, he pretended that she wasn't. He made his way to the bar, nodding at people as he went. He was wearing his Cornell baseball hat, and he felt, as he nodded, like a bird pecking at something. Ellen was behind the bar, smiling at him, watching him walk toward her, and when he got there, she stopped smiling and asked, "What's your problem?"

"I feel like a bird pecking at something."

"I was going to guess that," she said. She poured him a Saranac and handed it to him over the bar.

"Is it smoky in here?" he asked. It wasn't really a question. It was smoky in there, and Ellen was one of the people who had made it that way. *I thought you weren't going to smoke anymore,* was what he wanted to say next. Instead he asked, "Where's Kurt?"

"Out with his cronies." Kurt was their fourteen-year-old son. They were certain he was getting himself into some big trouble even though they had no hard evidence that he actually was getting himself into some big trouble. In any case, his grades were fine.

"Is everything OK?" they sometimes asked him.

"My grades are fine," he always replied.

"So, what are you doing here, Big Red?" Ellen asked. Because she knew Matty didn't like to come to the bar, especially on weekend nights, and she knew he didn't like it when she called him Big Red, which she did, not because he had red hair or because he was big, but because that was Cornell's sports teams' nickname—the Cornell Big Red—and Cornell was his alma mater, and Matty did like to wear his Big Red baseball hat, even to the bar, even on a weekend night, when there would be lots of drunk people with whom he'd gone to high school who'd be reminded, by the hat, that he went to Cornell and that they didn't go to Cornell, or anywhere else for that matter—all of this was in her opinion—and by his wearing his Cornell hat, Matty ran the risk of seeming like a superior jerk to these people, or of actually being a superior jerk, also in her opinion. And Ellen also knew he didn't like it when she expressed this opinion, whether directly, or indirectly by calling him Big Red.

Was this normal, he wondered, to be married to a woman who did all these things you didn't like? Did it make it better or worse that she knew you disliked them and did them anyway? Did it make it better or worse that you probably deserved it? Was it possible to still be in love with such a person? Was it possible for that person to still be in love with you? Am I really going to do this? he thought again, still.

"Whoa!" someone in the bar said. That was the lightning. A second later, there was the sound of someone falling and then glass breaking, and that was the thunder. Matty didn't even have to turn around.

"So there's your guidance counselor," Ellen said.

"So there *used* to be my guidance counselor," Matty said. Ellen raised one eyebrow, the way she did, and left it raised as she reached over, took off his hat, tucked it under the bar, and then disappeared into the kitchen to get a broom. Meanwhile, Matty rubbed his matted hair, then turned and walked over to talk to Sheilah. She was still on the ground. Her hair was wet now. Either someone had dumped a drink on her head and then she'd fallen, or she'd dumped a drink on her own head as she fell. In either case, someone had put another full glass of something in her hand. It looked like one of those vicious dark-colored drinks constructed of many different, competing kinds of liquor. Sheilah looked at Matty, or at least in his direction: she was looking either at him or at the stuffed moose head on the wall behind him. Whatever she was looking at, or thought she was looking at, her expression was vague and seemed only to be able to communicate something that would never be reassuring, something like, Hey, it's all good. In fact, this was what Sheilah often told the students who came to her with their problems: "Hey, it's all good." And when they said, "Really?" she usually shrugged and said, "Sure. Why not?"

No one would wonder why Matty had fired her. The only thing they would wonder was why it had taken him so long.

7

. . .

I t turned out Sheilah's brother, Ronald, wasn't in the Dominican Republic at all. He'd just gone to see a movie down in Utica.

"Did you ever go to a movie and then realize halfway through that you've seen it already?" Ronald said.

"You really weren't in the DR?"

"And I didn't even *like* the movie the first time I saw it," Ronald said. "That's the part I don't get."

"Why did I think you were in the DR?" Sheilah said.

"No offense," Ronald said, "but only stupid people say things like 'the DR.'"

"Oh *really,*" Sheilah said. It was Saturday, late morning. They were walking on the towpath, which used to run alongside the Watertown-Barneveld Canal. Now there was no more canal, and the towpath had been repurposed to be a surface on which people who don't really like to exercise could walk and call it exercise. *Repurposed* was an ugly word. So were *towpath* and *canal*. Especially since everything around them was so beautiful. Lovely, steep hills and deep ravines and creeks rushing over mossy boulders, and many different kinds of conifer—some runtish and scrappy, some tall and senatorial. There was even a bald eagle soaring overhead. Sheilah didn't know much about birds, but there was no mistaking its regal white head. A bald eagle! It was incredible that an animal really could come back from the verge of extinction. Life! Rebirth! Majesty! But all Sheilah could think was, *Repurposed, towpath, canal,* the world is so full of such ugly fucking words. God, she was hungover. "And what do the smart people say?" she wanted to know.

"They say, 'the Dominican Republic.'"

"You might be right," she admitted. Ronald was three years older than Sheilah. A couple of years before, he'd gotten his left hand kind of injured at the sawmill and somehow had parlayed that into a lifetime supply of workmen's comp, and all of that—his advanced age, his somewhat gnarled hand, his sinecure—made him seem wise to her in ways he hadn't when they were children. Truth was, she had no idea why she'd started saying "the DR." Possibly she'd heard one of the kids at school call it that.

"I got fired," she said.

"No offense," he said, "but I'm sure you deserved it."

"Meaning?"

"Meaning you sounded hammered."

"When?"

"On your phone message," he said.

"I didn't eat dinner beforehand," she said. "That was my main problem."

Ronald nodded. "I'm guessing your Bossman didn't enjoy

being called Bossman by his screaming-drunk guidance counselor."

"But it's not like that's the first time that's happened."

"Well, yeah," Ronald said.

But it *wasn't* like it was the first time she'd gotten drunk at
the Lumber Lodge and run into the principal, her boss, and
said something inappropriate to him. It had happened many
times; it was almost as though it *had* to happen, as though it
was *meant* to happen. After all, there were only two bars in
Broomeville, and the other bar was where the younger Broomevillians went, and no doubt if she went there, she'd run into
some of her former students, and if they were as drunk as she,
they'd no doubt remind Sheilah that, as their guidance counselor, she'd given them neither guidance nor counsel, and in
drunken response she'd say something inane, something she'd
probably said to them already, something like, "Hey, it's all
good," which was perhaps the most idiotic expression on the
planet, more idiotic even than "the DR," and she'd hate herself for saying it, ever, not to mention many, many times, and
hating herself, she'd get even drunker and maybe do something
even more self-hate-worthy, like end up trying to have sex with
one of these people, one of her former students whom she had
not successfully guided, had not adequately counseled, and either this person would refuse, laughing, or accept, laughing,
and in either case, the next morning she would wake up even
sadder and lonelier and more full of the hungover death wish
than normal. No, it was better to go to the Lumber Lodge
and make a fool of herself in the company of people her own
age, which was forty-seven, which she knew was ancient in bar

years and felt older even than that. And since Principal Klock's wife owned the Lodge, it was inevitable that Sheilah would see him there on occasion and make a fool of herself in his presence and end up insulting him in the bargain. It was fate, pretty much. She'd accepted that, and Principal Klock seemed to have accepted it, too. He'd never even given her a talking-to, never even given her a warning, in the eleven years of her employment, before he fired her, right there in the bar. That was the weird thing. And you know what else was weird? The look on his face after he'd pulled Sheilah to her feet and hauled her over and sat her down at the table under the moose head and delivered the bad news. It looked like he was going to cry; it looked like he hated himself. She recognized the look, because it was so often her own. His mouth said, "You've left me no choice," but his face and eyes said, I can't believe I'm really doing this.

Yes: the more Sheilah thought about it, the stranger it seemed, and the stranger it seemed, the more Sheilah had a sense that she'd been wronged. Fired! On a Friday night! In the bar! Nearly two months into the school year! For reasons that would have seemed obvious to anyone, but that Sheilah knew were not the obvious ones, even though she didn't yet know what the real, less obvious reasons were. She would definitely need help finding out.

Meanwhile, Ronald had stopped to tie his shoe. Sheilah watched him. He did it with only one hand, because of his accident. Before the accident, Ronald had been an ordinary guy who tied his shoes the ordinary way. But now, look at him! Look at him do this incredible thing! Life! Rebirth! Majesty!

The bald eagle was still soaring above them, too, showing them that anything was possible, even a return from near extinction, as long as you had a little help.

Ronald finished tying his shoe and stood up, and Sheilah said, "Ronald, I need help with something." She told him the story. He listened carefully. When she was through, he nodded and said, "You're right. Someone is missing."

"Someone?" she said. "Don't you mean some*thing*?"

Ronald stroked his bad hand with his good. His sister was wrong about most things, but she wasn't wrong about his hand. He really did believe in it. Some people got hurt and acted as though their injury made them better people. He was not one of those people. He got hurt and his injury gave him the power to see through the lies that other people told themselves when they got hurt. "No, I mean someone," he said. "Someone is definitely missing."

"The new guidance counselor?" Sheilah said.

"Obviously," Ronald said. But he needed to see what was not obvious. This was difficult, even with his one hurt hand. Sometimes he wished that both hands were crippled. But then how would he drive? "But there's someone else."

"Who?"

"I don't know," Ronald said. "Maybe the new guidance counselor can tell us."

8

. . .

It was Sunday night at the stone house. They were all there: Matty, Ellen, Kurt, plus Matty's older brother, Lawrence, who was definitely not Larry. Matty and Ellen were in one part of the kitchen, making drinks. Meanwhile, in another part of the kitchen (it was one of those ancient stone houses upstate that had been kept as close as possible to its original colonial condition except for the kitchen, which had been added onto and added onto until it began to resemble a house in miniature, with its own entrance and mudroom and bathroom and TV nook and sitting area and of course the woodstove, which in the fall and winter and spring was always vibrating with heat and the absolute center of everything and in the summer was covered in a shroud like the religious object it basically was), Kurt sat on the couch and watched football on TV, while his uncle Lawrence sat in an adjacent easy chair, reading the newspaper. Lawrence taught eleventh- and twelfth-grade history at the school, but mostly he thought of himself as something of a world traveler, and he found inventive ways to remind people of that fact. For instance, there was a town just to the north of Broomeville called Turin, and Lawrence was the person who *had* to call it Torino. In any case, Lawrence was reading the paper, making those clucking sounds designed only to make the person sitting with you finally ask, What? But Kurt refused to ask it. He was busy feeling melancholy. Watching football on Sunday made him feel this way. It wasn't that he cared so much for the game itself. It was just that on the other side of the game was Monday and school. It made him sad to the point of wanting to hurt someone. Exactly like a football player, come to think of it.

Anyway, his uncle Lawrence was clucking and Kurt was ignoring him.

"Syria!" Lawrence finally blurted out.

"What does that mean?"

"Fifteen people were killed in Syria!" Lawrence said. He sighed, dramatically, through his mouth and nose. Even his pores seemed to be exhaling. "Have I ever told you about my time in Amman, Jordan?" he said. "It was the summer, 1983. Oh, I'll never forget the *kubbeh nayyeh* I had there. Some people in this country call it *kibbeh* but that is incorrect." Lawrence looked at his nephew warningly: Do not be the kind of person in this country who mispronounces this word in this way, his look seemed to want to communicate. Kurt was still watching football and trying not to pay attention. But he thought: He's talked about the food. Now he'll talk about the people, how generous they are, especially the one who took him into his home. "And the people!" Lawrence said. "Such amazingly generous people! Ibrahim, for instance, the bead artisan I befriended in the market who took me into his home!" Lawrence had been taken by so many generous strange men into their homes that Kurt sincerely wondered whether his uncle was gay. He'd asked his father about this once: "Is Uncle Lawrence gay?" His father had thought about it for a long time before admitting, "I don't know *what* he is."

"Amman is so close to Damascus, too!" Lawrence was saying. "I was dying to go. I would have given a body part to go to Damascus. A vital organ, even. But of course, the political situation made that impossible." He sighed again, transparently thinking now about the political situation. Kurt continued to watch TV, although it was halftime, which meant he was even closer to Monday morning. Halftime! Kurt was so full of sadness he could sort of feel it around his eyes, like it was a sinus thing. If his uncle didn't stop talking, Kurt thought he might stick one of their heads into the woodstove. That would at least spare both of them the agony of Lawrence being Kurt's teacher in a couple of years. "Fifteen more people were killed in Syria," Lawrence said again, flapping the newspaper. "It drives me crazy!"

"What does?" Ellen asked. She had her glass of white wine, and she handed Lawrence a glass of raki, several bottles of which Lawrence had brought back from his tour of the Bosporus. To Kurt it smelled like sweet kerosene. It tasted that way, too. Kurt knew this because his uncle sometimes sneaked Kurt sips of it when he thought no one was looking. The stuff was awful, then it was terrible, and then it wasn't so bad, until finally, when you got used to it, you could pretend it was pretty good.

The room was full now, everyone with their drinks: Lawrence and his raki; Ellen and her white wine; Matty and his martini, which was really a vodkatini; Kurt and his Coke, into which Lawrence clandestinely poured a little of his raki.

"What drives you crazy?" Ellen asked Lawrence.

Lawrence didn't answer right away. He sipped his drink and then smacked his lips while regarding the contents of the glass as though actually having deep thoughts about what was in there. Kurt mimicked all this—the lip smacking, the regarding—without realizing it. When he did realize what he was doing, he was horrified. Am I turning into my uncle? he wondered. Was there a worse person in this room to turn into? Was that a rhetorical question?

"The recent massacre in Syria," Lawrence said, and then he described it. The government had killed a group of its citizens who wanted a new government. The citizens had been raped and beheaded. Their bodies had been burned and dumped into a pit. Everyone in Syria was horrified and outraged, including the government, which insisted that it had had nothing to do with the massacre. The citizens had done it to themselves. And seen a certain way—the government's—that was pretty much the case.

"Let them kill each other," Matty said. He was like a lot of off-duty educators: after years of pushing cultural enlightenment on his students, he allowed himself to turn nasty on occasion, especially if the occasion included his consumption of a martini.

"They're not killing each other," Lawrence said. "It's one group killing another."

"Yeah, Dad," Kurt said. "That's what makes it a *massacre*."

But Matty was having none of it. "I say let them kill each other," he said.

This then began a long argument that no one except the two main combatants much listened to. Ellen stood up, walked into the kitchen, and then returned with a full glass of white wine and the glazed, slightly detached look of someone who occupies the same room as arguing people whose arguments basically have nothing to do with her. She sat down on the couch next to Kurt and smiled at him. The smile was real. But also tired. Her eyes were bright, bright blue, as ever. But also tired. And old. Kurt could suddenly picture his mother's death—not the manner of her death, just the fact that she would die, and way too soon. He would not be ready for it, whenever it happened. I love you, he wanted to say. Please don't die. But Kurt hadn't drunk enough raki to say something like that. Instead he looked back at the television screen and thought, Monday, Monday, Monday.

"If they want to kill each other in the name of Allah," Matty was saying, "then I say let them."

"Oh great," Kurt said.

"Actually," Lawrence said, "the Alawite rulers of Syria have quite a vexed relationship with radical Islam."

"Actually, the Alawite rulers of Syria have quite a vexed relationship with radical Islam," Matty mocked. This was the way they argued: Lawrence would try to reason with Matty, and Matty would give Lawrence every reason to abandon his reason and say, Wow, I'd really like to punch you right in the face right now. They would argue like brothers, in other words. Brothers: to Kurt, an only child, being around them could make him feel very lonely, or lucky, depending.

"Matty," Ellen said. Because this was her role: to finally

distract the arguing brothers from their argument. No wonder she looked so tired. "Tell your brother about why you fired Sheilah Crimmins."

And then something weird happened: his father lost his grip on his martini glass and some of the booze spilled onto his lap, and then he said, "Shit," and stood up, thus spilling the remaining booze on his shirt. "Shit, shit," he said, looking mad and guilty, the way you do when you spill something on yourself, except even madder and guiltier than that.

"Napkin," Lawrence said, and he handed one to his brother. Matty took it and started wiping himself with it, still muttering, not looking anyone in the eye, like he'd done something really wrong. Kurt noticed it, and so did his mother. "Matty," she said, "what's your *problem*?"

"Nothing," he said, and only then did he seem to recover. Matty met Ellen's eyes and smiled, and then turned to his brother and said, "I fired Sheilah because she's a terrible guidance counselor and also because she's a drunk," and then all the adults took up the subject, talking about Sheilah's famously alcoholic ways, how they couldn't believe it had taken Matty this long to fire her, and how much better the new guidance counselor would automatically be, asking Matty whether he had any leads on a new guidance counselor, and in fact Matty did have some leads, he hoped to have someone new start next week, but his leads were all on people from out of town, they might have to put up whomever he hired in one of the rooms above the Lumber Lodge until the new guidance counselor found a place of his own, etc. Kurt didn't say anything during any of this. The moment his father had spilled his drink, the room had started to feel spooky, like something or someone had entered it. Kurt looked around. His family was all here. So who else *was* there? His English teacher, Ms. Andrews, in lieu of taking attendance, often just asked, "Is everyone here? Who is here? Who is not here?" Kurt sipped some more raki and Coke and wondered, Is everyone here? Isn't everyone here? Who is here? Who is not here?

9
. . .

Two days later. The plane was in the air. They were well on their way to New York.

"If you want to ask any questions," the agent said, "now would be the time." Jens couldn't believe how loudly she was talking. Apparently everyone, even secret agents, talked on airplanes as though everyone near them were deaf or in any case couldn't possibly be interested in listening to their private conversations. Then Jens noticed how tightly she was gripping her armrests. She was nervous, he realized, although he couldn't figure out whether it was flying that made her so nervous, or the prospect of going to New York, or something else entirely. Jens stood up slightly and acted as though he were just casually looking around the airplane. But of course he was really looking for people who might want to kill him. Three rows in front and to the right, there was a woman in a headscarf, sitting next to a dark-bearded man wearing a skull-cap. The man was reading a book; the woman was tapping the video screen on the back of the seat in front of her in an irritated way. She said something to the man in German. Jens didn't speak German, but he was fairly certain that what she was saying was not, Is that the Danish cartoonist we've been wanting to assassinate back in 24E? but rather, This stupid thing is broken. Why do I always get the broken one? Jens sat down again. He and the agent were sitting in the leftmost two seats of the six-seat middle row. The agent was in the aisle seat. Next to Jens were an older man and woman, Americans, who were having their own loud, oblivious conversation.

"I don't know what this is, Carl," the woman was saying, dangling a white packet over her cup of coffee. "But I do know what it is not."

"Helen, you know exactly what it is," Carl said. "It's sugar."

"But it's not Splenda," Helen said. "That's my point."

"Henrik Larsen?" Jens said to the agent. Because right before entering the airport, the agent had handed him his passport and ticket and said, "This is you." The name on both was Henrik Larsen, and the passport said that he was a citizen of Sweden. "Why Henrik Larsen?"

"Because your English is too good for you to be anything but a Dane or a Swede. And I thought it would be better for you to be a Swede."

"And why am I in America?"

"You met an American woman in Sweden. You fell in love. You married her. The two of you moved to the United States, to New York City. Then you did something stupid. She divorced you. You deserved it." All of this should have sounded mean, and in fact might have been intended to be mean, but the agent's voice instead sounded sweet, definitely sweet. She smiled at Jens in what seemed to him an oddly fond way. It was the way his wife had looked at him back when she thought of him as a lovable goofball, before she began to think of him as an unbearable and then dangerous-to-be-married-to goofball.

"What did I do?" Jens asked. "To make her divorce me?"

"I'm sure it won't be too hard for you to think of something," the agent said.

It wasn't too hard. Jens was already thinking about it. He never stopped thinking about Skagen, the cartoon, his wife, their burning house, their marriage, his fake death. His whole life, it seemed, was a series of mistakes that anyone else in the world but him would have recognized as mistakes in advance and therefore not have made them.

Then again, he told himself, this was probably true of everybody.

But then again, he told himself, not everybody was on the run from people trying to kill him because of that mistake that nobody else would have made. "Where is Broomeville?" Jens asked.

"It's in the sticks," she said loudly.

"The where?"

"The boonies." She said this more loudly yet, giving the word many long o's.

"I see," Jens said. "And are you from there?"

"I have some people on the ground there."

"What are they like?"

"Who?"

"The people in Broomeville."

The agent turned to look at him. Her eyes were black, dancing. She smiled at him, showing teeth. In the eight months she'd been guarding him, Jens had not once seen the agent smile.

"There shouldn't be any Muslims in good old Broomeville," she said, patting him on the knee. "If that's what you're asking."

"I'm not," he said, and in one sense he wasn't. But then again, in another sense, of course he was. He looked at the people sitting next to him, to see whether they'd heard what the agent had said, but they were still talking loudly, paying no attention to him at all.

"I thought that Hamburg had a very nice facility," Carl was saying. "Much better than the facility in Düsseldorf."

"Oh, Düsseldorf was a terrible facility."

"'Terrible' might be overstating it," Carl said. "But it's true that I've seen better."

"Will you write that in your report?" Helen asked.

"Only in so many words."

They clearly hadn't heard Jens and the agent talking. No one else seemed to be paying attention to them, either. Jens stood up slightly again, looked three rows in front of him and to the right. The woman and man had switched seats. The woman's screen was showing a movie, but she was looking incredulously at the man's screen, which was also now showing a movie. Jens sat back down. For the past two years, whenever he saw a Muslim in public, he was convinced they were looking for him, even though he was supposed to be dead. But he didn't feel this way on the airplane: apparently, to be on an airplane was to be in a place where the rules and fears that guided you had been suspended. This was what he hoped it would be like to live in Broomeville, too.

"I think I'm going to like Broomeville," Jens said to the agent.

"Yeah, you would think that," she said. Once again, this should have sounded mocking, mean, but didn't. Jens took a close look at her. She was still smiling at him, but it was as though she was amused not by him but by something way off in the distance; meanwhile her legs lazily wagged in and out in the manner of someone who is sort of sedated. You're on drugs! Jens thought, and decided to ask her something that he'd wanted to ask all the agents who'd guarded him, but hadn't had the nerve.

"What's your name?"

Her smile got wider, although again it seemed like it was directed at something far away. "Locs," she said.

"Locs?" Jens said. "How do you spell that?"

That seemed to do something to Locs. Her eyes focused and turned wary. "Why would you need to spell it?" she asked.

"Well," Jens said, "is it your first or last name?"

"Yes," Locs said. But before either of them could say anything else, the pilot came on the loudspeaker, promising a rough ride the rest of the way. The plane bucked, and the engines made that whining shifting-gear sound that ends up meaning nothing even though you think it must mean something. Locs closed her eyes and gripped her armrests even more tightly. "You'd better fasten your seat belt, Henrik," she said to him. And those were her last words to him until they landed at JFK.

10

• • •

fter they arrived at JFK, Jens and Locs took a taxi to the bus station, where he was to take a bus to Broome-ville. Alone. Locs told him that the usual precautions weren't necessary. She told him that in America, no one would ever look for anyone important on a bus, that in America no one who was anyone would even consider taking a bus, not even an assassin.

"And you're going to be there when I arrive?" he asked her, yelled actually, over the tumult of the New York City bus station. Port Authority, Locs had called it, although Jens didn't see a port visible, nor any authority: twenty feet away from them a man wearing what looked to be several layers of charred burlap sack was urinating into a corner; in the corner opposite, a man in a blue pin-striped suit and shiny brown wing tips was doing the same in, or to, his corner. But Locs wasn't paying attention to either of them. Jens could tell that whatever sedative she'd taken for the plane trip had worn off; she was all business now, again. She was wearing sunglasses, even though they were inside. Her head was like a security camera, panning to one corner of the bus station, then panning back, not seeming to see anything, but possibly not missing anything, either.

"Am I going to be where?" she asked.

"Broomeville," Jens said, and when he said that name, Locs's head stuttered to a stop. She and he had said the name Broomeville several times on the airplane, and it hadn't seemed to affect her then. But now there was an effect. "Broomeville," Jens said again, and Locs took off her sunglasses. Her eyes were as black as black licorice, and wide with horror, but also with wonder. It was the way the corners might look if they had eyes to see the men urinating on them. Then she put her sunglasses back on and resumed her scanning.

"Don't worry," Locs said. "Someone's always watching you in Broomeville."

Suddenly a bus driver called, "All aboard!" Then he took Jens's bags and shoved them under the bus. Jens turned to Locs. She took a step closer to him, put her left hand in his right jacket pocket, then withdrew it. "Have a good trip," she said. Jens nodded. He got on the bus. It idled loudly. He watched Locs through the window, repeating to himself the name and address of the place where he was to be staying in Broomeville, repeating what Locs had told him after the airplane had landed at JFK.

"Remember," she'd said. "You are Henrik Larsen. You have always been Henrik Larsen. Remember: you are no longer a cartoonist. You are a guidance counselor. Remember: do not tell anyone the truth about who you are. Remember: go to the Lumber Lodge and ask for Matthew." And Jens (Henrik) had asked, "But won't Matthew know who I am?" And Locs had said, "Matthew doesn't even know who *he* is."

Then the bus backed out of its parking spot. The driver hit the horn, twice. Henrik glanced quickly at the driver, then looked back to where Locs had been standing, but she was already gone.

Henrik put his hand in his jacket pocket and pulled out a bottle of pills. He didn't know what they were, but he was so terrified, being alone and unguarded for the first time in two years, that it didn't matter what they were. He took two of the pills; five minutes later, he was unconscious.

WHEN HE WOKE UP, it was four hours later. Henrik felt that pleasant, superior, invincible feeling one gets when one has just gotten up. It's the way cats must always feel. He stretched his hands to the ceiling, then looked out the window. He was sitting in the back of the bus, in a seat next to the window on the right side of the vehicle. Outside, he saw a body of water—either a canal or a calm, wide river. There were no boats. It was as though boats had yet to reach this country. On the other side of the water were green fields, green hills. Looking outside made him feel new and hopeful inside. But inside the bus, the seat was sticky. As far as Henrik could see, there were no people outside the bus. Inside the bus, across the aisle, was a man: he was wearing a red sweatshirt with the hood pulled over the back part of his head, tucked just behind his ears, but still Henrik could see his long, curly black hair, a beard that was struggling to really be one. The man was wearing large white headphones through which Henrik could hear random squawks. The man was making squawks, too, with his mouth, while his hands played what Henrik imagined was an imaginary guitar, right hand high up against his chest, left hand out in the airspace of the seat next to him, fingers moving furiously. The seat next to him was empty. Possibly the seat next to him was always empty. Through the man's window, out the other side of the bus, was a wall of black rock, a runtish tree here and there trying and mostly failing to take root, streams of water pouring down the face and onto the sides of the highway. Henrik preferred the view out his window, but before he could turn back to it, the man must have seen Henrik looking at him, because the man turned in his direction and said, yelled actually, "Stevie Ray's birthday!"

"I see," Henrik said but the man must have thought he didn't, because he elaborated: "It's Stevie Ray Vaughan's birthday!" And then he raised his imaginary guitar to his mouth, where he appeared to eat it.

"I see," Henrik said again. Because he did. He knew exactly what musician the man was talking about. He had heard this Stevie's songs played on the radio in Denmark, had seen him on TV. Henrik had read all about him in newspapers and magazines. Henrik knew Standard English from school, but he knew America from everywhere else. This was his first time in America—not because he'd never had the chance, and not because he'd never wanted to go, but because he never thought he'd needed to, because America was always coming to him, the way it always comes to you, whoever you are.

Meanwhile the man had stopped gnawing on his imaginary guitar and was looking at Henrik, eyes wide, possibly in expectation, possibly in fear, possibly both, waiting, wondering, possibly wondering the same thing Henrik was wondering about him, and about himself. Wondering, What kind of man is this? Friend or foe? Wondering, Is this a man I should trust or a man I should run away from? Wondering, Are you scared like me? Why do you wear your hood that way, half on, half off? Are you in hiding? Do you not want to hide anymore? Have you been alone for so long? Are you so lonely? Do you have anyone to talk to? Do you have anyone to sing with?

And that's why Henrik started singing. He sang, of course, one of this Stevie's songs, one of his most popular songs, a duet. "Ebony and Ivory live together in perfect harmony," Henrik began, eyes closed, singing both parts, but softly, embarrassed, because it was his first time singing to a stranger, on a bus, in America. Then he opened his eyes and saw the man looking at him, his eyes darting back and forth like little nervous pale blue bugs between Henrik and the rest of the bus. Henrik stood up slightly and looked over his seat toward the front; there were only a few other passengers on the bus, but their heads were turned in his direction, their faces pinched, wary, and Henrik remembered another thing Locs had told him: Never call attention to yourself. I've made a terrible, terrible mistake, he thought. This wasn't the first time he'd had that thought, but every time felt like it would be the last. But when Henrik looked back at the man across the aisle, his eyes were smiling. His mouth, too. He nodded, Go on, and so Henrik sang another line, and when he did, something incredible happened. The man pushed the hood off the back of his head, and then his headphones, which landed in the hood, so naturally that it made Henrik wonder if that's where he stored them when they weren't over his ears. Then the man scooted over to the seat next to the aisle, closer to where Henrik was sitting. Henrik had read and heard but never really understood that English word—*scooted*—and why it was preferable to, for instance, the word *moved* until he saw the man do it on his bus seat. He did not *move;* he definitely *scooted.* Henrik scooted closer to him, too. Then the man sang the next line. He sang the line after that, and then the next one after that, too, which was Ebony's. He seemed like he wanted to be Ebony, and Henrik let him. Individually, they sang loudly; together, they sang sweetly. When the song ended, they sang it again. Whenever they sang the chorus, the man grinned, reached over the aisle, and with his fist began walloping Henrik on the thigh, hard, not out of menace, but out of joy, joy, joy. Henrik knew he'd have bruises, but he didn't care. He did not care. Everything is going to be just fine, he thought, and he might have gone ahead and said it out loud if he hadn't already been singing. Henrik thought this because he felt safe; he felt like he belonged. Henrik felt like he'd come to the right bus, the right place, the right country. He felt, if his time on the bus was any evidence, like nothing and no one in America would ever hurt him, except possibly by accident or overenthusiasm.

Anyway, they sang the song again, and again, six times at least. They might still be singing it if the bus driver hadn't yelled, in the way of all bus drivers—fingerless gloved hands on the wheel, his eyes finding theirs in the large rearview mirror— "Quit it or you're walking!" In telling them to quit, the bus driver also called them by their last names. Not their real last names, of course, but the last names of the men who'd made the song famous, including the last name of the Stevie whose birthday it was. Henrik knew the bus driver wasn't comparing them favorably to the original singers, of course; Henrik knew the driver was being sarcastic. But that felt fine, too. It doesn't hurt to be insulted if you're not the only one being insulted. It felt safer to be insulted with a friend than to be kept safe by a safe-keeper. This was one of the things Henrik was learning, on his own, unguarded, on the bus, on the way to Broomeville. He looked away from the bus driver and back to his new friend. Except now the friend's smile was gone, his eyes were sad, subdued, his headphones over his ears, his hood half back on his head. And only then did Henrik truly hear one of the last names the bus driver had called them. It wasn't the last name of the Stevie whose birthday it was. Or was it? Had Henrik heard the bus driver correctly? Please tell me I'm wrong, he asked his friend with his eyes. Please tell me everything is going to be just fine. Please tell me we're talking about the same Stevie.

"No, you're talking about Stevie Wonder," the man said, and then he reached across the aisle and gently patted Henrik's left forearm. "But he's also quite a talent."

AFTER ANOTHER HOUR OR SO, the bus exited the highway and entered another highway. The bus began to labor as the road went up and up and up. The air in the bus changed, even though the windows were closed. It felt colder, and cleaner. The man across the aisle retreated even more completely into his sweatshirt. Henrik buttoned his coat and looked out the

window. It was a world of trees. Tall trees with unreal red
and yellow leaves. Taller trees thick with deep green needles.
Even the road was full of wood. Trucks hauling logs roared
past the bus. Henrik couldn't believe how fast they were going,
especially since the logs were restrained by straps that looked
just about thick enough to control a good-size mental patient
and not several thousand pounds of lumber. The straps made
Henrik nervous. Otherwise he felt good, and new inside. The
bus passed a series of billboards. One said WELCOME WOODS-
MENS!!! Another said CLAMZ THURZDAY. The billboards made
Henrik feel even better, like anything was possible, even new
ways of spelling old words.

Then the bus took a left, off the divided highway. It bumped
and rattled over some train tracks. The road narrowed. On the
right was thick brush and piles of discarded railroad ties. On
the left was a succession of three-story wooden houses, each
with chipping gray paint and rusted metal balconies on the
upper levels. The balconies leaned dangerously over the road,
and children leaned dangerously over the balcony railings. The
road narrowed some more, until it looked more like a chute
than a road. It was very dark, but there was definitely light
in front of them. It was like the bus was being born. Henrik
imagined a cartoon in which a tiny bus covered in oil emerged
from between the back wheels of a reclining larger bus. Maybe
he would draw that cartoon once he got settled in Broomeville.
But then again, maybe not. It might seem gross, even offensive,
if you looked at it in a certain way. Henrik could imagine his
wife looking at it in that certain way. Henrik could imagine
the person who'd tried to kill him looking at it in a certain

way, too. How would Broomeville look at it? Would Broomeville see things the way he did, or the way his wife did, or his
would-be assassin?

And then the bus driver honked his horn, twice, and suddenly they were out of the darkness and into Broomeville's
town square. In its center was a fenced-off grassy area with a
white gazebo and a statue. On the far end was a building that
looked like a Swiss chalet. To Henrik's left was a two-story red
brick building. The building was long and seemed, on its first
floor, to house several businesses—a restaurant, a tavern, two
beauty salons, a consignment shop (whatever that was). To
Henrik's right was an even larger three-story gray stone building with five white columns supporting a white balcony on the
third floor and a white balcony on the second, and hanging
from the top balcony were red, white, and blue half circles—
they weren't American flags (there were no stars on the fabric),
and Henrik wondered who or what they represented. Possibly
Broomeville itself. Anyway, at the very top of the pillars was
a piece of white wood with the black words LUMBER LODGE,
and on top of that a triangular peak with the black numbers
1792—the date of the building's construction, or possibly its
address. The building listed a little to the left, and some of the
stone had been patched, or smeared, with mortar.

Go to the Lumber Lodge and ask for Matthew. This was
what Locs had told him to do. "Broomeville!" the bus driver
was calling. But Henrik did not move. Suddenly this seemed
like a terrible idea; a moment earlier the new world had
seemed full of hope, but now it seemed full of mystery and
menace. Why would Locs send him to this strange place with

its strange flag? Why didn't she bring him herself? Who was this Matthew? *Matthew doesn't even know who* he *is*. That's what Locs had said. But what was that supposed to mean? And did that really need saying? Does anyone really know who he is? I do, thought Henrik. I'm Henrik Larsen. OK, but who was *he*? Was he any different from Jens Baedrup? How? Who was going to teach him how Henrik was different from Jens? "Who's getting off at *Broomeville*!" the bus driver yelled before exiting the bus.

The man across the aisle scooted toward him and whispered, "That's you." Henrik didn't know how he knew this. But the man was right. Henrik got out of his seat, walked down the aisle, down the stairs, picked up his bags from where the bus driver had placed them on the sidewalk, and walked toward the Lumber Lodge. He had to. There was absolutely nowhere else for him to go.

11

. . .

He did *what*?" she asked into her cell phone, and then she listened to the whole story again. At the end of it, she had two questions.

"Why did you say it was Stephen Ray Vaughan's birthday?" Locs knew it was Stevie, not Stephen, but she refused to refer to grown men, even dead grown men, by their boyish diminutives.

"Because it really is his birthday," the agent said. "And his name was *Stevie*. He hated to be called Stephen. His *mother* called him Stephen."

Jesus Christ, Locs thought, they'll let anyone be an agent nowadays. But maybe they'd always let anyone be an agent. The agent who'd recruited her, for example.

"And why did you say that about Stephen Wonder?" she asked. The agent didn't say anything back at first. Locs knew he was wondering whether he should correct her again, and if he did, whether she would have him fired or murdered.

"Because the guy looked so sad," the agent finally said.

"But hopeful," Locs said.

"That made it even sadder," the agent said. "I wanted to hug him."

"Or slap him," Locs said. "Either way, he failed the test."

"You knew he was going to."

"I didn't *know,*" Locs said. But she did. The test was for the agent to try to get Henrik to call attention to himself, to do something stupid, which she had specifically told Henrik not to do. And if Henrik failed the test, then Locs would have to go to Broomeville under the lame pretense that she and she alone could make sure he didn't do anything else stupid. In truth, she'd already gotten a rental car and was well on her way to Broomeville. She'd known Henrik would fail. And in knowing that, she'd known that she would fail, too.

"I don't know why you didn't just drive him to Broomeville in the first place," the agent said.

Because I wanted to give myself one last chance not to go back to Broomeville, Locs thought but did not say. "Because Capo wanted it to happen this way," Locs said. "It was his idea." This was untrue. Capo was her superior and the agent who'd first recruited her. As far as Capo knew, she was still in Berlin. And if Capo found out that she wasn't still in Berlin . . . well, Capo was well known for the manner in which he took care of people who weren't where they were supposed to be. But Locs didn't want to think about Capo just now.

"Capo—" the agent started to say, but Locs cut him off.

"You shouldn't be worried about Capo," she said with authority, because she was the agent's superior, the way Capo was hers. "It's me you should be worried about."

Then Locs went quiet and let him think about that for a while. The agent was still on the bus. She could hear its noises in the background—the in-bus movie, the people in the back softly debating whether they could do drugs right in their seats or whether they should repair to the bathroom. Where did the bus go after Broomeville anyway? Canada? Canada was its own country. It had sovereign rights. Nevertheless, she had people in Canada.

"Please don't have me fired," the agent said.

"Or murdered," Locs said, and she hung up. Two hours from now, she would be in Broomeville. It had been seven years since she'd last been there, eight and a half years since she'd first moved there, eight years since she'd first kissed Matthew. Locs back then was not yet Locs. She was still Lorraine. Lorraine Callahan. She'd moved to Broomeville to work for the national wildlife department's northern New York division. Her job: to look through binoculars. She was looking for American bald eagles on land that was owned by the federal government and leased to Broomeville Forestry Resources Management, a company that, had it been given a more accurate name, would have been titled Broomeville Lumber Company. Or better yet, Broomeville Tree Killers, Inc. It had been that kind of joke that had made Locs especially friendless during her first six months in Broomeville. Her job hadn't helped, either. If she saw an American bald eagle in one of the trees leased to Broomeville Forestry Resources Management, then she would report it to her superiors, and BFRM would no longer be allowed to manage resources in that particular part of the forest. So far, she'd spotted six eagles in six different parts of the forest. This was another reason she'd been especially friendless during her first six months in Broomeville.

Anyway, it had been early November. Snow was falling lazily, as though it mostly couldn't be bothered. Lorraine was in the forest, looking through binoculars, even though it was a Saturday, because what else did she have to do? "Locs," someone said from behind her.

"Jesus fucking Christ!" Lorraine said, wheeling around, dropping her binoculars. It was the principal. She'd of course met him. In a town this small, you couldn't help but meet the junior-senior high school principal. She'd even been to a party at his big old gloomy stone house out by the river. This was the kind of party to which anyone who was anyone was invited, and in Broomeville, if you were a new person, then you were someone, even if you were someone whom no one particularly trusted or liked or wanted to stick around for very long. Lorraine liked the principal, maybe because he seemed to like her. His wife, Ellen, she didn't like so much, maybe because Ellen called her husband Matty, which Lorraine hated, or maybe because Matty's wife didn't seem to like Lorraine much, maybe because Lorraine made a big deal out of calling him Matthew.

"Matthew," Matthew had repeated when she'd called him that at the party. He smiled, showing teeth. He was the Broomeville Junior-Senior High School principal, which was lame, and he was ten years older than Lorraine and also married, with a kid, which was lame, too. But Lorraine did like him when he smiled like that. "No one ever calls me Matthew," he said, smiling, and his wife looked at him in that way married people look at each other when they're promising to get into a really big fight later on, when there aren't so many people around.

Lorraine hadn't been invited over to Matthew's house since that once, but she saw him often enough around town, and each time, they talked and acted as though they'd known each other longer and better than they actually did.

Matthew bent over, picked up the binoculars, handed them to her. He was wearing clothes that you wore in the woods during hunting season, even if you weren't hunting—a bright red-and-black lined flannel shirt, a red hooded sweatshirt underneath, somewhat fouled jeans, work boots—but also a red baseball hat emblazoned with a white letter C.

"I was just out for a walk," he said.

"I like your hat," she said.

"I went to Cornell," he said.

"And that's why I like it," she said. "I went there, too."

He smiled at her in that way again, took off his hat, and put it on her head, and when she started to protest, he said, "Don't worry. I have lots of them." Then he looked around and said, "Beautiful, isn't it?" Lorraine looked away from him and back at the forest. It was snowing a little bit harder now. The maples and walnuts were stark and naked and tough-looking even without their leaves; the evergreens and their droopy branches caught and held the snow. It sounded like the wind was blowing somewhere, but it was not blowing there. It is impossible to feel warm and cold at the same time. But where they were standing felt warm and cold at the same time. It really was beautiful. How could Lorraine not have noticed this? You missed a lot when you spent so much time looking through binoculars. She turned back to Matthew, and he was looking at her the way she'd been looking at the trees, the snow.

"What did you call me earlier?" she asked, and he repeated it, a sheepish smile on his face.

"Short for Lorraine Callahan," he admitted. "I sometimes call you that, in my head." He was still smiling at her, but not so sheepishly now. Locs, Locs. It was, heard objectively, an unforgivably stupid nickname. But Locs did not hear it objectively. It was the first time anyone had ever given her a nickname.

"Are we really going to do this?" Locs had said. Matthew didn't say anything. He kissed her, but before he did that, he reached over and softly, softly, traced the marks the binoculars had made around her eyes.

12

. . .

The first thing Henrik noticed in the Lumber Lodge was the moose head on the wall opposite the entrance. Then the neon Saranac beer paraphernalia—neon signs, canoe paddles, T-shirts nailed to the walls—scattered everywhere. And then, finally, the large, beeping video game machine in the back corner. There were three teenage boys facing the machine; the one in the middle seemed to be the one playing the game, and the two on either side of him were spectators, or cheerleaders, or critics, Henrik couldn't tell which. "Get it!" the two kept yelling. "I'm trying!" the one in the middle kept saying, but this didn't seem to have much of an effect on his companions. "Get it!" they screamed. "Get fucking it!" After another half minute of this, the machine made a sound that was somewhere between laughing and dying, which caused the boy in the middle to smack the machine with the palms of both hands. "You didn't get it," the boy on the right said, and the boy in the middle struck the machine again.

"Easy, Kurt," said a woman's voice, coming from Henrik's right. He turned and saw her, behind the bar, where she hadn't been a second before. Behind her, on the wall, was a mural featuring hunters and large wild animals in snowy nature, nei-ther group paying attention to the other, both of them basically just hanging out among the pines and boulders and snowdrifts, everyone minding their own business.

"Soup!" the woman said in the direction of the boys. The first thing Henrik noticed was that she had yellow hair. This was not a problem with translation: the woman's hair was yel-low, not blond, the difference being that yellow is a color found in nature whereas blond is a color found in hair. Her face was ruddy, raw-seeming, but still somehow smooth and shiny. Her cheeks were round and high, and on them were brown freck-les, and above them were blue eyes, ice-blue eyes that looked as though they were melted. In other words, her eyes were wa-tery. Possibly because she'd come from the kitchen and was holding three bowls of steaming something. This might have explained the color and texture of her skin, too. But nonethe-less, to Henrik she looked rough, and beautiful: like a valuable rock cut with indelicate tools.

Henrik was obviously paying lots of attention to the woman, but the woman hadn't seemed to notice him, and the boys hadn't seemed to notice either of them. Instead they seemed to be having an argument about letters. "I-G-N," one of them said. "That me, that's my high score." And another said, "You're not an I nor a G nor an N, botard."

"Boys!" the woman yelled. "Soup. Now!"

This time, the boys paid attention. They scuffed over, heads lowered, and, without a word of thanks or any other word, took their bowls and retreated to a table adjacent to the ma-chine, where they commenced slurping.

That accomplished, the woman finally recognized Henrik's presence. This is not to say that she said anything to him. She merely tucked her hair behind her ears, then began taking dirty glasses from the bar surface and depositing them into a container of steaming water. As she did this, she looked directly at Henrik, not at the glasses or the water. This was something *he'd* learned to do in art school. His teacher made Henrik draw without looking at the drawing. "You can see the soul only when you are not looking," his teacher had taught. The teacher, with his gnarled hands and his whiskers, had seemed like the cartoon of wisdom, and so Henrik always listened to him, although Henrik never did learn whether he was supposed to be seeing the cartoon's soul or his own, or maybe his teacher's. Anyway, two by two, the woman whisked the glasses off the bar top and deposited them somewhere below, her eyes peering through the steam. Those eyes, those eyes. They really did make Henrik feel like she was looking into his soul. Her eyes were so beautiful they could make you forget who you were, or at least who you were supposed to ask for upon entering the Lumber Lodge. But Locs had given Henrik the impression that the Lumber Lodge was going to be his new home. Except it seemed to be only a tavern, not a hotel or pension or anything like that.

"Are there rooms here?" Henrik finally asked, and the woman raised her left eyebrow to say something with it, possibly, Why, yes, you're in one. So he clarified: "Are there rooms to let?"

"To *let*?" she said, with her mouth this time, although also with her eyebrow, which remained raised.

"Yes," Henrik said, trying to sound sure of himself, although he wasn't. He knew *let* was the word he wanted, but he wasn't sure whether it was the word the woman wanted or one she even knew. What other word might be the word he was looking for? *Sale,* possibly, but he did not want to own the room, and when he was done with it (he assumed he would be done with it eventually, and possibly sooner than that), he didn't want to have to sell it to someone else. *Rent* was another possibility, but didn't that word also mean "torn"? Did it *only* mean "torn"? Henrik didn't want to take the chance and end up asking the woman whether she had any torn rooms or whether he might tear one that wasn't already torn. Then she might never let him let a room. And once he thought that sentence, he wondered if *let* was the right word after all. But he decided to stick with it anyway. "*Let.*"

"Let," the woman repeated. "Let you do what?"

"Excuse me?'

"In the room," she said. "You'd want me to *let* you do *what* in the room?"

Henrik turned to look at the boys, but they didn't seem to be paying attention to anything but their soup. He then turned back to the woman, who was still peering at him through the steam. Was this an invitation? And if it was, would Henrik accept it or decline? On the one hand, he was married. On the other hand, he was dead. *You have to act like I'm dead,* he'd told his wife. *I can do that,* she'd said. She hadn't even needed to think about it. "Hey, wait," the woman said, her face brightening a little, "are you. . . " She seemed to want Henrik to finish the sentence for her.

"Henrik Larsen," he said.

"Right," she said. "Do you go by Henrik or just Henry?" The way she said "Henrik" left no doubt that he should go by just Henry.

"Just Henry," Henry said, and then he finally remembered what he was supposed to do, once in Broomeville. "Is Matthew here?"

"Matthew?" she said. She said the name like she'd said "Henrik."

"*Matthew*," said one of the boys, in the same voice.

"That's my son, Kurt, and those are his cronies," the woman said, gesturing behind Henry. Henry didn't know that word—*cronies*—but he guessed it referred to the two boys who had forsaken their spoons and were now drinking directly from their bowls. That meant Kurt was the thin, curly-headed boy with the spacey blue eyes who'd been striking the machine earlier. Now he seemed to be paying attention to Henry. He nodded at Henry, and Henry smiled in return, and the boy scowled back. Henry turned back to the woman.

"Matthew," she said again. There was an expression on her face that suggested she really wanted to punch someone. Henry took a step back from the bar. "Do you mean Matty?"

"Do I?"

"Matthew," she said. "No one calls him Matthew."

"No one?" Henry said. Because he'd been given very strict instructions. *Go to the Lumber Lodge. Ask for Matthew.* Meanwhile the woman still had that look on her face.

"Almost no one," she said.

13

...

Matthew, Matthew. Kurt's mother must have said "Matthew" about a thousand times, like it was more than just a name. It wasn't. It was just a name: his father's name. Although it was true that almost no one called him that, except for his mother, and only when she was mad at him. And even then, when she called him Matthew, it was like she was impersonating someone else who called him by that name. Like when he called Kevin and Tyler his cronies, which was not his but rather his mother's name for them.

"Cronies," he said to them, loud enough to be heard over their slurping but not loud enough for his mother or this weird guy to hear over all her "Matthews." Kurt gestured with his head in the direction of the door, and then wondered, Why do people do that? Because he was just going to get up and walk out the door anyway. And then his cronies would know what he wanted them to do, although that was perhaps overestimating their powers of cognition. Kevin and Tyler stared at him blankly for one beat, then another. They were fraternal twins, and also wrestlers, and wore that perpetually dopey look of people who are always trying either to starve or to stuff themselves. Also, they were often high. Anyway, they looked at Kurt, then at each other, then shrugged before returning their attention to their soup, which they were now drinking directly from the bowl. Jesus, maybe his mother was right to call them cronies.

In any case, he got up and walked out of the bar, daring his mother to notice. She didn't. *Matthew,* she'd been saying to the guy. *No one calls him Matthew.* Once outside, Kurt leaned against the building, waiting for Kevin and Tyler so they could go do whatever. A few minutes later, the stranger walked out of the bar. He looked one way, and then the other, before crossing the street and entering Doc's. In his fifteen years on earth, Kurt didn't think he'd seen anyone over the age of four actually look both ways before crossing the street. In fact, by the time he'd finished this thought, Kurt himself had already crossed the street, not having looked.

The stranger was standing just inside in the diner's doorway. Kurt watched the stranger from outside, watching him wait for Crystal, the waitress, to notice him standing there. There were no customers; it was the kind of place that almost never had any customers, and still, somehow, it stayed open. Crystal was standing behind the counter, reading the *Broomeville Bulletin,* but otherwise not doing anything, including noticing the stranger standing there. But still, the stranger didn't do anything. He just stood there. Like an idiot. Finally, Kurt couldn't stand it anymore. He crouched down so that no one in Doc's could see him through the window and bellowed, loud enough for the people inside to hear him, "Hey!" Kurt then waited a second before standing up. When he did, he saw that Crystal had come out from behind the counter and was standing next to the cooler labeled Les Desserts. She blew a stray piece of brown hair off her brown eyes, but then it just fell back to where it'd been. She didn't look happy. But then again, she never looked especially happy. Was it possible that no one Kurt had ever known had ever looked especially happy? *Matthew, Matthew,* he heard his mother say. As for the stranger, his back was to Kurt. His back gave away nothing: it looked neutral.

"Counter?" Crystal said to the stranger.

"Yes?" he said. It really did sound more like a question than an answer, as though he really weren't sure after all that he wanted to sit at the counter. In any case, the guy didn't move. He just stood there. Crystal had turned and walked back behind the counter. Still, the stranger just stood there! Kurt started to itch all over. Is there anything more embarrassing than someone who doesn't seem to know that he should be embarrassed? Please move! Kurt thought, and just then Crystal, seeing the stranger still standing there, took a menu off the stack, bowed, presented the menu with a little flourish before letting it drop *smack* on the counter, as though to say, Here's your frigging invitation. Only then did the stranger walk to the counter and sit on one of the stools. Kurt could see his face now. He didn't look embarrassed at all, although he did offer Crystal a baffled little smile.

"Coffee?" she said.

"Yes, please," the stranger said, although Crystal was already pouring it into a white mug.

"Black?" she said. And again the stranger sat there, not saying anything, with that confused, genial smile on his face.

Kurt was beginning to wonder whether he was retarded or something. Possibly Crystal wondered the same thing, because she didn't even bother to ask, Or do you want cream? She just reached into the pocket of her apron and withdrew two plastic containers of half-and-half, which she tossed onto the counter, dice-like. "Thank you very much," the stranger said, although he didn't bother with the half-and-half. His English was formal, definitely foreign sounding. Kurt wondered where he was from. The stranger took a sip of his coffee and said, "It is excellent."

"I'm so glad," Crystal said, not sounding especially glad. She was standing directly across the counter from him, holding a pad in her left hand and a pencil in her right. The stranger smiled at her again, still; he took another sip of his coffee.

"Just the coffee?" she finally said.

"Oh!" the stranger said, apparently getting it. Or maybe he was pretending not to have gotten it before. Kurt was starting to think of this guy not as possibly retarded but as a wild card. Maybe you could be both? Even though in his experience, adults were never wild cards. They were always totally predictable, even, especially, when they thought they were being mysterious.

The stranger opened the menu. Kurt watched his eyes travel down it. "Two eggs," he said, "with a side of hash?" He said these last words slowly, and definitely with a question mark at the end, as though he wasn't sure of their pronunciation or meaning. Or maybe he just wasn't sure he really wanted the hash. *That,* Kurt understood. Who knew what that stuff really was? Kurt could see Doc in the kitchen, baseball hat and gut straining, yellow-armpitted white T-shirt and no apron and no rubber gloves, dumping the hash out of the can and onto the griddle. The can looked rusty, too, although it *was* hard to distinguish between the color of rust and the color of hash.

"How do you want your eggs?" Crystal asked.

"How do I want them?" he repeated. On a plate, Kurt thought. Next to the hash, Kurt thought. "How *do* I want them?" the stranger asked.

"Scrambled," Crystal said. "Poached. Sunny-side up . . ."

"Sunny-side up," the stranger said. Crystal nodded, snatched the menu, stored it somewhere underneath the counter, and walked away from the stranger and toward the kitchen. When she did, Kurt watched the stranger look around the place: First, to his left, was the cooler labeled LES DESSERTS. Then the stranger turned to his right and regarded, at the far end of the counter, four analog clocks over the door to the men's bathroom. The clock labeled BERLIN said it was 10:10; the clock labeled CAIRO, 5:47; BROOMEVILLE, 4:59; MOSCOW, 1:22. There was no clock for London, just the word LONDON and an empty space where the clock should have been. Time was correct and moving only on the clock labeled BROOME-VILLE. The stranger looked at these clocks for a long time, as though he had never seen one before, just like he'd looked at the counter like he'd never seen one before, and the cooler, and the menu, and the Crystal. Kurt was starting to change his mind again: Maybe this guy was just retarded. Because there was nothing odd about any of these things. They were normal. They had been there for as long as Kurt could remember.

After staring at the clocks for a while longer, the stranger shook his head, then took a pad and pencil out of his jacket pocket and began scribbling. Soon, Crystal brought out his eggs and hash. The stranger looked at the food, shook his head again, and then started shoveling the eggs and hash into his mouth. This was about right, as far as Kurt was concerned: the food in Doc's looked disgusting, but Kurt knew from experience that it tasted delicious. When the stranger was finished eating, he pushed the plate aside and then resumed his scribbling. Kurt could hear the scratch of the pencil on the page. He could hear Crystal laughing with Doc in the kitchen. The lights dimmed in the restaurant. Or maybe it was just the sun going down. The stranger didn't seem to notice; he scribbled on, hunched over his pad, all by himself, looking lonely. It was the kind of loneliness so powerful that it was contagious.

I'm so lonely, Kurt thought, and then, to counter that thought, he thought, Fuck that shit. And then he thought, Counter. The stranger didn't seem to know what Crystal had meant when she'd said, "Counter?" Kurt had been taking Spanish for three years in school; he tried to think of the Spanish word for "counter." There had to be one. It was such a simple, common word. He must know it. What was the Spanish word for "counter"? And then he thought, Why *is* the cooler full of soda labeled LES DESSERTS? And what's with the clocks? Why do none of them work except for Broomeville? Why those four cities and not four others? What happened to the London clock? And for that matter, why was Doc called Doc? Because he definitely did not look like someone who had ever been a member of the medical profession. Why, why, why? Kurt thought. It wasn't the first time he'd asked why, of course, but it might have been the first time he'd asked why for a purpose other than being an absolute pain in the ass. For the first time, he really did want to know. Why, for instance, did the stranger order his eggs sunny-side up and not scrambled or poached?

Suddenly the stranger was standing in front of him. That smile still on his face, the pad of paper sticking out of his jacket pocket. The stranger didn't seem to be surprised to see Kurt there. It was impossible to tell whether he recognized Kurt from the bar, or knew he'd been standing there the entire time, or cared. Except for that goofy, hopeful smile, there wasn't anything on his face, not even a chunk of hash, a smear of egg.

"Why did you order your eggs sunny-side up and not scrambled or poached?" Kurt asked.

The stranger didn't hesitate. "Because it seemed the most optimistic and least violent of the three choices," he said. He then stuck out his hand and Kurt took it. "My name is Henry Larsen," he said. "I'm going to be your new guidance counselor."

"My name is Kurt. And I'm definitely going to be needing your guidance counseling."

Henry's face suddenly grew serious. But still goofy and hopeful. He patted Kurt on the shoulder and said, "Don't worry. I think everything is going to be just fine."

"I really hope you're right," Kurt said. But just in case, he sneaked the pad of paper out of Henry's coat before Henry crossed the street and went back into the Lumber Lodge.

14

...

Ellen was in the bar talking to Matty on the phone. In the background, she could hear the sounds of baseball. Not the game itself, which hadn't started yet, but the warm-ups. The lazy thud of a ball hitting a mitt. The ping of a metal bat hitting a ball. Someone apologizing for mishitting, or misthrowing, or miscatching. Someone complaining about how cold it was. Because it was *cold*. It was supposed to snow, too. Matty had told Ellen why this faculty-student baseball game had been played in October, right in the middle of football season. He had told her many times. But the specifics always eluded her. It had something to do with Cornell. A campus tradition. A morale booster. An official good-bye to summer. If it's good enough for Cornell, it's good enough for Broomeville. Something like that. She pictured rich white boys wearing red shorts and white sweaters with the big red letter C on the chest and drinking beer out of pewter steins in one hand while catching the ole horsehide with weathered old-timey leather gloves with the other and calling each other by their nicknames, which were all Tripp. Ellen sensed this mental picture was unfair and ridiculous. Which was not to say it was inaccurate.

"Your new guidance counselor is here."

"What's he like?"

"He asked for you."

Matty must have heard something in her voice. He didn't say anything at first. Ellen could tell he was trying to figure out where the trouble was and how he might steer away from it. That was marriage, pretty much. "Heads up!" someone yelled in the background. Ellen could hear the ball hitting someone or something. Then someone else yelled, "Hey, that fucking hurt!" And then the first person said: "I think you're over-reacting a little. But anyway, I'm sorry." That was pretty much marriage, too.

"He asked for you," Ellen repeated.

"Did he ask in Swedish?"

"He said, 'Is Matthew here?'"

"Because he's from Sweden."

This was news to Ellen: all Matty had told her was that the new guidance counselor would be showing up this afternoon, and to please have one of the rooms ready for him. "Sweden?" she said.

"Originally," Matty said. "I bet you're wondering how a Swedish guy ends up a guidance counselor in Broomeville." This was not what Ellen wanted to talk about. But yes, now that Matty mentioned it, she was wondering that. God, he made her hate him for sometimes making her forget why she still sometimes hated him.

"Yes," she said. "How?"

"Well, it's complicated."

"He called you Matthew."

"That is my name."

"Almost no one calls you Matthew."

"My mother sometimes called me Matthew."

"You didn't cheat on me with your mother."

Matty paused again. He might make a joke about how all men cheat on their wives with their mothers and how he learned that in his first-year seminar on Greek mythology or Freud or something at Cornell. And if he did that, Ellen would finally leave him. Or he might ask her whether she was by herself. And then she might also leave him. But maybe not. Because this was what it meant to be a junior-senior high school principal in a place like Broomeville. You had to be sure no one was listening to you and your wife talk about things that everyone already half knew about already.

"Are you by yourself?"

Ellen turned and looked at Kurt's cronies. They were oblivious to everything but their bowls of soup. They were already on their third. "Yes," she said. "I'm by myself."

"Where's the Swedish guidance counselor?"

"He was hungry," Ellen said. "I sent him across the street to get something to eat at Doc's."

"Couldn't he have eaten something in the bar?"

"No, we don't officially open until five," Ellen said, as though Matty didn't know that. And as though Matty also didn't know that Ellen often opened the bar earlier than its official opening time. To feed soup to their son and his cronies, for instance. Henry could have eaten some of that soup. There was no need to send him across the street to Doc's. But it was weird: She knew she was going to have this conversation with Matty. And she did not want Henry around to hear it. She did not want Henry to hear her being the shrewish, paranoid, needy, get-over-it-already wife talking to the husband who had cheated on her many years ago with that strange woman who was always walking around with binoculars in her hands and a scowl on her face. You swore you'd never see her again. I haven't seen her again; I don't even know where she is. You promise? I promise. Then why do I have a bad feeling that you're seeing her again? This was some of what Henry would have heard, had he stayed in the bar. And why shouldn't Henry hear it? Who was he to her? He was nothing to her; he was only Matty's new guidance counselor. Nevertheless, Ellen did not want Henry to hear her saying any of this. She did not even want to hear herself saying any of this.

"Is there anything you need to tell me?" she asked.

"Yes," Matty said. "I need to tell you to please bring the new guidance counselor with you when you come to the baseball game."

15

. . .

M r. . . . ," the voice started to say. Then it caught itself
and said, "Capo?" The connection was scratchy, the
voice teary. Capo remembered this about him. Even
as a student, he had always wanted to do the right thing, had
always been ready to cry at the first thought that maybe he
hadn't done the right thing.

"London?" Capo said. "Why aren't you in London? Where
are you?"

"Canada," the voice said. Between sobs he told Capo the
story, and when he was done, Capo asked him go through the
whole thing again. "But this time without the pitiful sniffling."

"I'm *trying,*" London said. He sucked in a wet breath and
then told the story again. Capo listened. How could I have
known something like this was going to happen? he thought.
And also: I should have known something like this was going
to happen. When the story was over, London said, "She called
me in London and said to fly to Kennedy, then meet her at Port
Authority. I had to do it," he said. "She's my superior."

"And I, hers."

"She said it was your idea in the first place," London said.

When Capo didn't respond to this, London asked, "What should I do now?"

"You should come home," Capo said. He hung up, then dialed again. He heard the voice say, "Doc's," in a tone that made it clear that she was really saying, What the hell do you want?

"Manners," Capo said.

"What the hell do you want?"

"Put London back on the wall," he told her.

"That all?" she said.

"No," he said. "Take Berlin down after you put London up." Then he told her why. When Capo was done with his story, Crystal laughed. That abrupt, barking smoker's laugh. Except she had never smoked. This was why she was such a good agent. She was so clearly one kind of person that it would never occur to anyone that she was actually another kind of person entirely. "You knew something like this was going to happen," Crystal said, and then she hung up.

16
· · ·

They took turns trying to say the word.

"Cock-en-BOARD-en-gord," Kevin said.

"Crack-er-GOS-borg-en," Tyler said.

"Come on," Kurt said. "Stop adding syllables." He was taking the pronunciation of the word seriously. Then again, it's possible that his cronies were taking it seriously, too. "It's KOOK-en-boord," he said, saying the word very deliberately and giving it too many long *o*'s but coming somewhat close regardless.

The word they were trying to pronounce was *køkkenbord*. It was written on the pad of paper Kurt had taken from Henry's pocket. Next to that word was an equal sign, and on the other side of the equal sign was the word *counter*.

"But what's it mean?" Tyler said.

"Idiot," Kevin said. "It doesn't mean anything. It's probably just a made-up word."

"Counter," Kurt said, still studying the word. They were standing in the parking lot between the Lodge and the Stewart's. There were many signs emphatically warning would-be parkers that the lot was not for patrons of either the Lumber Lodge or Stewart's convenience store and gas station, and that violators *would* be towed. But the signs didn't also say who *was* allowed to park there. In any case, the boys were standing right in the entrance to the lot, huddled around the pad, which Kurt was holding. "It means 'counter,'" he said. He then flipped the page. On the next page there were no words, just a pencil drawing of a man hunched over the counter, pencil in his right hand and poised above a pad of paper. An empty plate and coffee cup were off to the left side. Farther off to the left was the LES DESSERTS cooler; farther to the right were those clocks. And in the foreground was the front door, open, and to the left of that the window, and in the window was the very top of someone's head: hair, eyebrows, eyes peering over the sill. No nose. The eyes were enormous. They occupied almost the entirety of the face.

"Who's that supposed to be?" Kevin asked.

"Me," Kurt said.

"It doesn't look like you," Tyler said.

"No," Kurt said. Because it didn't. His real eyes were actually on the smallish side. But that was definitely Kurt in the drawing. It was incredible. The old guidance counselor had known Kurt for years and had never given him any useful advice, except for telling him that he was going to be late for his next class. And even *that* she usually got wrong. But somehow this new guidance counselor, in just a few minutes of being in Kurt's general vicinity, had managed to see into Kurt's soul, or essence, or whatever. Kurt felt something running up and down his spine. "But it's definitely me."

"Excuse me!" This was from a woman. She was trying to

pull into the parking lot. Her head was out the car window. She had black hair peeking out underneath a baseball hat like the one his father often wore—a red hat bearing a white C—and her mirrored sunglasses were the large kind that seemed designed to swallow the whole face. They dominated the woman's face like Kurt's eyes in the drawing had dominated his. "Excuse me!" she yelled again. And then, before they could excuse her, or not, they hadn't yet made up their minds, she hit the horn! She hit the fucking horn! The unbelievable arrogance of people and their fucking car horns! Which always caused the opposite of the intended reaction.

"I'm sorry, but you can't park here," Kurt said. He said this really, really slowly, as slowly as he possibly could. He often did this with his parents: he would talk slowly so that it would seem to them that he must be on drugs and so that they'd eventually ask, all worried, "Are you on drugs?" and he'd get to say, in his normal voice, "No, I can't believe you'd ask me that!" because even when he was on drugs, the drugs didn't make him talk that way. "I'm sorry, but you can't park here," he said, slowly, slowly.

"What?" the woman said. "What did you say?" And then she beeped again! Unbelievable, this woman and her horn. No wonder she couldn't hear. The horn had probably deafened her, the way she leaned on it all the time.

The three of them moved to the driver's window, Kevin and Tyler flanking Kurt. Kurt leaned over slightly, just barely entering the car's space. It smelled to him like Delray Beach, Florida, and also Telluride, Colorado, but really it only smelled like the rental cars his parents had rented to get them from the airport to those places. "I said," he said, "you can't park here."

"Oh," she said. "I thought you said something before that, too."

"Well, I didn't."

"No, hey, you did," Kevin whispered. "You said, 'I'm sorry.'"

"I didn't."

"You did," Tyler said. "You said, 'I'm sorry, but . . .' And then the rest of it."

Kurt all of a sudden felt tired, especially in the eyes. He wished he had this woman's huge sunglasses to rest behind. "I said, 'I'm sorry,'" he said to her.

"Apology accepted," the woman said, already backing out into the street. Fast, too. With Kurt's head pretty much still inside the car window! What a bitch! "Bitch!" they yelled, as the car drove west. Once the car was out of sight, they continued to talk about what a bitch the woman was. Who the hell did she think she was? And who the hell *was* she? She was a total bitch, whoever she was! Etc. And only when they were done with that did they notice that Kurt was no longer holding the stranger's pad of paper. It wasn't on the ground anywhere, and neither of the cronies could find it on their persons. It was gone. Their memory of the strange word that meant "counter" was gone, too. All that any of them could remember was that they'd probably all mispronounced it. This was the worst: they'd failed to remember anything about something except that they'd failed at it. This was a lot like school, of course, not to mention everything else.

17
· · ·

Henry entered the Lumber Lodge just as the cronies were exiting. He smiled and held the door open for them, but they did not thank him or even seem to be aware of his existence. He closed the door behind him, then entered the bar. It was empty. But Henry didn't feel like he was alone. He could hear footsteps overhead. Someone took four steps, then stopped, then took four steps back. There was a long pause. Then another four steps, another brief stop, then another four steps. It was like someone was trying to speak to him in code. He'd felt this way in the restaurant, too. Those clocks, for instance: what were they trying to tell him? He'd been in hiding in two of those places—Berlin and Moscow. Surely those clocks must be some kind of sign or clue. But then again, he'd never been in hiding in London or Cairo. And then there was the clock labeled BROOMEVILLE. It was the only one that was running, but did that mean that Henry had plenty of time in Broomeville, or that time was running out? He didn't know, but he felt strongly that someone probably did. He also felt strongly that someone was watching him. Locs had predicted this. She'd told him, *Don't worry. Someone's always watching you in Broomeville*. But he did worry. That's why he'd drawn that cartoon in the restaurant. It gave him some sense of control: Everything is going to be just fine, because I know you're watching me! was what the cartoon was meant to communicate. But to whom? When Henry had left the restaurant, there was only Kurt. He didn't think Kurt was the one watching him, and if he was, then that probably wouldn't be so bad: Kurt seemed like a good kid. He wouldn't mind if it was Kurt's mother watching him, either. Don't worry. Kurt's mother is always watching you in Broomeville. That sounded much better to Henry. Although it would sound even better if he knew her real name. He didn't like calling her "the woman" or "Kurt's mother," not even in his head.

Henry heard more footsteps overhead. Then a furious crashing of feet on wood, and then a door to the left of the bar flew open as though it'd been kicked, and Henry saw the woman jump from two steps up. When she noticed him looking at her, the woman smiled sheepishly, and girlishly, as though to say, My mother always told me not to run down the stairs.

"I was just getting your room ready," the woman said. She handed him a key. It was attached to a piece of plastic with the number 24 on it.

"I don't even know your name," Henry said.

"It's Ellen," Ellen said. "I brought your suitcases up there, too."

"Thank you, Ellen."

"I hope you don't mind," she said.

"Why would I mind?"

"Because I rifled through them a little bit, too."

Rifled? Henry thought but did not say. Then he did a quick mental accounting of the contents of his suitcases. Clothes, bathroom things. What else? Anything incriminating? The expression on Ellen's face said, Come on, we both know what I found in the suitcases, and Henry wondered whether he should be worried about her watching him after all.

"So, you're Swedish," she finally said.

She took my fake passport! Henry thought. But then he remembered it was in his inside jacket pocket, not in his suitcase. He patted the spot, just to make sure. Locs must have told Matthew he was Swedish or was pretending to be Swedish. And Matthew must have told Ellen. And Ellen had told Henry that almost everyone called him Matty, not Matthew.

"Matty told you," Henry said, and she smiled at him. Gratefully, he thought, and also a little sadly, he thought.

"Come on," she said. "He's at the baseball game."

BY THE TIME THEY got outside the Lumber Lodge, it was snowing. Snowing! Evidently, Ellen felt the same way. "Snowing!" she said. But then she looked up and got a snow-flake in the eye.

"Oh, wow," she said. She blinked rapidly and then began tugging at the underside of her right eye.

"Does it hurt?" Henry asked.

"It's only snow," Ellen said. "But yeah, it does hurt a little." She tugged her eye again, then blinked slowly, once, twice, three times. "I really should wear glasses."

"They would protect your eyes from the snow," Henry said.

Ellen blinked once more and then looked at him with wide eyes. "Instead of contacts," Ellen said.

Contacts? Henry thought. And then he thought: *Kontaktlinsers*. He wore them, too, special *kontaktlinsers* that helped correct his nearsightedness and also made his blue eyes brown.

Anyway, it had apparently been snowing for a while, because there was a rusty blue pickup truck parked in front of the Lumber Lodge and its windshield was covered with snow. Ellen got into the driver's side of the truck, and Henry into the passenger's side. Ellen then did several things in quick succession. First, she put the key into the ignition and turned it, which started the truck with a roar and then a rattle. Then she turned the windshield wipers on, but the snow was crusted on the glass and wouldn't wipe off. Henry offered to get out and scrape, but Ellen waved him off. "It's cold out there," she said. Then Ellen turned on the defrost, and cold air came blasting into the truck. Then she turned on the radio. A man's voice came out. He was talking about the weather. They listened for a few seconds, and then Ellen punched a button on the radio and another man's voice came out. Henry recognized it immediately: sports talk radio sounds the same no matter what language it's spoken in and what sport is being discussed. They listened to that for a few seconds, and then Ellen punched another button and another man's voice came out, talking about politics. After a few seconds of listening to that, Ellen turned off the radio. She lit a cigarette and smoked it halfway to the filter before glancing at Henry. The glance was half dare, half apology. "Matty doesn't like to see me smoke," she said.

Finally she put the car in gear. To Henry, all of this seemed like preparations for a very long journey. But not even a minute later, Ellen stopped the truck and said, "We're here."

In this way, Henry learned several things. That once Americans were out of the cold and in their trucks, they did not like to get back out into the cold, even if it meant making the inside of their trucks as cold as the outside; that American weathermen liked to refer to snow as "the white stuff"; that American sports talk radio announcers liked to say about something, "There's no doubt about it," before then expressing their many doubts about it; that American political commentators liked to preface their comments by saying, "No offense," before then saying something offensive (the political commentator on the radio had said to whomever he was talking to, "No offense, but you have to be the stupidest human being on the planet"); that Americans were very impatient people with very short attention spans; that Americans believed as long as they were inside their trucks they were invisible, and that as long as they smoked cigarettes inside their trucks they would not then smell like cigarettes once they exited their trucks, and that in general Americans thought their trucks were magic; that while Europeans tended to think of Americans as people who liked to drive incredibly long distances in their pickup trucks, in fact Americans liked to drive incredibly short distances in their pickup trucks as well. These were the lessons Henry learned about Americans during his first minute in Ellen's truck, and not once was he forced to reconsider them during all his days in Broomeville.

Ellen put the truck in park, but its engine was still running, its wipers still wiping. It was difficult to see anything but snow; the truck headlights were full of it.

"Does it always snow this much here?" he asked.

"Why? Doesn't it snow like this where you're from, too?"

"No," Henry said. He was picturing winter in Skagen, which rhymes with *rain* in English, although in Danish the word for rain—*regn*—rhymed with *pine* and not *Skagen* or *rain*. Regardless, it didn't snow much there, not even in the winter.

"Really?" Ellen said. "Because when I see Sweden, I see snow."

"Of course, of course," Henry said. "But then, I'm from southern Sweden."

"It doesn't snow in southern Sweden?"

"It does. But not often in October."

"It doesn't usually snow this much in October here, either," Ellen said. She turned off the truck and the headlights, too. But still, there was snow; still, there was light—not too far in front of them and much higher off the ground. A ring of light towers. Henry supposed they had something to do with this baseball game. In a moment he and Ellen would get out of the car and start walking in that direction. And what then? Something is about to happen, Henry thought. But what is about to happen? He wanted to reach across the bench seat to grab Ellen's hand. Instead, he said, "It's beautiful."

"Snow is always beautiful in October," she said.

"I really think I'm going to like it here," he said.

"OK, listen," Ellen said. "You shouldn't talk like that."

"Talk like what?" Henry asked. He seemed genuinely, almost pedagogically concerned. If he'd had a pad of paper, Ellen was sure he'd have started taking notes on the subject. In fact, he reached into his jacket pocket, as though looking for something to write on and with. And then he reached into the other jacket pocket. There was clearly nothing in either. Then he looked even more concerned. Ellen didn't think she'd ever seen a face like that, so wide open; Ellen didn't think she'd ever seen someone who clearly wanted advice, who wanted to be helped.

"Like you talk," Ellen said. "'I really think I'm going to like it here.' If you say things like that, these people will eat you alive."

"Even the students?"

"Especially them."

"What should I say?"

"Maybe you shouldn't say anything," she said. Ellen remembered when Kurt was younger. She would say something he didn't like, and he would just stand there with his arms crossed, frowning, evidently waiting for her to say something else. Which she inevitably did. She explained this to Henry. "You should just go like this," she said, and then she demonstrated. Henry did it back, and when he did, Ellen thought of a younger Kurt, and a younger Matty, and a younger self, and suddenly she became so lonely for that time and those people.

"Are you all right?" Henry asked.

"I've been a little lonely," she said. Henry didn't say anything back. He just frowned at her, as though he disapproved of the inaccuracy of her declaration. "I'm so lonely," she said. "I've *been* so lonely for a long time." Still, Henry frowned.

Ellen remembered this now: She remembered feeling that she would have done or said anything to get that look off Kurt's face. Even tell the truth. "I've been so lonely ever since Matty told me he'd been cheating on me."

The frown disappeared. That's more like it, Henry's face seemed to say.

18

. . .

"Turku!" Lawrence was saying, but Matty was barely listening. He was looking at Kurt, who was standing with his buddies against the fence. None of them were wearing coats. Instead they were wearing sweatshirts, with the hoods up and their hands in the pouches. God, Kurt looked so cold. Matty wanted to go over there and hug him. But then Kurt would say, What are you *doing*? and then Matty would feel hurt and then get on Kurt's case for not even being half smart enough to dress for the weather, and besides, it was possible the clothes Kurt *was* wearing would smell like pot, and Matty would either have to pretend he didn't notice or admit he did notice and then make a big scene about it in front of Kurt's friends, who were also, of course, Matty's students. If Kurt smelled like pot, then they would also smell like pot, and if Matty made a big scene about Kurt, then he'd have to make a big scene about them, too. Meanwhile, there was this baseball game to be played. Everyone had told him to cancel it. There had been no school that day, because of state-mandated teacher workshops. That would mean that students would have to come back to school for the game. Plus, there was supposed to be a big snowstorm. But it was a tradition: they always held the faculty-student baseball game on the first Wednesday in October. And besides, it was only the first Wednesday in October. They would never actually end up getting that much snow. And yet, it seemed like they really were getting that much snow.

"Turku!" Lawrence was still saying.

"What does that mean?"

"So much snow!" Lawrence said. "It reminds me of that December I spent in Turku." And then he was off, talking about that December he spent in Turku. Wherever that was. Someplace where there was snow in December, evidently. Just one of many stops on what Lawrence called his "grand tour" and what everyone else thought of as his more than ten years of fucking around after college before settling down and getting a real job back in Broomeville. Although he couldn't have been entirely fucking around: he must have had a job somewhere doing something to pay for all his traveling. But finally, Lawrence must have run out of money or gotten bored or something, because twelve years earlier he'd come home and Matty had given him a job teaching twelfth-grade history. It had worked out, too. It turned out that Lawrence was a pretty good teacher. He'd even become the Civics Club adviser; the club met down at Doc's every Friday after school. The students in the club loved him and in fact were younger versions of him: conscientious, smart, eager, not quite right, but not demonstrably wrong, either. Matty sometimes dropped by Doc's and watched the students listen with big eyes as Lawrence told them about all his travels to all these places where this man and that had welcomed Lawrence into their homes. A few of them even kept in touch with Lawrence after they graduated, would meet him for coffee at Doc's when they were back in town visiting. Matty thought the whole thing was very sweet; it made him hopeful: everyone finds the people, or person, they're meant to find, eventually.

"I have missed you," Matty had told Locs on the phone.

"That's the second thing," she'd said.

So he'd agreed to hire this guy—whoever he was, whatever kind of trouble he was in—as his guidance counselor. "Is he going to come here by himself?" Matty had asked. He waited for Locs to answer. But she didn't. She was waiting for Matty to tell her something. Either: Because I want you to bring him. Or: Because I don't want you to bring him. And before he could ask himself, again, Am I really going to do this? he'd said, "Because I want you to bring him."

"Maybe I will," Locs had said. "But then again, maybe I will not."

And then she hung up, leaving Matty with two visions of the future. Both of them gave him a bad feeling.

"I have a bad feeling," Matty said.

"Well, as I was just saying, I had a bad feeling that December in Turku as well," Lawrence said.

"Uncle Lawrence!" Kurt yelled, and then he waved at Uncle Lawrence to come over.

"I'm being paged," Lawrence said, and he walked over to his nephew. Matty then turned in the opposite direction and thought, Where are they? And a second later, there they were: Ellen and a man walking toward him through the snow. The man looked tall—taller than Matty—and thin; he had gray hair and had lost most of it except for on the sides, but he was one of those tall, fit men who cut their remaining hair very short, and so he looked youthful even though he was not young. Locs had described the guy—Henrik Larsen—as a goofball. But he did not look like a goofball. Matty, on the other hand, was dressed in his ridiculous homemade umpire uniform. The uniform was supposed to be a joke, but now he wondered whether he'd succeeded a little too fully in making it so. He was wearing Kurt's old soccer shin guards, and the pieces of black plastic barely covered half the length of his shins. He'd also stuffed a pillow into his red sweatshirt for a chest protector. And while his mask was a genuine umpire mask, it was ancient, and several bars had been broken, so that the ones that remained were too far apart to stop anything—a ball, a rock—from reaching his face. He'd dressed like this for the fourteen years he'd umpired this game, but today, for the first time, he felt like a man who was absolutely ill equipped to go into battle.

Matty shook the guy's hand when he got close enough, and said, "So you must be my new guidance counselor."

The guy didn't say anything. He just took his hand back, then crossed his arms and frowned. Locs was supposed to have told this Henrik that he was going to be the new Broomeville Junior-Senior High guidance counselor. Did this frowning and arm crossing mean she hadn't told him? Although she *had* told Henrik to call him Matthew. What *else* had she told him? Locs, Locs. He felt her nearby. She might even be sitting in the stands, watching him. He looked at Henrik, making sure he didn't look anywhere else. "Henry," Ellen said. "This is Matthew."

Henry? thought Matty. "I go by Matty," he said to Henry.

"Or Big Red," Ellen said.

Matty felt his face turn unhappy. He wondered whether Henry could see it behind the mask. Henry was still frowning; his arms were still crossed. "I went to Cornell," Matty explained to Henry.

Henry let his frown disappear. For now. It felt so good, knowing he could and would be able to return to it. Earlier he'd wondered whether there was a difference between Jens and Henry. This was the difference: Jens was always a little out of control, even though he insisted that he was in control, that everything would be just fine. But Henry had a method. And Ellen had given it to him. Henry had known her for only a couple of hours, but already she seemed like the most incredible woman he had ever met. How could Matty have cheated on her (Henry had not asked with whom, and Ellen had not volunteered the information, but he had a hunch it was Locs, because Locs had said, "Matthew doesn't even know who *he* is," and you don't say something like that about a person unless you're in love with him), Matty who apparently went to this Cornell? Henry had never heard of it, but the way Matty had said the word—"Cornell"—made it sound like some mystical, faraway place. Timbuktu. Kathmandu. Atlantis. "I went to Cornell," Matty had said.

"And when did you get back?" Henry asked.

Ellen laughed. But Matty did not laugh. He lifted the mask up off his face and seemed to be prepared to say something unpleasant when a woman and a man walked by. The woman was dressed like an Arctic explorer with her fur-lined and hooded anorak. The man was wearing what seemed just to be a lined, checked shirt and a tasseled hat with the word SKI-DOO ringing its perimeter.

"Hello, Bossman," she said to Matty. "Hello, Me," she said to Henry. The woman smelled strongly of alcohol. She might once have had other smells, but the liquor had eradicated them. The man didn't say anything. He just extended his hand in Henry's direction and Henry shook it. There was clearly something wrong with the hand—the fingers seemed fused together and hard, so that it was like shaking a closed frozen lobster claw with human skin on it—but Henry shook it anyway, the man looking deeply into his face, seemingly daring Henry to in some way acknowledge the claw. Henry didn't; he didn't even need to frown, since the man wasn't actually saying anything. Finally the man retracted his hand, and he and the woman walked away, past a group of sweatshirted teenagers standing next to a chain-link fence, whispering conspiratorially and not even trying to hide the fact that they were pointing at Henry. It was easy to read their pointing: it said, Who the fuck are you?

"I fart in your general direction!" someone yelled in what seemed like a French accent. Henry looked in the direction of the voice. It clearly had come from a large man wearing a very colorful short-sleeved shirt who was looking—but as far as Henry could tell, not farting—in Henry's direction. A woman descended the bleachers behind the man, long braids trailing out of her ski hat. She had a martial look on her face, and sure enough, she struck the man in the arm, then ran back up the stairs. The man rubbed his arm but otherwise seemed unaffected by this sudden violence. Although he did seem cold; he wrapped his arms around himself and yelled in Henry's and Matty's direction, "Hey, chief, play ball already!" Henry looked at him. Henry looked at all of them, the whole crowd. And what did he see? What did he not see? He did not see one Muslim in the crowd. He did not see one person who by evidence of their skin color or headgear or dress or *anything* seemed likely to want to kill him. Henry did not like himself for noticing this. But neither did he like himself being around people who might be trying to kill him. He turned back to Matty, who was busy feeling that crushing combination of shame and defiance known only to people in small towns who are forced to welcome an outsider into that small town. I know this place is awful, was Matty's feeling, and also: But don't even think about telling me how awful it is. "I apologize for the freak show," Matty said.

"I really think I'm going to like it here," Henry said.

"You do?"

"Yes," Henry said. "I think everything is going to be just fine." He allowed himself to say these things one last time, as a way of saying good-bye to Jens, the way Matty's baseball game was his way of saying good-bye to summer. Then Henry crossed his arms again. Now that he'd started truly being Henry, he couldn't imagine ever wanting to be anyone else. Meanwhile, Matty was looking at him in amazement. He wasn't sure he'd ever heard anyone say "I think everything is going to be just fine" before. And Henry had sounded like he'd *meant it*, too. Was he talking somehow about Matty and Locs? Matty felt sure Henry was. He glanced at Ellen, who was now

talking to Lawrence and Kurt, and then said, "How is everything going to be fine?" Henry didn't respond to that, except
with his frown, which communicated, to Matty, Oh, you know
how. Matty did. He'd known it last time, and he knew it this
time, too. He just needed someone else to remind him.

Meanwhile, Lawrence had walked over and was now standing in front of Matty and Henry. Lawrence said several things
in a language that Matty didn't know and that Henry didn't
seem to know, either: he stood there, arms crossed, frowning.
"So you're from Sweden!" Lawrence said, in English. "Or as
you say, Sverige! I'll never forget the fall I spent in Stavsnä! . . ."
And then Lawrence said several more typically Lawrence
things. None of which appeared to have any effect on Henry:
he was still frowning and crossing his arms. Finally, Lawrence
seemed to give up, and said simply: "I'm Lawrence Klock. I
teach eleventh- and twelfth-grade history. Welcome to Broomeville." Introducing himself! Like a real person! This new guidance counselor really was incredible. I know how, Matty
thought. I know how everything is going to be just fine. And
then he pulled down his mask, strode back toward the snow-
covered field, and ordered everyone to play ball.

19

· · ·

Matty had ended up giving Henry a tour. He couldn't help himself. After the game (the students won; the students won every year; every year, the faculty insisted that they wanted the students to win, that it was important that the students win, that it was important for the students to feel good about themselves; every year, the faculty ended up doing everything they could to win and ended up losing anyway), all Matty had intended to do was walk Henry back to the Lumber Lodge and tell him what to expect tomorrow at school and maybe ask him whether he knew where Locs was, whether she was in Broomeville or somewhere else. But here he was, giving a tour of Broomeville. This was another burden for people from small towns: they couldn't stop themselves from giving an out-of-towner a tour and then at the end of the tour saying, I know it's not much, and then daring the out-of-towner to agree.

"And this was where Dietrik Broome lived," Matty was saying. They were standing in front of the chalet. The snow was still falling, falling. There was at least a foot of it already on the ground and it was piled high on the roof and the gables, making the house look even more Swiss than usual. Although Broome himself had emigrated from Holland. "He emigrated from Holland, in 1789," Matty was saying. "No one lives in the house anymore, of course. It's more of a museum than a house."

"May we go in?" Henry asked.

"It's open only by appointment." Matty hoped Henry wouldn't ask with whom he could make that appointment. Because honestly, Matty had no idea.

But Henry didn't ask anything. They kept walking, past the gazebo and monument, which memorialized Broomeville's war dead, and then they were in front of the Lumber Lodge, which was alive with drunk people. Matty could hear them from where he was standing, even though the bar windows were closed. Ellen had left the game early; she was inside now, tending bar. "Snowstorms make people want to drink," Ellen liked to say. "As does extreme heat. Not to mention a light drizzle."

"So that's the tour," Matty said. "I know it's not much . . ."

"You haven't yet told me what a guidance counselor does," Henry said. He sounded tired. Which made sense, since he'd traveled who knew how far to get there.

"No one really knows," Matty said. "Don't worry. You'll do just fine."

"Just fine," Henry repeated. And then: "I think I'll go to bed now."

"Fair enough," Matty said. "See you at school tomorrow." Then Henry turned and walked toward the Lodge. Matty watched him. The door opened. Matty heard a boozy roar. Then the door closed, and the roar disappeared. Matty looked through the bar windows. His teachers and staff were in there. They always went to the Lumber Lodge after the game. Matty really belonged in there, too. He always made a speech after the game, thanked his troops, bought them drinks. But tonight he ignored that tradition. Matty started to walk. This was one of the ways that he was different from Ellen. Locs, too. Both of them liked to drive, anywhere, always. But Matty liked to walk. He told people it helped him think. It also had the virtue of helping him postpone having to do the thing he was thinking about.

20

...

It was after eight o'clock, and Locs didn't know what to do. Matthew might be down at the Lumber Lodge. But she couldn't go into that terrible place, because his wife might be there. He might be at his house or at the baseball game (The first Wednesday in October! she remembered), but she couldn't go to those places, either, for the same reason. And Matthew wasn't in his office at school. She knew that because she'd checked. He wasn't there. He was not anywhere. She didn't want to risk using her cell phone to call his, because if she used her cell phone, then she could be tracked by her cell phone, and right now she knew the people who might be trying to track her. London, she thought. Crystal. Doc. *Capo.* Jesus Christ. His ridiculous nickname and his ridiculous clocks to remind him of the whereabouts of the rest of his ridiculous people. But just because they were ridiculous did not mean she wanted them to know where she was. But what exactly *do* I want? she wondered. What am I *doing* here? But that was a rhetorical question. She was here because she was lonely; she was here because she loved Matthew. She loved Matthew so much that she couldn't stop thinking about him, even after he'd dumped her, even after she'd left Broomeville and joined the CIA just so she could put several thousand miles and several large bodies of water between them. She loved Matthew so much that she'd brought that cartoonist thousands of miles under the ludicrous pretense that this was the best place for him to stay hidden, forever. She loved Matthew so much that she'd convinced herself that Capo would somehow not discover that she'd brought Henrik to Broomeville, even though Capo lived in *that same fucking town*. She loved Matthew so much that she'd convinced herself that if Capo *did* discover that she'd brought Henrik to Broomeville, then Capo would see the enormity of her love for Matthew and would be so moved by that love that he would forgive her for bringing the person she was supposed to be guarding to Broomeville, without his permission, and not kill her, as he had done to other agents who had gone rogue and done things without his permission. She loved Matthew so much that she'd convinced herself that after Capo had forgiven her for going rogue, he and she and Crystal and Doc and London would look after Henrik together, like a family or something, while she simultaneously started a family of her own with Matthew, even though Matthew already had a family and even though Matthew had already shown a pretty clear resistance to leaving his family for Locs, even though he supposedly loved her so much. "Fuck, fuck," she said to her rental car, which was a dark blue Chevy Cruze or something ridiculous like that. Everything about the car was slightly wrong, in the way of rental cars. The steering wheel, for instance, was too low. It felt like it was practically in her lap. And she couldn't find the knob or lever to raise the thing, either. It was an awful car in which to drive aimlessly around the town you hated, hoping to find the man you'd come so far to see.

And it was snowing, too, because of course it was, because it always snowed. It *was* pretty. But there was always something that ruined it. For instance, the insolence of people who, during or after snowstorms, walk in the road instead of on the sidewalk or the shoulder. There was someone in front of her doing just that. He was practically in the middle of the street, too. And it wasn't even a street; it was Route 356, where you could and wanted to drive fifty-five miles per hour. Yet this bozo was walking pretty much down the center of the road, not anywhere near the shoulder. There was snow in both places: it was calf deep on the shoulder, while it was only shoe high on the road itself. But there was snow, and the cars had to drive on it, and cars were known to sometimes skid on snow, were they not? Was this not common fucking knowledge? Had this guy really weighed his options? Had he examined the two possibilities—getting his shoes and pants a little snowy, a little wet, while walking in relative safety on the side of the road, or keeping his feet somewhat dry while being struck by two thousand pounds of hurtling steel—and chosen the latter? He apparently had. And she knew exactly what this guy was thinking: Oh, I hate it when my pants get all snowy, so I'll take my chances with the road, the cars will move over, they always move over, they have always moved over. God, she hated these people. One of these days, maybe this day, she really would hit someone, and when that happened, she would get out of her car and stand over one of these arrogant bozos who had finally gotten his due, and before she would be able to get a word out, he would say, if he wasn't already dead, I can't believe you actually hit me.

She pulled around this guy, but she did not give him a wide berth, just to see what he would do. Sure enough, he gave her a look that said, Hey, what's your problem, you almost hit me! And only after she'd pulled back into her lane and driven maybe a hundred feet farther did she recognize him as Matthew.

21

. . .

It was after eight at night when Henry returned to the Lumber Lodge. The tavern was full now—full of big people and the big sounds they made—but he didn't join them. He was tired. Besides, there'd be time to join them on some other day, at some other hour. Odd: Henry didn't know them but was already thinking of these Broomevillians as family, family being the group of people you look forward to spending more time with later.

Anyway, he waved to Ellen as he skirted the barroom, climbed the stairs to room 24. He turned the key and opened the door. The first thing he noticed was that the room, using the expression his students would teach him in the days and weeks and months and years to come, "smelled like ass." The walls were painted dark yellow, and nailed to those walls were several faded prints of families being transported through the snow by horse-drawn sleighs. The carpet was yellow like the walls, and there were NO SMOKING signs everywhere, even though there were cigarette burn marks and holes in the carpet. The bathroom was visible from the rest of the room; the sink was white, but the porcelain was stained blue under the tap, as though the tap released not water but antifreeze. Henry sat down on the twin bed, which creaked and buckled but did not break. Home, he thought, and then he thought it might be easier to think of room 24 as a home if he turned the lights off. He did that. Then he got into bed, fully clothed, without taking off his contact lenses. Downstairs he could hear the big happy sounds of the big happy people. There was music playing, and the people were shouting to be heard over it, making both the music and the shouting unintelligible. Henry put his hands over his ears, but he could still hear the sounds—of the people and the music, but also of Ellen and Matty and Kurt and his cronies, and of the man on the bus and their singing, and Locs telling him to go to Broomeville, and Ilsa in Aarhus, and his editor in Skagen, and the man who'd burned down Jens's house, and that strange man at the baseball game (Lawrence was his name), who had started talking to Henry in what was probably Swedish, and the people on the television and in the newspapers and on the Internet, talking about Jens's cartoon, his death, whether it meant the end of something (*civilization*, maybe) or the beginning of something, or whether it meant anything at all—all these sounds and voices and faces gathering around Henry, and he thought, If I were still a cartoonist, I would draw a cartoon of a man in bed with his eyes squeezed shut and his hands pressed over his ears surrounded by faces with their mouths open, little sad or happy or angry lines coming out of their mouths. But Henry wasn't a cartoonist anymore. He was a guidance counselor, and in ten hours he had to get up and find out what it meant to be one.

He pulled the scratchy covers up to his neck and fell into a deep sleep, a sleep so deep that he didn't even hear, three hours later, someone opening his door, didn't sense her standing over him, breathing hard.

22
...

Generally speaking, to be in love is to be embroiled in an endless internal conflict between world-weariness and stupidity. I am in love, Locs thought, I have been in love before, I have been in love before with the same person, I know that that same person had been in love with me, and yet that love did not work out so well, that love ended up terribly, all love ends up terribly, why deny that all love ends up anything other than terribly, that is what it means to live in the world, it is so wearying to live in the world, this is why the world makes us weary, it makes us weary so that we're too weary to love again, and yet the world also gives us another chance, and now I have another chance to see the person I love, because I still love this person, I still love this person so much, and since I still love this person so much, after everything that has happened between us, that must make this love different from all other loves that ended up terribly, including our own love that ended up terribly, that only *seemed* to end up terribly, because true love never really ends, love, love, love, love renews the world, it changes people, it changes the world, the world gave me the name Lorraine Callahan, but you gave me the nickname Locs, which is a terrible nickname, a nickname I should have loathed, but I loved it because you gave it to me, I loved it because I loved you, because love makes you act out of character, it makes you feel like doing things you never wanted to do before, it makes me feel like doing something ridiculously domestic, like tidying up this rental car, like it's a home or something, please forgive the mess, my love, here, sit down, but first let me take this notebook off the passenger seat of my Chevy Cruze, the notebook I lifted from your son, who lifted it from your guidance counselor, a notebook that has, inside, an incriminating cartoon and also an incriminating Danish word, can you believe that that cartoonist could be so stupid, sweetie, to draw this cartoon and write this word in this language, sweetie, you look just as handsome as ever, sweetie, is everything all right, sweetie, why do you have that look on your face, sweetie, I haven't seen you in so long, sweetie, but the last time I saw you, you also had that look on your face, you mean I came all this way just to see this same look on your face, Jesus, I'm so stupid, Jesus, I'm so weary.

"You're wearing my hat," said Matty. Because that's really what he was. She wanted him to be a Matthew. But he would always be a Matty.

"Do you love me?" Locs asked.

"I really do," Matty said. "But I just can't."

Locs didn't listen closely to the rest of it. Matty wasn't really saying anything he hadn't said before. Locs stared out the windshield while Matty talked. It was still snowing. The snow made everything seem out of time; it was night, but as long as it was snowing like this, would the day look much different?

"I know this hurts," Matty said. "But I also know that everything is going to be just fine."

Locs was suddenly paying attention. "What did you just say?" she asked, and Matty repeated what he'd just said. Locs knew the words weren't Matty's. She was sure that he'd never said anything like that before in his life. In fact, even when he said, "Everything is going to be just fine," his voice sounded tragic, like nothing would ever be all right again, like he desperately wanted to be saying something else.

"What did he tell you?" Locs demanded.

Matty didn't even bother to pretend not to know whom she was talking about. "Henry said I knew how to make sure everything would turn out fine." And then he repeated what he'd already said. "And the only way to make everything turn out fine is to let you go, once and for all. I need to stay with Ellen and Kurt. It's the only right thing to do."

Henry, Locs thought, hating him even more. "He said that?"

"In so many words."

Somewhere in the distance, Locs could hear the roar and scrape of a snowplow. A minute earlier she would have wanted to throw herself into the path of that plow. Now she was thinking of throwing someone else.

"Please tell me what you're thinking," Matty said.

"I'm not thinking anything," Locs said. In truth, she was thinking that she was going to kill that cartoonist. But that was an imprecise thought: she had actually never killed anyone. This was a common misunderstanding about secret agents: sometimes they protected people from getting killed, and sometimes they got people killed, but rarely did they do the killing themselves. No, Locs would not kill the cartoonist; she'd get someone else to do that for her. She *would* leave him something, though, just a little hint of the huge fucking disaster he'd made for himself. But first, she needed Matty to go away.

"Please just go away," Locs said. Matty seemed to want to protest. He opened his mouth. But then he closed it, opened the door, said good-bye, I'm sorry, etc., and shut the door. Locs watched him walk away in the rearview. The idiot was walking pretty much in the middle of the road again. A car appeared in the snow and almost hit him. It drove past where Locs was parked, slowed down enough for Locs to see that the car was, like her rental car, a blue Chevy Cruze. The car turned around, drove very slowly past Locs again, and then suddenly sped up. Too suddenly: it fishtailed, spun, ended up stuck bumper-first in a snowbank. Matty didn't seem to notice: he kept walking, head down, while the car spun its wheels and spun its wheels, trying and failing to get out of the snowbank. Please hit him, Locs thought. And also: Please don't. Those mixed feelings were the worst. Love, love: it was never as pure as you needed it to be. That was the good thing about hate. If you hated someone, really hated him, then you could wish him dead and never once worry that you would change your mind about it.

23

· · ·

What? Ellen was in his bed. No. That was just a dream. Henry knew it was a dream, because his pants were off, and in reality he'd fallen asleep with his pants on. And in the dream Henry knew his pants were off, not because he'd taken them off in the dream, but because he could feel Ellen's bare legs rubbing against his.

"You took off my pants," he said in his dream.

"I took off mine first," she said, not in his dream.

Henry sat up, opened his eyes wide. His dried contact lenses made the room looked crinkly and bleached out, even in the dark. He'd neglected to close the window shades before falling asleep, and could see that it wasn't snowing anymore. "What time is it?"

"A woman without pants is in your bed and you want to know what *time* it is?" Ellen said, and Henry lay back down again. Ellen smelled like cigarettes and dish soap and something else that Henry couldn't identify. Her right leg was touching his left; he could tell that he still had his underwear on, and he wondered whether she had hers on, too. What else? Henry was suddenly desperate to know what he should do with his hands. He placed them on his stomach, but he'd seen corpses in coffins do that. He then tried to reach back and clasp them behind his head, but in doing so, he almost hit Ellen in the head with his left elbow. Finally, Henry did what he'd been wanting to do the whole time anyway: he placed his left hand on Ellen's right thigh, and Ellen put her hand over his and left it there. Henry thought he could feel her thigh vibrating, humming.

"Anyway, it's not even midnight," Ellen said.

"You're in my bed," Henry said.

"I decided to close the bar early."

"I can't believe you are in my bed."

"Two hours early," she said. "Do you know what drunk people hate?"

"What?"

"When you close their bar two hours early."

Henry didn't know what to say to that. He guessed "I'm sorry" wasn't the right thing, especially since he wasn't. I am so happy right now, is what he wanted to say, but he worried that maybe that wasn't the right thing, either. "I'm not a drunk person," is what he ended up saying, even though that sounded much lamer than either of the other two things.

"I want to have sex with you in a minute," she said.

"I am so happy right now!" he said, and they both laughed. But then Ellen abruptly stopped laughing.

"Listen," she said. "I am married to Matty, and after you and I have sex I'll still be married to him. I might still be married to him for a long time; then again, I might not. But either way, I also still might want to have sex with you again."

Henry didn't say anything to that. He had the sense that

Ellen was talking to herself more than to him. So he did what she'd taught him to do. He didn't say anything; he just lay there, frowning, touching Ellen's hand and thigh in the dark.

"I'm just telling you the truth," Ellen said.

"OK."

"Don't ever lie to me."

"I promise," he said.

"Are you married?"

"I used to be," Henry said immediately. He did not want Ellen to think he was lying. Besides, was he? Was he still married? What was your marital status if you've been declared dead and your wife knows you've been declared dead and has agreed to act like you're dead, even though she knows you're not? At the very least, he was divorced in spirit—"in spirit" being the small lie people tell themselves in order to get to do the thing they really want to do before getting in big trouble for it later on.

"Please get over here," Ellen said.

Henry thought he was already over here. "I thought I was already over here," he said.

"Well, you're not," she said, and then she rolled over onto his chest and kissed him. Ice skating. That was her smell. The smell of someone who's been out ice-skating—cold air and dried sweat and wool.

"hey," ellen said. They were back to lying side by side in Henry's bed. Ellen hated it when she asked someone a direct question and that person answered, "Well, yes and no." But had Henry asked her the direct question, Are you happy?

her honest answer would have been, Well, yes and no. But he wasn't asking her anything. Maybe he was thinking yes and no, too. "These were on your floor when I came in."

"When you broke in," Henry said.

"It's not breaking in if you use a key," she said. "Besides, I did knock first." She reached over to the end table, picked up and handed Henry two pieces of paper. On one was his drawing of himself being watched while at Doc's; on the other was KØKKENBORD = COUNTER. Someone had scratched a big black X through Henry in the drawing; the other paper was untouched. Neither page was attached to the notebook.

"Did you draw that?" Ellen asked, and Henry said that he did. "It's pretty good," she said. "Although apparently you didn't think so." Henry realized that she thought he hadn't liked the cartoon and had drawn the X himself, and he let her think that. "Is that the word you taught Kurt?"

"What's that?"

"I heard Kurt talking to his uncle Lawrence at the baseball game. Something about not remembering a foreign word for 'counter.' I figured it had something to do with you."

Kurt. Either Henry had dropped the notebook and Kurt had picked it up, or Kurt had stolen it from him. Either way, it must have been Kurt who had ripped out the pages, Kurt who'd defaced the cartoon with that big black X, Kurt who'd slipped the pages under his door. But why? What was Kurt trying to tell him? What had he ever done to Kurt? Besides have sex with his mother, that is. But the X had been made before that. Anyway, he would have to keep his eye on Kurt.

"Is that word Swedish?" Ellen asked.

Don't lie to me, Ellen had told him, and he had promised not to. But then again, he had no idea what the Swedish word for "counter" was. Besides, the languages were pretty similar; everyone always said so. If the Swedish word for "counter" wasn't *køkkenbord,* it was probably something very close. "Yes," Henry said. "That is Swedish."

"I probably have to go," Ellen said.

"Please don't," Henry said. He meant it. But he knew that Ellen really did have to go, and once she did, he would destroy those pieces of paper. It had probably been very stupid of him to draw that cartoon, and write those words, in the first place. It was exactly the kind of thing Locs had warned him not to do.

24

. . .

Capo was sitting at Doc's counter. The lights were off. Doc was in the kitchen, making corned beef hash and scrambled eggs in the dark. London was sitting in a car outside Matty's house; Crystal was across the street in the Lumber Lodge. In front of Capo, on the counter, was an open laptop. A cell phone was plugged into the laptop. Capo was certain of four things. He knew that Locs had rented a blue Chevy Cruze, because she'd paid for it with her agency credit card. He knew that Locs was in town, because at the baseball game Kurt had described to him the woman who had taken the cartoon from him, the cartoon that Kurt himself had originally taken from the cartoonist. He knew that Locs would find Matty, or Matty her. He knew that Matty would, at the last minute, suffer a failure of nerve, again, and that he would walk away from Locs, again. After that, there were a number of possibilities. Locs might decide to murder Matty. Locs might decide to murder Ellen. Locs might decide not to murder Matty or Ellen but instead to murder their marriage by calling Ellen at the Lumber Lodge and telling her that she and Matty had seen each other again. This was why London and Crystal were stationed where they were stationed. This was why the laptop was open in front of Capo: if Locs used her cell phone, the laptop would tell him where she was using it, and if someone called the Lumber Lodge, the call would be routed into Capo's computer and he could answer it on his cell phone.

But there was another possibility. That Locs would do something else, something even Capo hadn't yet thought of.

Meanwhile, Capo watched, on his laptop, the barroom of the Lumber Lodge as seen through the camera he'd placed in the eye of the moose head. There was no sound because the microphone wasn't working, again. Every year Capo, Doc, and Crystal replaced the camera and the microphone, and every year the microphone stopped working immediately after they replaced it. Capo had wanted to put the camera and the microphone there in the first place, not because he thought the Lumber Lodge worth spying on, but because he didn't want his and his agents' bug-planting skills to get rusty. Anyway, a little after eight, Capo watched Crystal get off her barstool, walk across the room, look up the stairs, and then walk back across the room to her barstool. From there, she gave the moose head a thumbs-up. This wasn't as conspicuous as it seems: Capo had noticed that the bar patrons tended to gravitate toward the moose head. The drunker the patrons, the greater the gravitational pull. They stared at the moose head, toasted it, talked to it, confided in it; once, a man had propositioned it sexually. The microphone hadn't been working that time, either, but the man had made a series of vulgar hip thrusts so there was no way the moose head, or Capo, would mistake his meaning. Good Lord. Sometimes, Capo wished that the camera didn't work, either, or that it had been placed in a different stuffed animal head, in a different bar, in a different town.

But regardless, Crystal's thumbs-up meant that the Danish cartoonist was safely in his room above the Lumber Lodge.

A little after that, he heard from London: Matty was safely inside the old stone house.

A little after that, the phone rang. The call was not from Locs's cell phone. It was a local number. But it was from someone calling the Lumber Lodge. Capo raised his eyebrow at Doc and then answered the phone. "Lumber Lodge," he said in Ellen's voice.

"Yeah," the voice said. It was a woman's voice. It was muffled, slurred. The woman sounded drunk. But it was Broomeville. That could mean it was lots of people. "I just saw your fuckin' husband. With that Lorraine chick. The bird woman. You know who I'm talkin' about. In a blue Chevy Cruze out on Route 356, by the power lines."

"Who *is* this?" Capo asked in Ellen's voice. But the woman had already hung up. Capo hung up, too. He closed his eyes and tried to picture the scene: Matty and Locs together in the car on Route 356. Matty telling her the inevitable. Matty getting out of the car. Matty walking home. Locs sitting in the car, and sitting there, and sitting there, not believing that she had let this happen to her again; trying to figure out whom to blame; trying to figure out where she was going to go; trying to figure out what she was going to do next.

Capo opened his eyes and called London. London was already in his car. He was closer to Route 356 than any of the rest of them. Besides, he had helped make this mess. It made sense that he be the one to clean it up. Capo gave London the information, told him what to do. Then Capo hung up. Five minutes later, just as Capo was about to tuck into his eggs and hash, London called. Crying. Really crying. Not as though he was afraid he had done something wrong, but as though he *knew* it. The poor boy. Perhaps Capo had been wrong after all to recruit him. This was the dangerous part of recruiting among the young. You never knew how much they weren't going to change when they got older.

"Drive away," Capo said. "Calmly, calmly. The roads are treacherous. Don't worry. The county coroner is on his way." At that, Doc took off his apron, withdrew his black bag from under the counter, and ran out the door. Not many people knew that Broomeville County even had a coroner, let alone that Doc was that coroner, let alone that that's why Doc was called Doc.

That was that. London had killed the wrong woman. Locs was gone. Who knew where? She was an excellent agent; they probably wouldn't be able to find her. They would probably have to wait until she decided to come back to Broomeville again. In the meantime, Capo, Doc, Crystal, and London would keep watch over the cartoonist. No one else in Broomeville would know his true identity. But what about Matty? Doesn't Matty know who the cartoonist is? Capo asked himself, and then quickly answered, No, Matty doesn't even know who *he* is. Matty doesn't even know who *I* am.

That decided, there was nothing left for Capo to do except eat Doc's eggs and hash. He did love Doc's eggs and hash. He often rhapsodized about them during his time away. "Broomeville! Oh, I'll never forget the eggs and corned beef hash at Doc's!" he would say. Since his return, he'd spent as much time there as his other job allowed. In fact, he had been there that Saturday morning, seven years earlier, drinking his coffee, in the company of his clocks, looking out the window. Matty had just gotten out of the car and walked away, but Locs was still sitting inside. Capo knew what she was doing: she was trying to figure out whom to blame; trying to figure out where she was going to go; trying to figure out what she was going to do next. Capo finished his coffee, walked outside. Locs's head was thrown back against the seat; her eyes were closed. He tapped on the window and her eyes sprang open and she gave him a calculating but still furious look. A very promising look. Although also a very dangerous look. He gestured with his hand for her to roll down her window, and she did that.

"What the fuck do you want, Lawrence?" she said.

"Lawrence," he repeated. "Some people call me by another name."

"Creep?" she suggested. "Asshole?"

Capo tried to ignore that. "I *am* sorry my brother"—and here Capo paused, pretending to search for just the right word— "*dumped* you. But you should have known something like that was going to happen." When Locs didn't say anything to this, he asked, "What will you do next? Where will you go?"

"What do you care?" she said. And then, in a different, lonelier voice, she said, "I really don't know."

"Don't worry," Capo said. "I know some people who will take you into their home."

25

...

Broomeville Bulletin, October 12, 2009

Sheilah Crimmins, age 47, was found dead in her automobile on State Route 356 early Thursday morning. The county coroner has ruled that the deceased died of a self-inflicted gunshot wound. According to reports, Ms. Crimmins had a history of substance abuse and was distraught over recently losing her job at Broomeville Junior-Senior High, where she'd been employed as a guidance counselor for eleven years. She was a lifelong resident of Broomeville and is survived by her older brother, Ronald, also of Broomeville.

Well, that was bullshit, as far as Ronald was concerned. This was what he'd told Doc the day the newspaper report had come out, which was the day after the police had told him what was going to be in the report, which was a week after Sheilah had died. Ronald was sitting across Doc's counter from Doc. Doc, in his early sixties, was about fifteen years older than Ronald. He was from

Broomeville, too, but Doc must have gone away at some point in his life, because then he'd come back with Crystal, grouchy Crystal. But anyway, as far as Ronald could remember, Doc had always been on the other side of that counter, with his spatula and his greasy apron and his yellow-arm-pitted T-shirt. This seemed like the only thing there was to know about him. But now, Ronald had just discovered another thing.

"You're the coroner?"

"Elected."

"I didn't vote for you."

Doc nodded. He picked up the coffee pot and refilled Ronald's cup. There was no one else in the place. There was basically never anyone else in the place. "Well, somebody did," Doc said.

"My sister never owned a gun," Ronald said, "let alone fired a gun."

"I am sorry," Doc said.

"If she killed herself," Ronald said, "then why was the window blown out?" Because this was what the police told him: a bullet had gone through the passenger's side window, destroying it. Meanwhile his sister's dead body had been found in the driver's seat.

"There were two bullets fired," Doc said. "One through the window, and then one into her head."

"Why would she fire a bullet through her own window?" Ronald wanted to know.

"Why was she stuck in a snowbank? Same reason she shot out the window before she shot herself. She was really drunk, Ronald," Doc said. "I'm sorry, but she was."

"But she was always really drunk," Ronald said. "Why would she kill herself?"

Doc shrugged, as if to say, Hey, I'm just the coroner. "She'd just lost her job," he said. "Maybe she was distraught."

"That's bullshit," Ronald said.

"What part?"

"*All of it.*"

And it was. Ronald knew this because of what had happened earlier that night. The new guidance counselor had shaken Ronald's fucked-up hand at the baseball game, and it'd bothered the new guidance counselor not at all, and later on Sheilah had said, "Your hand didn't work."

"I'm sorry," Ronald had said.

"Hey, it's all good," Sheilah had said. They were sitting in the kitchen in the house they shared, which before that had been the house they'd shared with their parents. Sheilah was drinking vodka out of a juice glass. No ice or mixer or fruit or anything. At least she wasn't drinking it straight out of the bottle. "I wasn't much good as a guidance counselor anyway."

"Maybe you'll end up being good at something else," Ronald had said, and Sheilah had lifted her glass in his direction.

"Maybe I already am," she'd said. It'd made Ronald so sad to hear his sister say this. But Sheilah *had not seemed sad saying it.* She did not seem like a person who three hours later, after all the vodka in the house was gone, on the way to doing more of what she was good at at the Lumber Lodge, would decide, You know, maybe I will kill myself, and then somehow, somewhere, from someone, get a gun and then drive herself into a snowbank and then shoot a window and then herself.

It was bullshit and Doc was bullshit and the county that had elected him was bullshit and the town in the county and everyone in it was bullshit, including the principal who had fired his sister for bullshit reasons and then hired this guidance counselor, this bullshit Swede or whatever he was, and the bullshit principal's wife, who was bullshit herself if for no other reason than she'd served Ronald's sister so many drinks and made so many people laugh at Sheilah and not love her the way Ronald, her bullshit older brother, had loved her, and he, Ronald, was the biggest bullshit of all with his bullshit hand, which was not magic or any bullshit like that, it was just mangled and disgusting and weak and pathetic and it did not *tell* him anything, it did not *tell* him, for instance, not to have a funeral for Sheilah, he *decided* on his own not to have one, because he was afraid that no one would come to the funeral and how awful that would be, and can you *believe* that bullshit, oh God, he had not even had a proper funeral for his sister, his only sister, instead he had had her cremated, which is the bullshit term for what you do when you don't know what to do with a dead person's body, and then after he did that, he did not know what to do with her ashes, either, there was no special enough place for him to scatter her ashes, no place she loved, and so he just kept the urn on the top of the kitchen cabinet with the dust and that fondue pot, and sometimes when he tried to remember her, to remember her when they were young, for instance that time when their mother was reading a book to them, maybe Sheilah was three and Ronald was six and the book had an armadillo in it and Sheilah said, "What means armadillo?" and Ronald and their mother laughed, it was cute, how she'd said that, and so they laughed, and Sheilah didn't know why they were laughing *or* what armadillo meant, and so she said, really mad now, "What *means* it?" and then they laughed even harder, but whenever he tried to think of that person, of that time, the urn and the supposed self-inflicted gunshot wound to the face and the shot-out passenger's side window and the car in the snowbank and the alcohol in the bloodstream and all that *bullshit* got in the way, and the only way he knew to get that bullshit out of the way was to find out who murdered his sister, and it was probably one of two people, either the principal or the new guidance counselor, or maybe it was both, either way, he would find out, he would prove it, and if he couldn't prove who killed her, then maybe he would just go ahead and kill both of them, and while he was at it maybe he'd kill *all* of them, maybe he'd kill every single human being in this town and then let the coroner deal with that *bullshit,* unless Ronald decided to kill the coroner, too.

26

· · ·

"Good morning." This was Matty, talking to Ellen. It was three in the morning. It was after three in the morning. She'd just gotten home, had tiptoed into the room, and had slipped into their bed. Now she was just lying there, hands clasped over her chest, staring at the ceiling, in the way of married people who have slunk into bed too late and think they've gotten away with it and are now wondering, Now what? Matty knew this because he'd been, and somewhat still was, the slinker, the wonderer.

"Good morning."

"Jesus!" Ellen said, sitting up straight. "I thought you were asleep."

"Well," Matty said. "I'm not."

The wind roared. It would be even colder tomorrow. It would snow some more, too. The wind roared, the windows rattled in their frames. Matty had grown up in this house; he'd bought it from his parents right before they moved to Florida and then died—not on the beach or the golf course, as is the dream, but from a carbon monoxide leak in their condo while they watched television in the middle of the afternoon.

Anyway, Matty had lived in this house his entire life, more or less. When the wind was up, the windows had always rattled in their fucking frames. His father had never done anything about it, and so neither had Matty. God, it sounds like the glass is going to break. But no, the glass won't break, because the glass has never broken. God, I should have lived somewhere else, Matty thought. Anywhere else. But where?

Ellen lay back down. Matty was on his back, too. She was as close to touching him as she could possibly be without actually touching him. Matty remembered when they were in high school and they'd gone to see a movie and their elbows were on the same armrest and Ellen was as close to touching him as she could possibly have been without actually touching him. This was exactly the opposite of that.

Still, they didn't talk. Matty's mind was nervous. It flitted from Locs to Ellen, Locs to Ellen. Where are you? his mind asked Locs. Where have you been? it asked Ellen. He turned a little and watched his wife watch the ceiling, watched her watch the ceiling for an unbearably long time, thought of the most irritating question one person can ask another person, remembered how Ellen had reacted to his asking that particular question many times over the years by answering as truthfully and pain-givingly as possible, tried to stop himself from asking that question, failed.

"What are you thinking?" he asked her.

"That I want a divorce."

"Seriously?" he said, and Ellen nodded, still looking at the ceiling, and then Matty rolled onto his back to look at it, too. Why did people look up in times of great distress or sadness?

Matty could imagine a student paper on the subject: *Through-out the history of mankind, in times of great famine or strife or war, people of all faiths and persuasions would look to the stars for guidance and comfort.* That paper would probably get an A–, despite the gross generalizations. But he and Ellen weren't looking at the stars; they were looking at the ceiling, which needed some serious replastering. Not much comfort there. The whole thing might fall on their heads at any time. Maybe then they could see the stars. Of course, they might already be crushed dead by the fallen ceiling. And possibly *there* was your comfort.

"Wow," Matty said.

"You asked," Ellen said.

"Fair enough," he said.

"I'm sorry, Matty," Ellen said, and she sounded like she meant it. She even put her hand on Matty's forearm and left it there for a little while, and by the time she moved the hand, Matty felt like he was married again, marriage being in this case something you feel like fighting for only after you've already lost it.

"Am I really going to lose you?" Matty asked.

"Yes," Ellen said. "I'm going to sleep now." Then she rolled away from Matty and did that.

I am not going to lose you. I am going to fight for you! Matty thought but did not say—mostly because of the transparent emptiness of the sentiment, but also because he wasn't totally sure whether he was thinking it about Ellen or Locs. And in either case, with what weapon would he fight? And at whom would he aim it?

PART FOUR

• • •

27

. . .

I have blood on my hands, Søren had decided to say to Jens Baedrup's widow.

"I'm going to tell her I have blood on my hands," was what he said to his friend Tarik.

"Not literally," Tarik said.

"Well, I might not use that exact phrase."

"No, I mean you don't literally have blood on your hands."

"Gasoline."

"And not even that anymore," Tarik said. He'd had gasoline on his hands, too. But not blood, literally or figuratively. And in any case, it had been four years ago. Tarik's general feeling on the matter was, Come on, that was four years ago.

"That's easy for you to say," Søren said. "You don't have blood on your hands."

They were walking along Skagen Havn. It was a Saturday, early fall, which felt a lot like early winter. The cold wind was making the sailboats wag and bobble and strain at their moorings. The light was low and giving shine to the dull tankers as they chugged in and out of port. Søren and Tarik had worked all day at the boatyard. Their jobs were decent, decent jobs they hadn't had four years ago. Four years, four years. The wind gusted and the white awnings flapped over the red fish houses.

Tarik said, "Why do we paint the fish houses red when we paint every other building in this town yellow?"

Søren didn't miss the "we." Four years ago, Tarik would not have said "we." That was why they both had gasoline on their hands now, except that Søren had more than just gasoline. That's why he needed to go see Jens Baedrup's widow.

"*We*," Søren repeated.

"Just keep my name out of it," Tarik said.

"You wouldn't say 'we,'" Søren said, "if you had blood on your hands."

28

• • •

Søren thought it would probably be difficult to find the address of the widow of a cartoonist whom he'd murdered in what the newspapers had called a terrorist firebombing, but that was not the case. It hadn't been difficult to find the cartoonist's address, either. It hadn't been difficult for Søren to burn down his house, or for Tarik to burn down the newspaper's offices. It hadn't even been difficult for them to escape capture after the firebombing, after the newspapers had reported that the cartoonist had died in the fire Søren had set. No one from the police or the Danish Security and Intelligence Service had ever questioned them, even though there were barely any Muslims in Skagen, and even though it had been the only murder committed in Skagen that year, and the year before that, and so on. Murder, murder; blood, blood. *That* was the difficult part: having the words *murder* and *blood* crawl through his head for the past four years. Although he supposed the murder hadn't been easy for the cartoonist, either. Not to mention his widow.

Anyway, she lived in Aarhus, just a couple of hours south. The newspaper reports had given him her name. The Internet had given him her address and then directions how to get there. But first Søren had to borrow his dad's car.

So he went home, which was less than a mile from the boat-yard where he and Tarik worked, right across the street from OC Trawl, where his father worked, making fishing nets. His house was the house in which Søren had grown up and in which he still lived. It was yellow, of course, and had a red tile roof, also of course. His parents' names were Faruk and Benan, but they'd named him Søren, although their last name was Korkmaz. As far as Søren was concerned, they might as well have just named him Dane, Son of Turks.

Søren walked in the front door. His father was sitting on the couch, watching professional handball on TV. Handball was his father's favorite sport, even though he didn't understand the rules, because pretty much no one understood the rules. You were allowed to run and leap and catch and hurl the ball, except, in some circumstances, for some mysterious reasons, when these activities were forbidden.

"Kolding and Aalborg," Søren's father said. "Don't tell me who won."

"What?"

"It was actually played last night," Søren's father said. "They're replaying it on TV now. Don't tell me who won."

Søren sat down next to his father, who smelled of salt and fish, even though the nets he made hadn't yet touched the sea. Or maybe it was Søren himself who smelled that way. He watched the handball for a minute, but then it started to hurt his eyes, and so he looked out the front window. It was dark, and darker still with the fog, which came right up to the window. A deep-throated horn blew out there somewhere, and the fog seemed to get somehow even thicker against the pane. It was one of those times when it was difficult to imagine that it wasn't six o'clock everywhere in the world. Søren turned back to the TV and saw a bunch of rangy white men in knee and elbow pads hugging each other.

"Goal?" he said.

"I believe so," his father said.

"I don't know how you can watch this stuff."

His father shrugged. "It's better than making nets." This was the way Søren's father talked. Something was always better than something else. When his wife, Søren's mother, had died several years earlier of breast cancer, he'd gone back to work making nets the day after, and when someone had asked him how he could go back to work making nets so soon after his wife's death, he had shrugged and said, "It's better than sitting at home."

"Can I borrow the car tomorrow morning?" Søren asked. And then he added, "Don't look at me like that."

"Look at you like what?" Søren's father said, still looking at him like that. His father's look: it had always been there. But it had gotten more intense, more squirm inducing, more *knowing*, since Søren had accidentally murdered the cartoonist. Or was that just Søren's imagination? In any case, Søren didn't know how much longer he could take it, the look, the look, the look that was made up of a litany of don'ts: don't disappoint me, don't make me look bad, don't make your people look bad, don't you know we moved to this country so you could be your own person, don't be someone else's person, don't forget that you're my son, don't do anything stupid, don't hurt the car, don't hurt yourself, don't you know that your mother told me before she died not to let anything happen to you, don't you know I'd die if something happened to you, don't make me die, don't kill me, don't kill yourself, don't kill anyone else, don't get caught if you do, don't do anything terrible, don't you know that I love you no matter what terrible thing you've done, don't forget that, don't do it again, don't make it worse, don't you know I know everything about you, don't cry, for crying out loud, don't cry because then I'll cry, just don't, don't, *do not*.

"Just don't forget to put gas in the car," Søren's father said, and he turned back to his handball.

29
· · ·

I sn't it Saturday?" the imam said. Søren was looking into the tiny eye at the top of his computer but was also looking at the screen itself. On it was a man his father's age with a long gray-black beard grown high on his cheeks, wearing thick-framed glasses with slightly tinted lenses and a white turban and white robes. At least Søren assumed they were robes: Søren had only ever seen the imam from the shoulders up. "Isn't it a Saturday night?" the imam asked.

"Please, I know," Søren said. There were no mosques in Skagen; there were no Muslim prayer groups in Skagen, either; there were no Muslims in town at all except for Søren and Tarik and their families. Before Søren had killed the cartoonist, he had not been religious; he had not felt religious; he had not felt the need to feel religious. But ever since then, ever since he had committed a crime that everyone seemed to think was a crime that could only be committed by a religious zealot, Søren had felt the need to feel something else, something greater that might keep him from feeling something worse than what he already felt. So he went online. The problem with going online was that the kind of people who wanted to give advice online tended to be people who were big advocates of things like burning and killing, and Søren had already done that. But finally, a few months earlier, Søren had received what seemed like a mass e-mail from this imam, a Turkish Dane from Copenhagen who claimed to be all the things Søren wanted—he was wise, he was gentle, he was measured, he was compassionate, he had a reliable Internet connection and the ability to skype—and it turned out he was all those things, although he could also be a bit of a nag when it came to the subject of how Søren spent his Saturday nights.

"It's a Saturday night," the imam said. "You should be out with your friends."

It is not Saturday night in my heart, Søren thought but did not say, because the imam tended to get very impatient with Søren when he said this kind of thing. "I don't really have any friends," Søren said.

"What about . . . ," the imam said, searching for the name of the friend Søren had mentioned before.

"Tarik," Søren said.

"Yes," the imam said. "Him."

"He's probably out with his friends."

"Is there a reason his friends can't be yours?"

Søren thought about this. He'd been out with Tarik and his friends on previous Saturday nights. Tarik's friends were all white Danes—people with whom he and Søren had gone to school, people with whom they worked down at the boatyard, random people from around Skagen, friends of friends. They often gathered at Tarik's apartment before they went out and did whatever. After work, Tarik would tell him, "Go home, shower, then come to my apartment. It'll be fun. Don't be such a mope." Søren would go home, shower, walk to Tarik's apartment. And then he would be such a mope. He couldn't seem to help himself. Every time Søren caught himself having even a little bit of fun, he would think, But I'm a murderer. Whenever one of Tarik's friends seemed to be looking at him even a little bit funny, Søren would think, I bet you think I killed that cartoonist. And then he would add, And you're right: I did. "You're such a mope," Tarik would say. "What's your problem?" But Tarik knew his problem.

"Yes," Søren said. "There's a reason."

"Is it a good reason?"

Søren shrugged. He'd never come close to telling his father what he had done, but several times over the past month Søren had come close to telling the imam. The urge is great among those guilty of serious crimes to confess to relative strangers who nevertheless seem, in some obscure way, trustworthy. But Søren never could quite do it. The imam might be affected by the confession, but he hadn't been directly affected by the thing to which Søren wanted to confess. He would confess to the imam, and still he would feel the need to confess to the cartoonist's widow. Søren shrugged again. "They just don't seem like my kind of people," he said. The imam just stared into the screen, waiting, and so Søren added, "I don't think they like me very much."

"And why is that?" the imam asked. When Søren shrugged again, the imam said, "Sometimes, in order to understand our enemies we must put ourselves in their place; we must try to see ourselves from their point of view."

"Is that from the Koran?" Søren asked. The imam had seemed shocked that Søren had never read the Koran, not once in his twenty-two years. So he made Søren buy a copy, suggested he read a page or so a night. Søren had done that. Perhaps it was wrong to say, about reading a holy book, that you were kind of enjoying it, but Søren was kind of enjoying it, although it also had the effect of making much of what the imam said seem like he might be quoting from the Koran.

The imam smiled. "No, that's all mine," he said. And then: "What about your father? What's he doing tonight?"

"He went out for a walk." This was true, although it was also true that Søren had no idea where his father went when we went for his Saturday night walks. After dinner on Saturday, Søren's father often went out for walks and then didn't come back until an hour or two later. Søren suspected that his father had a girlfriend, a suspicion that made him feel happy and also made him feel like the loneliest person in the world.

"Poor Søren," the imam said. "Everybody is out doing something. Everybody but you."

This was the kind of tough love the imam practiced when pushed. He could be kind, and gentle, and patient, but he also liked to mock Søren when those things didn't seem to be working. Usually Søren just shrugged and took it, because he didn't want the imam to give up on him. But not tonight. Tomorrow Søren was going to confess to the cartoonist's widow, and everything was probably going to change then anyway. So why not start changing things tonight? "Not everybody," Søren said. "It's a Saturday night for you, too. You're just as pathetic as I am."

The imam blinked once, twice. He smiled sadly at the computer screen. "Maybe you're right," he said. He leaned forward, into the screen, reached out his right arm, and then disappeared.

30

. . .

The next morning, Søren stopped at the gas station near Gammel Skagen, on the way south out of town.

Gas stations were the worst, in Søren's opinion. A guy with Søren's skin color could go into a supermarket in Skagen to buy a loaf of bread without being especially scrutinized. But the minute you tried to buy something potentially explosive or flammable, you were suddenly terrorist material.

But then again . . .

Anyway, he went inside to prepay. At the counter, there was an American in front of him. Søren had seen only a few Americans in Skagen—they didn't seem to ever make it this far north—but he'd seen lots of them on TV. The Americans on TV talked basically like an exaggerated version of the way this woman talked, and both were less refined versions of the way Søren himself had been taught to speak English in school. The woman wore a baseball hat, with a big white letter *C* against a bright red backdrop.

"No, I don't need a PIN," she was saying to the clerk, who was holding the American's credit card.

The clerk just shrugged. His head was somewhat like the

American's hat. His hair and eyebrows were so blond they were almost white, and his face was ruddy. He swiped the card, then swiveled the card reader so that the American could read it. "It says to please enter your PIN, please," he said in English.

"But I don't *have* that," the American said. It seemed to Søren like she was trying not to cry. She took off her baseball hat, mussed her black hair, and then put the hat back on. Meanwhile the clerk smiled. The smile seemed genuine; the smiler, imperturbable. Everything about him, his hair, his eyes, his soul, communicated, Don't worry, we'll figure this out. "I bet you can just push a button or something so I don't need one."

"You don't need one what?"

"A PIN," the American said. "P-I-N."

"Yes," the agreeable clerk said. "That spells PIN. That is what you need."

The American looked down at the machine. She hit four numbers in a hurry, not even seeming to try to guess what might be the right ones, just getting it over with. The machine made known its displeasure. And the American then reached into her purse, pulled out a bunch of kroner, gave the cash to the clerk, and then retreated to her automobile.

Then it was Søren's turn. He smiled in comradely fashion at the clerk, who was busy counting the kroner and then putting each bill in with its denominational kin. When he was done, the clerk smiled at Søren until he lifted his head and actually saw Søren. Not that he then stopped smiling. But the smile changed. It was the way that white Danes tended to smile at Søren: with equal parts accusation and apology. He turned the machine in

Søren's direction. Søren swiped his card, entered the PIN. The machine beeped in affirmation. But still, the clerk then asked to see Søren's credit card, and also his driver's license, all the while still smiling that smile, which said, I am truly sorry, I recognize you're a human being, and a Danish citizen, just like me, except that I am a Danish citizen who doesn't get asked to show my driver's license when buying gasoline, but then again, I'm not a religious extremist who has used gasoline to blow up or burn up people, places, and things, but then again, you probably haven't, either, odds are very strong that you've also not committed arson or murder, and what a shame it is that I'm even for a moment thinking of you as someone who has committed arson and murder, it's actually worse than a shame that I'm thinking of you in that way, it's actually a crime, but not a crime like arson and murder are crimes, I think we can all come to an agreement on that topic, and I think we can also all agree that this is a great, civilized, open-minded country, and that is why you came here, or your parents came here, because it's such a great, civilized, open-minded country, and I'm sincerely glad, we're all sincerely glad, that you came here, because just by your mere presence you're confirming our sense that it is a great, civilized, open-minded country, or at least it was until you people started with your burning and killing and basically making it a little less great, a little less civilized, a little less open minded, but hey, I see from your credit card and driver's license that your name is Søren, how funny, good for you, here's your receipt, Søren, have a great day, drive safely, don't forget that we'll probably be watching you.

Or maybe that was just the guilt talking. Søren couldn't be

sure. That was why he had to go confess to the widow. Murder, murder, he reminded himself. Blood, blood.

Søren took his receipt and exited the building. On the way to his car he passed the American, who was still filling her car, and also talking on her cell phone.

"You said I didn't need a PIN," she was saying. "Well, if it wasn't *you*, it was someone like *you*." The second time she said "you," she was looking directly at Søren as he walked by.

31

. . .

The cartoonist's widow's house in Aarhus wasn't as pretty as the one Søren had burned down in Skagen. It wasn't even in Aarhus proper, but rather just outside the city; it looked pretty much the same as any place just outside any city in northern Europe. It was a two-story box among other two-story boxes—sleek, metallic, energy efficient, soul deficient, with lots of louvered windows that wouldn't even open far enough for you to jump out of them, if there happened to be a fire.

Am I really going to do this? thought Søren, and then he rang the bell before he could think it again. He heard footsteps from within. The door opened. A very pretty woman—white-blond hair, slender, attractive squinty sun lines in the corners of her pale blue eyes—appeared in the doorway. She was wearing workout clothes—black tights that ended just above the ankle, and a tight-fitting bright blue warm-up jacket—although she was also wearing clogs. These were clothes meant to communicate, I'm just hanging out, being myself, being comfortable, but also only a quick change in footwear away from launching into a really strenuous cardiovascular workout. "Hi, hi," she said, without noticing it was Søren standing there. But when she saw it was Søren, her eyes went wide. Søren recognized the look. It was the look white Danes sometimes had when Danes who were also probably Muslims knocked on their door. But with Ilsa, Søren guessed, even more so.

"Ilsa?" Søren asked, although he knew it was she. He'd seen a picture of her on the Internet. It was a picture taken by a newspaper, directly after he'd killed her husband. In the picture she looked so sad, so horrified, and she looked that way now, too. What have I done? was what Søren had thought when he'd seen the picture, and he thought it now, also. Nothing had changed: Ilsa was still a widow, Søren a murderer; Ilsa was still sad, Søren was still guilty. Things had to change. This was another reason he had to confess. No matter the consequences, which, honestly, were so overwhelming and awful that Søren hadn't really allowed himself to consider them. "Ilsa Baedrup?" he said.

"Oh no," Ilsa said. She took a step back into the house, and Søren took a step closer.

"Please forgive me," Søren said, and he was about to explain for what when Ilsa blurted out, "I don't know where Jens is! I promise!"

"What's that?" Søren said. But Ilsa had already slammed the door shut. He could hear the lock click and then a bolt *thunk* into place. "What are you talking about?" Søren said. "Jens is *dead*." Ilsa didn't say anything, but she didn't need to: she'd said enough already, enough to make Søren feel as if he could finally *think*. For four years it had been as though there'd been a door in Søren's head constantly banging shut

and then opening, making too much noise, letting things in
that he wanted out. But now, a bolt *thunked* into place in his
head, too. The cartoonist is not dead, he thought. I did not kill
the cartoonist. I did not kill anyone at all. I am not a murderer.
That made him so happy, but then he also thought: Four years,
four years, I've wasted four years thinking I was a murderer.
And that made him so angry that suddenly he really did want
to kill someone. Søren started banging on the door. "He's supposed to be dead," he yelled.

"I'm calling the police!" Ilsa shouted from inside the house.

"Your husband is supposed to be dead!" he said, and then
he kept banging and shouting, "Supposed to be dead!" loudly
enough and for long enough that some of the neighbors started
louvering their windows closed, or open, depending on the
previous state of their windows and depending on what kind
of people they were.

"You really don't want to be here when the police come,"
a woman's voice said behind him. She spoke in English. Søren
turned and saw it was the American from the gas station in
Skagen, the one who couldn't get her credit card to work. She was
still wearing her baseball hat with the letter *C* on it, but otherwise she looked almost completely different. Not so helpless
anymore. She smiled at him, the way people do when they want
you to know that they know something that you want to know.

"How do you know?"

"I just do."

"I don't care," Søren said. "I want to know where her husband is."

"I know that, too," the woman said.

32

. . .

Søren followed the woman back to Skagen, to a house, a holiday cabin, snug in the dunes of Gammel Skagen. Søren got out of his car, looked up, and saw smoke coming from the chimneys of all the other houses nestled in the dunes. Otherwise, it seemed like they were alone, alone with the gulls and the distant sound of the waves and the blowing sand.

Søren and the woman walked inside the house, into the kitchen, where they sat across from each other at a scarred wooden table. The house had other rooms, and they'd passed through a couple of them on the way to the kitchen, but the kitchen was the only room that contained furniture. "Do I know you?" he asked.

"I know you," the woman said. "You live on Lochersvej with your father. Your mother is dead. Your little buddy lives just down the street from you."

"Tarik?" Søren said.

"No need to thank us for getting you and your little buddy those jobs at the boatyard."

Søren thought about that. Neither Tarik nor he had had

any experience making boats, or fixing boats, or taking care of boats, or even being passengers on boats. And yet they applied for jobs and their applications were immediately accepted. "We had no experience," Søren said.

"You didn't have any experience burning down buildings, either," the woman said. "And yet . . ."

Søren just looked at her in amazement. You know everything about me, he thought, and then he wondered whether she knew that he was thinking that. Was this what meeting Allah would be like? Søren wondered. You lived your life thinking that you had some control over it, that you were the one making important decisions, and then you met Allah, who said, Well, actually . . .

"Why didn't you arrest me?"

"I knew you were thinking that."

"I hate you."

"And that's why we didn't arrest you. Because there's lots of people who already hate us. If we arrested you, then other Muslims would have rallied around you. There might have been more fires. Someone might have actually been killed this time. We thought it would be better for everyone if we pretended the cartoonist was dead."

It wasn't better for me, Søren thought. But was that even true? Was it worse to go to prison for arson or to stay free and believe you were a murderer? But it was impossible to say definitively, because he had only had experience staying free and believing he was a murderer.

"Plus," the woman said, "you didn't seem all that bad. We didn't think it was likely that you'd be killing anyone else."

"That's true," Søren said, before he remembered. It was difficult to instantly recall that everything you'd believed about yourself for four years was an absolute lie. "But I didn't kill anyone in the first place!"

"That's right," the woman said, chuckling. "Sometimes I forget that, too."

"I hate you so much," Søren said.

"Well, yeah," the woman said. "But I bet you hate someone else even more."

Søren thought about that. He knew she was talking about the cartoonist. How much *did* Søren hate him? On the one hand, he hated that the cartoonist was still alive. On the other hand, Søren loved that he had not killed him. Meanwhile the woman was watching him think. "Because he definitely hates you," she said. "Just in case you were wondering."

"Why are you telling me all this?"

"I want you to kill him," the woman said.

"Why don't you do it yourself?"

"That's a common misunderstanding about secret agents. We don't usually kill people ourselves. We usually try to get other people to do it for us."

"We," repeated Søren.

"What's that?"

"You said 'we.' 'We don't usually kill people ourselves.'"

"OK."

"But before that you said 'I.' 'I want you to kill him.'"

"I meant 'we,'" the woman said.

Did you? Søren thought, carefully considering her, and also the table between them. The table really was scarred—big random furrows crisscrossing the surface—and faded, too, like it had been left too long out in the weather. This was a table that had been abandoned, not sold or bought. The house seemed abandoned, too: it was cold in the kitchen, Søren could see his breath. The lights weren't on, either. The woman seemed to see him assessing the room; she adjusted her hat, then adjusted it again. "You didn't even know the PIN for your credit card," Søren said.

"Listen, Søren," she said, putting both hands on the table. It wobbled a little when she did that. "Are you going to kill him or not?"

Søren sat back in his chair to think about it. He thought about how awful it had felt when he'd actually believed he was a murderer and how he never wanted to feel that way again. But then Søren thought of that cartoon, and then of the cartoonist, out there somewhere, having a good laugh over how he and this woman and who knows who else had tricked Søren into thinking he was something he was not for the past four years, and suddenly Søren was overwhelmed by a sense of the world's injustice: he could actually feel the injustice, in his head and around his eyes, like it was a sinus thing. It was the kind of feeling that you would do almost anything to get rid of. But did that include murder? "I just don't know," Søren said, and the woman nodded as though she'd expected that answer. She took her cell phone out of her jacket pocket and said, "I wonder what your father will think when I call and tell him about his terrorist-arsonist son."

"No!" Søren said. Because suddenly he could see his father's face, the look on it making the journey from disbelief to disappointment to shame. The only thing worse than your father finding out about the terrible things you've done is thinking about your father finding out about the terrible things you've done. "I'll do it," Søren said.

"I knew you would," the woman said. She smiled quickly, showing no teeth, and then talked, in detail, about how Søren was going to do what she wanted him to do.

PART FIVE

• • •

33

...

One o'clock, the first Wednesday in October. Henry's office. Kurt, sixteen years old, fresh from driver's ed, confiding in his guidance counselor, who in three days was also going to be his stepfather.

"Dad seems lonely," Kurt was saying, and Mr. L. crossed his arms, frowned. Kurt tried again. "Dad *is* lonely," he said, and Mr. L. stopped frowning, as though to say, That's more like it.

"And that makes you feel . . ."

"Like shit," Kurt said, and then he waited to be reprimanded for his language. His mother and his father would have done exactly that. But Henry just looked at him, quizzically, the way he sometimes still did when confronted with the American vernacular.

"And then I come here and talk to you and feel better," Kurt said. He felt about Henry the traditional way you feel about your mother's boyfriend, and also your guidance counselor: you didn't want to trust him but ended up doing so anyway, although always with an eye toward returning to your original feelings. But the more time went by, the more distant those original feelings seemed, the more Kurt genuinely liked and trusted his almost stepfather, and the more he liked and trusted Henry, the more guilty he felt about his father being so lonely. "And that makes me feel worse than shit," Kurt said.

Henry frowned. "Worse than shit?" he asked. "Can one have that feeling?"

Kurt shrugged. "One can. I can. My dad can." Then he stared baldly at Henry. Sometimes he did this when the subject of his parents came up. Kurt did not really believe Henry was the cause of his parents' breakup. Kurt knew, mostly because they'd tried so desperately to hide it from him, that his parents had been in the process of breaking up ever since he was old enough to pay attention. Still, sometimes he liked to stare accusingly at Henry to see whether he could make Henry act guilty. He never did. Kurt stopped staring. "I feel sad for him," Kurt said.

"He has you," Henry said.

"Ugh," Kurt said.

"He has his brother," Henry said, and Kurt said, "Ugh," again, and this time Henry seemed to almost laugh. His uncle Lawrence was of course a well-known freak, but Henry's almost laughing made Kurt turn perverse and want to defend his uncle.

"Uncle Lawrence isn't so bad," Kurt said. He remembered a conversation his parents had had once, back when they were still married. Kurt's mother had been getting on his father's case for the way he treated his brother during one of their regular Sunday cocktail hour arguments. "You act like you don't even love him," she'd said. "Oh, I love him," his dad had said. "I don't think that I trust him, but I do love him." "Although

I don't think that I trust him," Kurt said now to Henry. And then he stared baldly again at Henry, just for kicks. But Henry shocked him this time by answering his stare, out loud.

"You can trust me, Kurt," Henry said. And wow, Kurt wanted to hug him right then. Instead he said, "Ugh," one more time and then got up to leave the office. But before he reached the doorway, Kurt turned and looked back at Henry.

"That was a good talk," he said, and Henry nodded gravely, as if he somehow knew it was the last good talk they would ever have.

34

. . .

Just before three o'clock, Henry looked up and saw a stout, dark-bearded, sleepy-eyed man standing in the doorway. On the door, which was open, was a sign that read MR. LARSEN, GUIDANCE COUNSELOR. On the other side of the cramped room was a metal desk, and on the other side of *that* was Henry himself. The stranger looked at the sign on the door and smirked. Then, still smirking, he looked at Henry's face, and most carefully, too, like he was committing it to memory, like a traveler might read an itinerary, which, of course, in Henry's case would have said Skagen, then Copenhagen, Stockholm, Oslo, Saint Petersburg, Paris, London, and so on and so on until finally here, in his office at the Broomeville Junior-Senior High School in Broomeville, New York.

"Larsen," the man finally said. "That's a Danish name."

In response, Henry did what by now came naturally: he frowned. Because this was what you did as his patient, or student, or whatever you called the person who came to see the guidance counselor: you uttered a declarative sentence. And this is what he did as your guidance counselor: he frowned to let you know he disapproved of the inaccuracy of your declaration.

Whereupon you tried again. This was Henry's method, for which he was famous throughout the school, and into the town of Broomeville, too, a declarative sentence that, had he heard it, would not have caused him to frown. In fact, just before the stranger appeared, Henry had sat down with Pete Schuyler, a crooked-toothed tenth grader who'd gotten into a fistfight after the football game against Lowville the Friday before. It was Monday, and the cut below Pete's left eye was still raw, still glistening with ooze. The fight had been with a senior at Lowville High, and when Henry asked Pete about the reason for the fight, Pete said, "Because he was a retard farmer."

Henry just frowned in response, as Pete must have known he would, as most anyone in Broomeville would have known he would. "If you're from Lowville, then you're automatically a retard farmer," Pete protested. "Everyone knows this. It's just common knowledge."

Henry frowned at that, too. He knew he was locally famous for his frown, for his method, and didn't mind, because after all, he had been internationally famous for something else, and that, he had minded. That, he still minded. Now, Henry was forced to think of the other people who might mind learning about his international fame—oh God: Ellen, Kurt, not to mention the stranger, who might do more than just "mind."

"Larsen, that's a Danish name," the stranger had said a few seconds earlier. The stranger then repeated the statement. But before Henry could respond again with his famous frown, someone said, "Mr. L.?" A second later, Jenny Tallent stepped into the office. As usual, everything about Jenny seemed to be wrong on purpose. Her hair was cut lopsidedly and dyed a color somewhere between red wine and mud. Her pants were black and baggy, and off one of the belt loops hung a chain that wasn't attached to anything. She was wearing a heavy, oversize black hooded jacket even though it was an unusually warm October afternoon; there were two strings hanging from the jacket on either side of her neck, and one of them was considerably longer than the other and looked wet. Henry guessed Jenny had been sucking on it, again. Her ears weren't pierced, nor was her nose or either of her eyebrows or her lips, but there was a metal rivet lodged in the left side of her neck, at the center of a tattooed bull's-eye. The bull's-eye and the rivet seemed to do something to the stranger. He got up and, without saying any last thing to Henry or any first thing to the girl, walked briskly out of the office.

"Who was *that* guy?" Jenny asked. Normally, her bull's-eye and rivet spooked him, too. But just now, he didn't think he'd ever been so relieved to see anyone in his life.

Help me! Henry said to Jenny in his mind. Shut up! he said to himself in the same place. He'd been telling himself to shut up for two years, since he first moved to Broomeville. That he'd managed to do so was a major part of his happiness, not to mention his method.

"I don't know," Henry told Jenny. Before she could ask him any more questions, he said, "What going on, Jenny?"

"Principal Klock sent me to tell you: *baseball*." She said "baseball" the way the stranger had said "Danish": "Larsen, that's a *Danish* name." The stranger had said it twice: the first time he'd spoken in Danish, and the second in English, even though Henry had understood the Danish perfectly well.

35
· · ·

Wednesday, October 6, 2011, 11:32 p.m.
From: undisclosed sender
To: undisclosed recipient
Subject: Broomeville

My first encounter with "Mr. Larsen" in his office was interrupted
by one of his female students. Nothing to worry about. I will visit
Larsen again tomorrow and begin the next stage of our plan.

36

. . .

*B*aseball meant it was time again for the annual student-faculty baseball game. Henry had never completely understood why this game took place during football season, nor why it was called a student-faculty baseball game when the only students who played in the game were already on the baseball and softball teams, and the only faculty who played were the faculty who coached baseball or softball. The only thing that made sense about the game was that everyone—students, faculty, staff—was required to go to it: in the case of an out-of-season, inaptly named student-faculty baseball game, you had to require attendance if you wanted people to attend.

The game had already started by the time Henry and Jenny arrived. Jenny went to lean against the fence with the other kids who dressed like something was wrong with them. Henry went to sit by *Dr.* Vernon, who was sitting by himself halfway up the bleachers. He was wearing a blue-and-yellow Hawaiian shirt with parrots perched on either end of a branch. The branch was supposed to span the shirt wearer's pectorals, but

Dr. Vernon was hunched over in such a way that it looked as though the parrots were feasting on his nipples.

"Hello, Henry."

"*Dr.* Vernon."

Dr. Vernon (his first name was Barry, but no one at the school ever called him anything but *Dr.* Vernon, with the italics) was the school's long-term sub. If you went to Broomeville Junior-Senior High School, then sooner or later *Dr.* Vernon would be your long-term sub, but he would never be your regular teacher because even though he (supposedly) had his doctorate in something or other, he couldn't be bothered to get his teacher's certificate. He was that kind of guy. He was also the kind of guy who always wore loud Hawaiian shirts, including to the student-faculty baseball games, where he would announce loud, possibly comic, play-by-play calls of the game to the crowd. For instance, just as Henry sat down next to him, *Dr.* Vernon had yelled out, "Jared Johnson hits a scorcher to short," when in fact Jared had hit a dribbler that had barely made it to the pitcher's mound. It was unclear to Henry whether *Dr.* Vernon's commentary was meant to be optimistic or sarcastic, but in any case it was found by almost everyone within earshot to be incredibly annoying. "Why don't you deck him?" Grace Vernon shouted to Henry. Grace was sitting several rows behind them. She was a home ec teacher at the school, and like so many who've had that calling, she seemed as though she'd blown in from some prairie in her long-sleeved sundresses and heavy braids and her crafty ways of making a little go a long way. She was also *Dr.* Vernon's wife. "Why don't you deck him already?" she asked Henry.

"Why don't you?"

"He *likes* it when I deck him," Grace announced. "It only encourages him."

Dr. Vernon turned in her direction. "That's true, sweetie," he said, beaming. Then he turned back to the field and said, in response to a lazy pop fly to the first baseman, "A Ruthian blast to right field. Going, going, going . . ."

That was it: Grace charged down the stairs, the metal bleachers bonging and vibrating in her wake, punched her husband hard in the upper arm, and then ran back to her seat, where she was greeted with cheers. Meanwhile, *Dr.* Vernon rubbed his arm, still beaming, encouraged.

"See?" Grace said to everyone. Then to Henry she said, "How you can *stand* to sit next to that fool anyway?"

Stand to sit? Henry thought but did not say. Instead he waited a few seconds, then leaned closer to *Dr.* Vernon. The urge is great among those in hiding to casually test other people's knowledge of the events that necessitated their going underground in the first place. Henry had resisted the urge for so long. For the past two years he'd resisted it so expertly that he didn't really feel the urge anymore. But now that the stranger had shown up, Henry felt it again, more strongly than ever.

"Do you remember a few years ago," Henry said, whispered actually, "the controversy about the Danish cartoonist Jens Baedrup?"

"Your mother was a hamster and your father smelt of elderberries!" *Dr.* Vernon shouted—not at Henry but at the umpire. This was another thing he did at these baseball games: he insulted the umpire—Matty—by way of quotes from Monty

Python movies. Matty took off his mask and looked in the direction of the insult. He smiled at *Dr.* Vernon, then stopped smiling and gave Henry a more complicated look, a look meant to communicate, among other things: I'm watching you, buddy, don't forget that, and don't forget that I know your secrets, or at least I know some of your secrets, or at least I know what someone else has told me about some of your secrets, or at least I know you have secrets, otherwise you wouldn't be here, not that you're the only one around here with secrets, God knows, and maybe one day you and I will drink some beers and talk about them, and Jesus, that would feel *good,* wouldn't it, wouldn't it feel fucking *great* to finally stop lying, to tell the truth, not to everyone, just to one person, just to have one person you can sit down next to at the bar and rip open your chest and reveal your terrible secret heart to and have that person sitting next to you at the bar not judge you or hate you for what's in that heart, for what you've done, a buddy, a true friend who will say, after you've shown him your heart, I'm so glad you just did that, I understand, we all have our secrets, this is what makes us human, this is what makes *me* human, now it's my turn, now I'm going to rip open my chest, etc., and so hey, let's get those beers someday soon, although speaking of beers, I know that in three days you're going to be marrying Ellen down at the bar, and I'm glad, or at least I'm going to act like I'm glad, because I know you make her happy, and also because the other day she told me, when I said, casually, like your marrying her didn't bother me, because it doesn't, I said, Hey, don't you think you're making a terrible mistake marrying this joker, and when I said that, she told me not to be a jealous dick, that I, of all people, have no right to be a jealous dick, and so here I am, not being a jealous dick, no, this is me being glad you're going to marry my ex-wife, but make no mistake, every time I think about you touching Ellen, even accidentally, I want to murder you, but hey, I hope you're enjoying the baseball game. Then Matty put his mask back on and squatted back down behind the catcher.

After that, neither *Dr.* Vernon nor Henry spoke for such a long time that Henry started to forget that he'd ever asked *Dr.* Vernon the question about the Danish cartoonist, the way, before the stranger had shown up, he'd almost managed to forget that he'd ever been anything but a public-school guidance counselor in upstate New York.

"Danish cartoonist, huh?" *Dr.* Vernon finally said. "That *might* ring a bell. Remind me."

But Henry did not end up reminding *Dr.* Vernon. Instead he started looking at the students sitting down near the fence. Specifically he was looking at Jenny, who seemed to be telling a crowd of students—including Kurt and his two cronies—a story. Henry assumed, and was afraid, that it was a good story, because for once, people actually seemed to be listening to her.

37

. . .

Wednesday, October 6, 2011, 11:43 p.m.
From: undisclosed sender
To: undisclosed recipient
Subject: re: Broomeville

What do you mean, "encounter"? What do you mean, "visit"?
What do you mean, "next stage of our plan"? There's only one
stage. That one stage is the whole plan. If I were to write out the
entire plan, it would read, "Kill him."

38

...

And then he went *ga borg ga borg ga borg gya*," Jenny was saying. "And when Mr. L. didn't say anything back, the guy said in English, 'Larsen: that's a *Danish* name.'"

"And then you walked in and the guy took off," Kevin said. This was the fourth time Jenny had told the story. She'd had to tell it a second time because no one listened to her the first time, because no one ever listened to her the first time. She'd had to tell it a third time because too many people had mistaken the moral of the story to be that Jenny was so unbelievably gross that her mere entrance into a room would cause anyone else in that room to flee, even a mysterious stranger. She'd had to tell it a fourth time because after the third telling, everyone realized that something truly strange was happening and that it'd be useful to hear the facts from Jenny one more time. Now, after the fourth telling, everyone seemed to understand the facts of the story, and they were ready to reach a conclusion.

"He's a gay," Tyler said.

"Wait, who is?"

"Well, they both are, obviously. Both Mr. L. and this guy. His lover."

"His *lover*? Did you just use the word *lover*?"

"What? It's a word. *Lover*. Someone *who loves*."

"What makes you think Mr. L. is gay?" Jenny said.

"There's lots of reasons," Tyler said, and he proceeded to list them: that Mr. L. had always acted in a secretive, gay-like manner; that this man, whom no one had ever seen before, was therefore logically part of this secret; that when you catch two men alone in a room and one of them then flees, that is more or less definitive proof of their homosexuality; that the stranger had spoken to Mr. L. in gay code.

"It wasn't code," Jenny said. "It was a language."

"What language, since you know so much?"

"Danish?" Jenny guessed. "Isn't Mr. L. from Denmark?"

"He's from Sweden," Kurt said.

"Aw," Tyler said, waving his hand dismissively. "Norland."

"He's from Sweden," Kurt said again, but he wasn't really talking to them. He was simply going through the facts, going through them in his head but also out loud, as though he were studying for a test. "But according to this stranger, he has a Danish name."

"*And* he's gay," Tyler said.

"He's not gay," Kurt said.

"How do you know?"

"How do I *know*?" Kurt said. "Because he's getting married to my mother on Saturday. *That's* how I know."

No one responded to that information immediately, though Kurt could sense how much everyone resented him for using this basic point of fact to destroy their fantastic hypothesis.

"Well, what is he, then?" Tyler finally said.

"I don't know *what* he is," Kurt admitted. He looked up at the stands. A moment earlier Mr. L. had been sitting with *Dr.* Vernon. But now *Dr.* Vernon was sitting by himself. No wonder, since he was wearing that ridiculous shirt and yelling those ridiculous things at Kurt's father and supposedly having the ridiculous degree of doctor of philosophy and the ridiculous title of permanent substitute teacher. He was pretty close to unbearable. The only thing that prevented him from being totally unbearable was that he sold pot to Kurt and his cronies whenever they needed it. Before Jenny had walked over, in fact, Kurt and his cronies had been talking about how much they needed it. Kurt waved hello at *Dr.* Vernon as a way of saying not hello but, We need to buy some pot from you later on, and *Dr.* Vernon waved back as a way of saying, Yeah, you do. Sometimes that's all Kurt could think about: how much he needed to smoke some pot. Although now he was also thinking about something else. *You can trust me, Kurt,* Mr. L. had said. That had been only an hour ago. He'd believed him then. Now he didn't know what to believe. "I don't know what he is," Kurt said about Mr. L. "Maybe he's a spy or something." Kurt had intended that as a joke, but the moment he said it, he felt he'd hit on something close to the truth and didn't want to talk to them about it anymore.

39

• • •

arsen, that's a Danish name," he'd said, first in Danish, and then in English. Although that was not part of the plan that Søren had made with the American secret agent. That plan was simple: Søren would find the cartoonist, and he would kill him. The American agent had wanted Søren to kill the cartoonist with a gun, but Danes, even murderous Danes, are famously opposed to guns, and Søren said that he'd rather use something else. A knife, for instance.

"A *knife*?" the American agent had said. Her face was pinched, as though she found the idea of using a knife to kill someone particularly distasteful.

"I don't know how to use a gun," Søren had explained.

"Jesus, a *knife*?" the American agent had said. "Why don't you just hit him with a *rock* or something?"

"But where would I get a gun?"

"Oh, I could tell you where to get a gun," the American agent had said.

"But could you tell me where to get a knife?" Søren had said, and the American agent had had to think about it for a long time before saying, "You know, I'm not even sure. I guess at the knife store?"

In the end, Søren had purchased the knife at something called a superstore, which the bus had passed on its way into Broomeville. In the superstore you could buy enormous tubs of mayonnaise and blinking shoes for your children and lawn mowers and boxes of cereal and prescription drugs and also, in a section right next to the other store sections, lethal weapons, including guns and also knives. The knife Søren had bought was a big-bladed thing with smooth edges and a deep, deep groove. The man who sold Søren the knife seemed to think that Søren was missing an excellent opportunity. He cocked his head in the direction of the wall lined with mounted pistols, rifles, shotguns, and semiautomatic weapons of all kinds, and asked, "You sure you don't want something else? It doesn't have to be a knife."

Anyway, Søren had bought the knife, placed it in its protective sleeve and attached the sleeve to his belt, made sure it was obscured by his jacket, and then walked to the high school. The American agent had told him where to go. "Just walk in the front door, like you've done it every day of your life. No one will stop you if you do that. Find the stairs that lead to the basement. They always put the guidance counselor in the basement."

"What's a guidance counselor?" Søren had wanted to know.

"He's the jerk you're going to kill," the American agent had said.

Søren had found the cartoonist in the basement. But then

he immediately began to have doubts about his mission. For instance, this guidance counselor was a white man and the cartoonist was a white man, but other than that, they did not strongly resemble each other. Was this man the same man? Was this man even Danish? He did have a Danish name. Which lead Søren to make his statement, first in Danish and then in English. But this Larsen didn't respond to either language: he just sat there, arms crossed, frowning, as though asking Søren, Are you really going to do this?

And then the girl with the disturbing neck had walked into the room and Søren realized that he was not really going to do this. So he'd fled, out of the room, past a janitor mopping the hall floor, up the stairs, glancing nervously from side to side as he ran, looking very much like he was someone who had *not* entered and exited the Broomeville Junior-Senior High School every day of his life. He opened the school's front door and thought the same thing so many other people exiting that building had thought before him—Freedom!—and then someone pulled Søren's arms behind his back and quickly bound them with something and then a black four-door sedan pulled up in the circular drive outside the school and the person behind Søren reached around him and opened the back door and pushed Søren in so that Søren fell facedown on the seat. "Scoot over," the man said. Søren did that. The man climbed in next to him, slammed the door shut. Then the car, which smelled strongly of kitchen grease and potatoes, drove off. There were two people in the front seat. Søren could see only the back of their heads but could tell nonetheless that the driver was a man and the passenger a woman. He turned and looked at the man sitting next to him. He was approximately Søren's age and was holding what looked to Søren like a black bag or sack.

"Can I put this on his head now?" the man asked the people in the front seat. The driver didn't speak, and would not speak, but the woman laughed. It was a dry, barking, mirthless laugh. A smoker's laugh if Søren had ever heard one.

"I don't know why you need to put it on at all," the woman said. "What's he going to see? Who's he going to tell?"

"Just in case," the man said, and the woman laughed again. It made Søren's lungs hurt to hear it. Otherwise he felt calm, maybe because the conversation was so obviously meant to make him feel scared. Suddenly he saw himself at his father's house. He was finally telling his father that he was the one who'd burned down the cartoonist's house. He pictured his father listening carefully, the look on his face making the journey from disbelief to disappointment to shame to relief as Søren told him the story of how he had not killed the cartoonist after all, that he'd only been manipulated into thinking so, and then manipulated by the American agent into going to America to kill the cartoonist for real, which he ended up not being able to do, and then, once he told these three American agents this, told them where in Skagen the other American agent was living, they would let him go. Søren would tell his father all this, and his father would say, "Don't worry, Søren, everything is going to be just fine." How had Søren not known he would say this? How had he not seen that everything really was going to be just fine?

"It would make me feel better, OK?" the man next to Søren said, and the woman sighed. And only then did the man turn to face Søren. He was holding the bag with his left hand. With his right hand he ruffled the back of his head, the way you do when you're trying to get used to a new haircut. "I'm sorry," the man said, and before he put the bag over Søren's head, Søren thought he saw the man's eyes watering a little, and that ended up being the last thing that Søren ever saw.

40

. . .

Wednesday, October 6, 2011, 11:48 p.m.
From: undisclosed sender
To: undisclosed recipient
Subject: re: Broomeville

The plan has changed. As yours did for me. Plans change. Is this
the nature of plans?

41

. . .

The Lumber Lodge wasn't even officially open. The front door was unlocked, but the beer lights were off. The chairs were still on the tables, the barstools still upside down on the bar. The floor was still sticky from the night before. Why, Ellen wondered, is the floor sticky even though I mopped it? And then she remembered that she hadn't mopped it. She'd been too tired to mop it. But she'd not been too tired to put the chairs on the tables and the barstools on the bar. Even though she knew that she was not going to mop the floor, even though she had no intention of mopping the floor, she had still put the goddamn chairs and stools up. And why? Because she always put the goddamn chairs and stools up before she mopped the goddamn floor. And you really did have to mop the floor before you went home. Because if you didn't, then the next day you would hate yourself, and your floors, and your bar, and your *life*. Ellen's feet made a disgusting sound as she walked. It sounded like a mouse getting stuck in something over and over again. Saturday, she thought, smiling. Saturday, I am getting married on Saturday, and maybe after that I will sell this bar, and Henry and Kurt and I will . . . But she didn't get to finish the thought. Because just then, Ronald Crimmins walked in. He must have just come straight from school, because he was wearing his janitor's uniform and smelled faintly of chemical disinfectant. His bad hand was sort of snuggled into the mouth of his pants pocket while the other was bouncing against his thigh.

"We're closed," Ellen said.

"Then let me help you open," Ronald said. He walked over to the nearest table and with his good hand took the three chairs off it and put them on the floor. Then he worked his way around the room, taking chairs off the tables, placing them around the tables. He did this quickly, but not carelessly the way Ellen herself sometimes did. Sometimes, Ellen just dumped the chairs wherever, which gave the impression that a tableful of people had gotten up in a hurry and probably also run out on their bill.

Now the chairs were around the tables. Ronald had taken the barstools down, too, and was sitting on one of them, legs extended. The toes of his brown work boots were so scuffed they were almost white, and the laces were double-looped and knotted and still they were too long. Ronald was staring at Ellen, head cocked, as though to say, What else?

"I'm not hiring, Ronald," Ellen said. Because she knew this was how Ronald had gotten his job at the school: he'd basically hung around the school on a volunteer basis, emptying trash cans and erasing graffiti and basically making himself useful until Matty had just gone ahead and hired him.

"Why'd you do that?" Ellen had asked him. This was a year and a half ago, a couple of months after Ellen had moved out, but before the divorce had officially gone through, and so Matty still had hopes of proving to her that she shouldn't leave him after all and that he was a good guy.

"Because I'm a good guy," Matty had said. That was part of it. But the other part of it was that Matty felt guilty about firing Ronald's sister, who then killed herself. That was Matty all over. When he wasn't being a good guy, he felt guilty for not being such a good guy.

"I'm not hiring, Ronald," Ellen said. Which was true. But that's not to say she couldn't stand some help tonight. Other than the nights before and after Christmas and Thanksgiving, her busiest night at the Lumber Lodge was the night after the baseball game. The faculty and staff always seemed very thirsty then, possibly because Matty always bought them several rounds. He sometimes made a toast, too. The toast often included some kind of classical allusion—Virgil, Shakespeare, Patrick Henry, the fifth president of Cornell University—which always made everyone drink even more desperately, and it was sometimes hard for her to keep up. Plus, she was worried about Henry and Matty being in the same room together. They were in the same room together at school often enough. But tonight in the same room with them there would be alcohol and also her, the ex- and future wife. Besides, Ellen was getting married in just three days, and like so many people in that particular state of limbo, she couldn't shake this sense of impending doom. If I can just get married, then I know everything will be just fine, was her feeling. This, of course, is a common feeling among people about to be married, even among people who have already been married.

"I already have a job," Ronald said. "In fact . . ." And he made a big deal of looking around the bar for someone, even though clearly they were the only two people in it. "Is Henry here?"

"No. He's probably at the baseball game." Ellen looked at Ronald. It was perhaps wrong to so dislike a guy who was crippled and whose sister had killed herself in such a spectacularly awful way. But Ellen did dislike Ronald. Ever since his sister died, Ronald had seemed as though he was up to something. "Why?"

"Oh, just wondering."

"You seem like you're up to something, Ronald."

"That's funny. Because I saw someone running out of Henry's office today. *I'm* not up to *anything*. But that guy, *he* seemed like he was up to something."

"That guy?" Ellen said, thinking, Married, married. Thinking, Doom, doom. Thinking, I'm going to marry Henry in three days. Please let me marry Henry in three days. "What guy?"

"That's what I was going to ask Henry. Me, I'd never seen him before."

"He was a stranger?"

Ronald nodded. "A mysterious one," he said, and then he looked around the bar again as though just realizing he was in one. "Hey, I could use a drink. You open yet?"

42

...

Matty was in his office, taking off his ad hoc umpire's gear, when someone knocked on the door. It was Kurt, standing there with a look on his face. Matty recognized it: it was the look you gave your principal when you needed to talk to someone about something important but didn't know who to talk to and then you remembered the mnemonic about the principal being your *pal* and so you decided to go talk to your principal. Except of course that Kurt wasn't only Matty's principal; the two of them had ample time outside school to talk as well. For instance, the night before, Kurt and Matty had eaten dinner together, during which Kurt hadn't said a word to Matty, or at least not a word that consisted of more than one syllable. After dinner they'd sat silently in front of the TV, Kurt flipping through the channels at superhuman speed until Matty had said, "Hey, buddy, slow down, I'm starting to worry about the well-being of your thumb," and then Kurt had sighed, dropped the remote on the couch between them, and gone up to his room. And neither of them had talked during breakfast, nor during the ride in to school, which had ended not ten minutes ago. But at *school*, Kurt felt like he could talk to Matty. So this meant that Kurt trusted Matty as his principal, but not as his father? Wow, that was depressing, if you looked at it from one point of view. But if you looked at it from another point of view, hey, at least Kurt felt he could talk to his principal.

"What's up?" Matty asked, flinging his shin guards and his mask into the bottom drawer of his file cabinet. Kurt didn't answer at first. He wandered over to the wall where the extra bathroom passes hung on a hook, took one down, and began fiddling with it. Each pass was a wooden block with a chain hanging from the block, and a key attached to the chain. Nobody knew what the keys were for. The bathroom doors didn't even have locks. Matty himself had used these passes when he was in high school, in a different building, with different bathrooms. And even then the wooden blocks had seemed ancient, the keys meant for locks that obviously hadn't existed in forever. That meant that generations of Broomeville schoolchildren had been holding these things while going to the bathroom. The more you thought about it, the more disgusting it was. But that was school pretty much: you got through it, not by changing the things that were gross, but by not thinking about them too much. Which was of course the opposite of what they taught you at Cornell. Think, Cornell had taught him. Think about how everyone else thinks and then think harder and better than they think. But Matty was thinking less and less of Cornell these days. And when he did think of Cornell, he mostly thought of Locs wearing his Cornell hat, of whether she was still wearing it, wherever she was.

"You need to go to the bathroom or something, buddy?"

Matty said, trying to tell Kurt to stop messing around with the bathroom pass but also trying to keep his tone light, making sure he called Kurt "buddy," which was what Matty called him these days when he was trying to keep his tone light. He wasn't sure it was working: every time he called Kurt "buddy" he felt as if he was acting like someone else's father talking to someone else's son. Although maybe that was the point.

Anyway, Kurt put the pass back on its hook, sat down in the red plastic chair next to the door. "What's up?" Matty asked again.

Kurt told his father about how Jenny had interrupted Mr. L. and the stranger in Mr. L.'s office the day before; how the stranger had fled; how Jenny had told them the story at the baseball game; and how the cronies had come to one conclusion about Mr. L., but Kurt himself had come to another.

"A stranger?" Matty said.

"A stranger who was speaking another language," Kurt said.

"A spy?" Matty said in a tone that was intended to let Kurt think that Matty didn't quite know *what* to think about this difficult-to-believe plot twist. By now, this tone came easily to Matty: over the past two years, he'd fired his guidance counselor, who had then killed herself; his new guidance counselor was internationally wanted for Matty didn't know what reason and had been sent into hiding in Broomeville by a CIA agent who'd been Matty's lover before he'd rejected her and turned her into a CIA agent and whom Matty then rejected *again*, regretting it the minute he had done so and then most minutes after that, too; and finally, Matty's wife had divorced him and in three days was going to marry this guidance counselor, who also was a fugitive of some kind or maybe even, as Kurt thought, a spy himself. For Matty, this last was the most difficult-to-believe plot twist of them all. This was what he'd been trying to say to Henry at the game today with his eyes: I cannot believe my wife is now my ex-wife, I cannot believe you are marrying my ex-wife, I can't believe I am not murdering you for marrying my ex-wife, I cannot believe I am not at least firing you for marrying my ex-wife, even though you are the best guidance counselor Broomeville Junior-Senior High School has ever had, by far, and I know that, and everyone knows that, and so everyone would know that I was firing you just because you were marrying my ex-wife, and if I were to tell everyone, You know, it might seem as though I'm firing him because he's marrying my ex-wife but in fact I'm firing him because he's not really a guidance counselor but instead an international fugitive of some kind and maybe even a spy, then you would have no reason not to tell Ellen and Kurt and *everyone* about why I hired you in the first place, and if you told them that, then you would tell them about Locs, and if you told them about Locs, if you told Ellen about Locs, if Ellen heard that I was *thinking* about Locs, let alone that I'd talked to Locs, let alone that I'd agreed to hire you as a guidance counselor because Locs wanted me to, let alone that I'd seen Locs, even though I'd seen her two long years ago, and only then to reject her again, which right after I'd done it I wished I hadn't done it, but even so, that wouldn't matter to Ellen, it would not matter, she would never take me back, even if she dumped you for lying to her about what you are, who you are,

which admittedly would give me no little satisfaction, since she
dumped me for being what I am, who I am, but even so, even
if she did that, she would still never take me back, and then
what would be the point, what would be the point in her not
ever taking me back unless I could figure out a way to get Locs
to take me back, Locs, wherever she is, however she is, how is
she anyway, is she thinking about me, does she ever mention
my name, do you think she's ever coming back to Broomeville, she's probably never coming back to Broomeville, and
if you're not here anymore, then she's *definitely* never coming
back to Broomeville, and if I fire you and Ellen dumps you,
then you won't have much reason to be here, either, and then
you'll leave, and if you leave, then Locs would never have a
reason, a professional reason, to come back to Broomeville, to
come back to me, her personal reason, and how awful would
that be, for me to never see Locs again, Locs my love, Locs my
true love, probably my truest love, and so maybe I wouldn't
fire you after all, besides you're probably as decent and great a
guy as everyone says you are, including my ex-wife, including
my students, including my son, including everyone else, and
since you're such a great guy, couldn't you do me at least one
favor, couldn't you tell Locs that I'm thinking about her, that
I still love her, that I want her to come back to me, depending
on how everything else shakes out, and see, that's why Locs
should never come back, why would she come back to me if I
don't know how I really want everything to shake out, do you
know what I need, I need someone who I can talk to, someone
who can sit down with me and help me figure out how I really
want all this to shake out, you know, a buddy, I don't have a

buddy, maybe that's why I'm calling Kurt "buddy" now, because I'm grooming him for this job, this job as my buddy, although can you imagine a worse job than the job of being my buddy, Jesus, what an awful future to wish for my son, my only son, my God, any job would be better, even a principal, even a bartender, even a guidance counselor, even a spy, although speaking of being a spy, you know, Kurt is probably right, you probably are a spy, I can't believe I'm letting a spy counsel my students, I can't believe I'm letting a spy stepfather my son, I can't believe my son's stepfather-to-be is a spy, I will not let my son have a stepfather who is a spy.

In this way, the thought solidified in Matty's mind, became a fact: Henry was a spy. And then it was joined by another fact: Locs was not coming back; Locs was never coming back. Matty now knew that to be true, and therefore he resolved to put an end to all this and finally come clean about Henry to Ellen, but to do so carefully, in a way that would reveal Henry's true self but would somehow not incriminate Matty himself in the process.

"A *spy*," Matty finally said, in a tone that was intended to let Kurt think that Matty really was starting to see things from his son's point of view.

"The minute I said it out loud, I knew it was true," Kurt said. "It was my come-to-Caesar moment."

Matty had heard this kind of thing from so many students during his time at Broomeville Junior-Senior High. A kid heard some adult say something, and tried to act as though it was something the kid himself said all the time, and then mangled the saying, thereby making himself sound even more like a kid.

It was pretty cute, but you could not tell the kid that, and you could not correct his mistake, either. At least not if you were the kid's father. At least not if you were Matty. As a divorced father trying to convince his son that he loved him more than anything in the world, Matty could not afford to correct Kurt's innocent mistake. He had to just let it slide. And yet, as a principal, as an *educator,* could Matty just let something like that slide?

"You mean 'come to Jesus,'" Matty said.

"Huh?"

"You mean, 'It was my come-to-Jesus moment,'" Matty said, and then he smiled in a way that was meant to communicate, But hey, buddy, I like *your* saying, too, and anyway, don't let my setting you straight ruin our father-son time together. But too late: Matty watched the look on his son's face go from embarrassment to resentment to defiance, and could tell that Matty's setting Kurt straight had ruined their father-son time together.

"I don't believe in Jesus," Kurt said.

"But you do believe in Caesar?" Matty said.

After that, they didn't say anything. The wall clock ticked loudly in the way of school clocks. It was getting late. Matty needed to get down to the bar to address the troops, give the toast, buy the drinks. He could picture everyone waiting for him: *Dr.* Vernon; his brother, Lawrence. Henry, Ellen. Matty was kind of dreading it. He'd even considered skipping the whole thing. But now, he was reconsidering. At the very least he'd ask Henry about this mysterious stranger. Who knew? Maybe the mysterious stranger would be there, too. "I promise I'll look into it," he told Kurt.

"Sure, OK," Kurt said, getting up, obviously not believing his father would look into it.

"I mean it," Matty said.

"Sure, OK," Kurt said, again. He had turned his back on his father and was now walking out the door.

"You can trust me, Kurt," Matty said. He could hear how lame that sounded. But maybe Kurt had heard it differently. Because Kurt turned and looked at Matty like he really wanted to believe it.

"OK," Kurt finally said.

"Good," Matty said. "I promise I'll figure out what's going on here. But I could use your help."

"What kind of help?"

"I don't know," Matty said. Because really he had no idea. He searched for the vaguest phrase, the one most easily reached for, then reached for it. "Just keep your eyes open." More lameness. But Kurt nodded seriously. "I can do that," he said.

43

· · ·

Wednesday, October 6, 2011, 11:49 p.m.
From: undisclosed sender
To: undisclosed recipient
Subject: Re: Broomeville

"Is this the nature of plans?" You're pretty philosophical for a terrorist-arsonist-murderer.

I hope you know what you're doing.

44

. . .

enry entered the Lumber Lodge just before six o'clock. He'd been walking around town—west along the river, south on the logging roads through the quasi national forest, north on the old canal that was now a walking path, then finally east, back to town, walking in only barely lit darkness through the neighborhood adjacent to the railroad tracks where the poor people lived, the neighborhood that, for some reason, was called the Flats, even though the whole town was flat—walking for almost three hours, trying to figure out how he was going to tell Ellen the truth about himself. No matter how he conceived of the plan, it began with his saying, My real name is Jens Baedrup, and it ended with Ellen saying, You lied to me. Now go away forever. He had made himself so exhausted with his lack of options and his future grief that he didn't think he could go on contemplating them without seeing Ellen first. This, Henry thought, is how you know when you're in love: when you're so worn out thinking about the woman you love leaving you that you need to be in the restorative presence of the woman you love before you start thinking again about her leaving you.

When Henry walked into the Lumber Lodge, it was full. Normally when the bar was full, it was a chaos of spilled drinks and yelling and darts and someone playing music on the juke-box and someone complaining about the music playing on the jukebox and people cursing at each other as though they were in a cursing competition—in general the noise of people who might have done some real damage to each other and the bar had they been just a little bit younger. But there was none of that now. There were forty or so people in the place. Most of them were Henry's colleagues from school. There were Matty and his brother, Lawrence. There were *Dr.* Vernon and Grace, his wife. There were Ms. Andrews, the English teacher, and Ron Ferraro, who taught music and band. There was even the janitor sitting across the bar from Ellen, that strange Ronald Crimmins with his strange hand and his dead sister, Ronald who was clearly watching Henry, watching Henry, watching him, always watching him, so obviously spying on him that Henry wondered whether he actually *was* a spy. Had Locs put Ronald in charge of keeping Henry safe? Henry had wondered many times over the past two years. In a few seconds he would no longer wonder that. But anyway, Henry saw that Ronald was watching him now and so was Ellen; she waved him over. He walked slowly toward them, and as he did, Henry felt a prickling around his collar; he had the distinct feeling that they had just been talking about him.

"Henry, we were just talking about you!" she said. Her eyes

were wide, like she was trying to tell him something. But what? On the one hand, it might be: I am so happy to see you. Or, on the other: I can't believe I used to be so happy to see you. "Where've you been?"

"I took a walk."

"With your friend?" Ronald said.

"My friend."

"Ronald said he saw someone walk out of your office today."

"A stranger," Ronald said. "And actually, he didn't walk. He ran."

The two of them waited for Henry to say something, and when he didn't, Ellen said, "I was wondering who he was. Was he someone you invited to the wedding?" They'd agreed to keep the wedding small, but still Ellen couldn't quite believe how small Henry was keeping his side of the wedding. He hadn't invited anyone. His parents were dead; he had no siblings. There was no one from his previous life that he cared more about than the people in the present, no one from his past that he wanted at the wedding. That was what he told her. It was all true enough.

"No," Henry said.

"See, I didn't think so," Ronald said. "He didn't seem like a guy who was about to raise a toast to the happy couple." But Ronald did seem happy, and so did Matty: he was sitting at a table with his brother, Lawrence, watching Henry with great interest, his eyes smiling as he took a sip of his beer. Matty worried Henry even more than Ronald. As an ex-husband of his future wife who also knew something—Henry didn't know

exactly what—about Henry's past, Matty was uniquely quali-
fied to do great harm. I'm watching you, Matty's eyes seemed
to say, but pretty soon I'm going to do more than just watch
you.

And that's when Henry knew that the time had come to tell
the truth. Henry knew this because he couldn't think of anything else to tell.

"I was going to tell you," he said to Ellen, but she was already gesturing to *Dr.* Vernon, who had just walked up with
two empty glasses. Ellen took them and said, "But Barry here
had his own nutty idea."

"Not nutty," *Dr.* Vernon said. His eyes were red; he smelled
somehow both earthy and clean, as though he had just tilled
the patch of dirt where toothpaste grows. He took the two
full beers back from Ellen and drank the head off one of them
and then the other. "I was just saying that you'd mentioned
a Danish cartoonist at the baseball game. And then later on I
was talking to some of the kids, and they said they'd heard you
were talking to a guy in your office, and that he spoke Danish.
Or said he was from Denmark. Anyway, I figured that's who
the guy was."

Everyone looked at Henry, and he frowned, not because he
didn't understand *Dr.* Vernon's nutty idea, but because he suddenly had his own. Am I really going to do this? he thought,
and then, before he could ask himself that question again, he
did it.

"That's right," Henry said. "The man told me he was Jens
Baedrup, the controversial Danish cartoonist."

"Oooh," someone said softly. It was the sound you make

when someone hits you in the stomach: more air than word. It had come from the part of the room where Matty was sitting with Lawrence. Lawrence had a carefully trimmed blond beard, which he would stroke in times of contemplation. He was stroking it right now. Just stroking that beard, and stroking it, and staring at Henry, as though assessing his worth. Lawrence had always seemed to distrust Henry; Henry knew this from students who said that Lawrence sometimes referred to him as "the *Swede*," with the italics. But then again, Henry was marrying Lawrence's brother's ex-wife. Of course he would treat him that way. There was a good reason for everything. Meanwhile, Matty was looking completely baffled. There was a good reason for that, too. Perhaps Matty had made that noise, and perhaps the noise was not "Oooh" but "Who?" That question made more sense. In any case, Henry repeated the name, "Jens Baedrup," and when he said it, he could feel a ridiculous, optimistic smile commandeering his face. Henry recognized it by feel. The smile was his. Or had been when he was still Jens Baedrup.

45

...

arsen, that's a Danish name," Ellen repeated. She and Henry were sitting in their room above the Lumber Lodge. It was just after one in the morning. Ellen had finally kicked the drunk stragglers out of the bar and closed up without mopping the floor, without even putting the chairs up. Henry had just told Ellen the story of the stranger visiting him in his office.

"How did he say it?" she asked. Ellen was now holding her phone, which was also something of a computer, and with her left hand she was doing gymnastic things to the face of the phone.

"How did he say what?"

"Jens," she said, pronouncing it improperly. It is *Yents,* not *Jenz,* Henry thought but did not say. "How did he say, 'Larsen, that's a Danish name'?"

"With an emphasis on the word 'Danish.' "

"What kind of emphasis?"

Henry pretended to consider this for a moment. "Unhappy," he said.

Ellen nodded again. "But you're from Sweden," she said. "Larsen is a Swedish name."

"That's true," Henry said. "But Larsen can also be a Danish name. You could hear the name Larsen and you wouldn't be wrong to think that it was a Swedish or a Danish name."

"And he spoke to you in Danish first and then in English," Ellen said, thinking about it. "You know how to speak Danish?" It was a very good question. Henry couldn't believe he hadn't thought of it himself.

"Danish isn't so different from Swedish," Henry said. "If you speak one, you can generally at least understand the other."

"But why is he here in the first place? Did he really hear that in Broomeville there was a guy with a Danish last name and thought, I should go there and talk to him?"

It was another excellent question. Henry didn't answer it. His thoughts drifted toward other excellent questions that he had not anticipated, other excellent questions people might yet ask and he might not be able to answer. This was a serious violation of his method. His method demanded that, when in the company of someone else, his thoughts remain on that person and only on that person. Because when your thoughts were somewhere else, then so were your eyes, and eyes could be read. Eyes will be read. Henry's thoughts and eyes returned to Ellen, who was looking at him, reading him.

"You look like you want to tell me something," she said.

"I do," he said. "I love you," he said. But she wasn't paying attention now; instead she was back looking at her phone.

"Does he look anything like the guy who was in your office today?" she asked. Jens looked over her shoulder. There was a picture of Jens Baedrup on her phone; it filled up its tiny screen. The picture was now six years old; it had been taken before Jens had drawn the cartoon, etc. The Jens Baedrup in the picture had a large, grisly black beard. He was sloppily dressed and tubby, with receding black hair in front and a wiry fan of hair over his ears and down to his shoulders. He wore thick red-framed glasses, too. Jens had always liked those glasses, even though Ilsa had thought they made him look like a clown. "Do clowns wear glasses?" he'd asked her. "They do if they're also cartoonists," Ilsa had said. She was right. A man who looked like that could be only one of two things: a clown or a cartoonist. And Ellen was right to ask her question, too: the stranger looked nothing like Jens Baedrup. But then again, Henry realized, neither did Henry. Over the past four years his hair had gone completely gray, and he'd lost so much of it, and he'd lost so much weight, too. He'd lost the clownish glasses, as well. You could stand Henry next to the guy in the picture and you would have a hard time arguing that they were even related, let alone the same human being.

"Somewhat," Henry said.

"Somewhat?"

"Yes," Henry said. Ronald hadn't said how closely he'd examined the man coming out of Henry's office. Ronald, Ronald. For two years, Henry had thought that Ronald was looking out for him. Now he was thinking that Ronald had it out for him, if that was the proper use of the American expression, and Henry wasn't sure that it was. Had *what* out for him? Anyway, Henry decided to describe the stranger as he was, just in case Ronald had also seen him as he was. Stout, dark bearded, with tired eyes. The tired eyes made it difficult to tell how old the stranger was. Ellen listened, looking dubiously at the picture of Jens Baedrup on her phone.

"Maybe it's not really him," Henry said.

"It's a weird thing to lie about," Ellen said.

"Maybe he had surgery," Henry said.

"Maybe he had *a lot* of surgery." Ellen stroked the phone face, and the picture of Jens disappeared and a newspaper article took its place. Ellen read it, frowning. "But then again, maybe he needed a lot of surgery."

Henry leaned back against the wall, crossed his arms over his chest, thinking of what he should say next. Now, back in their room, after seeing Ellen see the picture of the real Jens Baedrup, who looked nothing like the stranger, Jens's plan seemed even more clearly doomed to fail. Tell her! Henry said in his mind. Shut up! he said in the same place. These were his two paths. The first seemed to lead directly to disaster. The second probably would lead there, too, but only probably, and not as directly. Plus it was the easier path to take; all he had to do to take that path was to do nothing.

"Jens Baedrup," Ellen said again.

"Not *Jenz. Yents,*" Henry said. Ellen just looked at him, as though expecting more, so Henry said, "That's the correct pronunciation."

"Yents," Ellen repeated. "So you'd heard of him before today?"

Henry shrugged. "The Copenhagen cartoons were more famous. But yes, I'd heard of him."

"And what did you think?" He frowned at her, and she

said, "About the cartoons." Henry shrugged again but didn't say anything, and Ellen didn't seem to notice: she was back to reading her phone. "I mean, on the one hand," Ellen said, "what was this guy thinking?"

He was probably thinking that everything was going to be just fine, Henry thought but did not say.

"But on the other hand," Ellen said, "someone *killed* him. For *this*?" At that, she held up the phone so Henry could see. There was the cartoon. He had managed to not picture the cartoon since he'd been in Broomeville. Once, Henry had seen a monster movie in which the only way to keep the monster from killing you was to not think of it, to not allow the image of it into your mind. That had been Henry's approach to his cartoon. But it had found him anyway. What are *you* doing here? the cartoon seemed to be saying to him.

"But I guess he's not dead after all," Ellen said.

"Unless it's not really him," Henry said.

"I still don't get what he's doing in Broomeville," Ellen said. "It's a long, long way to Skagen," she sang, in a tune Henry didn't know, but in any case, in singing it she'd mispronounced the name of his hometown.

"Skane," he said.

"What now?"

"You said 'Skaw-gen.' But it's pronounced 'Skane.'"

"Skaw-*gen*," Ellen insisted, drawing out the *aw,* daring Henry to correct her again, and also letting him know she wasn't crazy about the way he'd corrected her the first time. This was the closest they'd come to fighting in their two years together. It reminded him of fighting with Ilsa, how they'd never fought until the day they'd started fighting, and from then on it felt like the most natural thing in the world. This was the worst thing about fighting with someone you loved: it taught you how easy it would be to just keep on fighting. "How do you know how it's pronounced anyway?"

"I went there once," he said. "On vacation." Then Henry described it: Skagen, the town between two seas; the town with the pretty yellow houses with the red tile roofs and the neat yards; the town with the wet wind and the cold sand; the town that painters in the nineteenth century made famous for its light; the town where the eastward-moving waves from the North Sea crash into the westward-moving waves from the Baltic Sea, and the spectacle is so great that even the skeptical end up taking too many pictures; the town so orderly and good that even the hulking tankers from Sweden and Norway and England and Germany patiently wait in lines that stretch from one sea to another before easing into the docks at Skagen Havn. The town with the big white church with the little white clipper ships dangling from the ceiling in between the chandeliers. The town that I loved, even though I went there only once, on vacation.

"That sounds nice," Ellen said when Henry was through, clearly not peeved anymore. She tossed the phone onto the bed and leaned back into him. "Skagen," she said, getting the name right this time. "Maybe you can take me there someday."

"Yes, I will do that," Henry said, thinking, How am I ever going to do that? He was still thinking that a minute later, when Ellen said, "We're getting married in three days," and then, before he could respond, she said, "I wonder when this *Yents* is coming back."

"Who knows?" Henry said. "Maybe he's never coming back." And in this, of course, Henry was right, but later he would have reason to wish that he hadn't been.

46
• • •

S o we got three things," Crystal said. "This." And then she handed Søren's knife to Capo. This meeting was taking place in Doc's. The blinds were drawn, and the lights were off except in the kitchen, where Doc was preparing the stove. London, who was now just called Joseph, was in the bathroom, running the water, thus drawing attention to his vomiting, which the running water was meant to obscure. Capo was sitting on a stool, back against the counter, facing Crystal, who was standing, violently chewing on something. Gum, Capo guessed, although he would not have been surprised if it were broken glass, or barbed wire, or human gristle. She really was terrifying; if there was a room where Crystal would not be the scariest person present, then Capo really did not want to be in it. He extended his right hand and she handed him the knife, handle first. He examined it briefly, then placed it on the counter behind him.

"And also this," Crystal said, and she handed Capo a cell phone. He idly fiddled with it as Crystal told him what they'd learned from Søren. That Locs had found him at the cartoonist's ex-wife's house; that she had brought him back to the house in the dunes in Skagen; that she had coerced Søren to come to Broomeville to kill the cartoonist again, finally, once and for all. The one thing that Søren had not been able to tell them is why Locs wanted him to kill Henry. Others would have made more sense. Matty, for instance. Ellen. Capo himself. But why Henry?

"Don't know," Crystal said. "But he wasn't going to be able to actually do it anyway."

"Is that your opinion?"

"I don't have an opinion," Crystal said.

"But if you were required to have one."

"I don't have an *opinion*," Crystal said. "I have a *knife,* which I took off the terrorist-arsonist-murderer who said he really wasn't one. But he—"

"Søren," Capo said.

"Yup," Crystal said.

"Søren Korkmaz."

"That guy," Crystal said. "He was sent here to kill our little guidance counselor, but he wasn't going to be able to actually do it. That was his opinion."

It's mine, as well, Capo thought but did not say. The griddle hissed, the toilet flushed, and Joseph emerged from the bathroom, eyes red, face wet. He saw Capo looking at him, and tucked his nonexistent hair behind his ears. It'd been two years since Capo had removed Joseph from his London post; two years since Capo had convinced his brother to hire Joseph as a security guard for the school when in actuality he was there to guard not the school but Henry Larsen; two years since Capo had made Joseph cut his ridiculous hair and then ordered him to keep it cut. And still, the child acted as though his mane had just been sheared.

"I was thinking," Joseph said. Crystal laughed. Joseph tried to ignore her. "We should send someone to Locs's house in Skagen," Joseph said, and again Crystal laughed.

"Locs won't be there," she said. "She's not stupid enough to still be there."

"I don't suppose Locs told Mr. Korkmaz where she might go next," Capo said, and Joseph shook his head.

"She never even told him her name," Joseph said. "Go to Broomeville, and kill the guidance counselor who is really the cartoonist. That's all she told him."

"How he reached the guidance counselor's office in the first place, I'll never know," Crystal said. Chewing, chewing, she pretended to think about it. Then she turned to Joseph and looked at him blankly. "Never mind," she said. "I know."

"I went to the *bathroom*," Joseph said. "Can a man not go to the *bathroom*?"

"A *man* can, sure," Crystal said.

"Fortunately," Capo said, "Jennifer intervened."

"Now, Jenny's a good girl," Crystal said.

"Jennifer *is* surprisingly capable," Capo agreed. "I've taken the liberty to invite her to my weekly summit with the students Friday afternoon." Here, Capo grew thoughtful. "Although she will have to be taught to keep the news of her good deeds to herself." And then Capo told them what he'd learned, beginning with Jenny telling Kurt and his cronies about what she'd seen and heard in Henry's office, and ending with Henry informing everyone at the Lumber Lodge that Søren had told Henry that his name was actually Jens Baedrup.

"He said *what*?" Doc said. He was bearing three plates laden with eggs, hash, English muffin for Capo, dry toast for Crystal, no toast for Joseph. Doc placed the plates on the counter, and Joseph and Crystal sat down on either side of Capo. "Eat," Doc said, standing behind the counter. No one ate. Capo watched them think about this new bad news, watched them try to go back in their minds, determine who was responsible, how it could have been prevented. The cartoonist drew the cartoon, Søren burned down his house; that was not their fault. Locs was crazy, but that was more Capo's brother's fault than Capo's. And besides, they could not have anticipated that she would bring the cartoonist to Broomeville. They could not have anticipated it, but that did not mean they had to facilitate it. Joseph had helped Locs bring the cartoonist to Broomeville; Joseph had killed the old guidance counselor, Sheilah, instead of Locs; Joseph's killing of the old guidance counselor had gotten her brother involved, her brother with the stricken hand and the murderous eyes. Ronald. Doc had told Capo that they should be worried about Ronald, that Ronald knew that his sister had not killed herself. Now, Ronald had seen Søren run out of Henry's office. And whose fault was that? Whose fault was it that Søren had made it to Henry's office in the first place?

"Hey, at least you killed the right person this time," Crystal said to Joseph.

"Crystal, no more," Capo said, but by then Joseph had

already gotten up and run to the bathroom. Capo sighed and said, "I assume Mr. Korkmaz's body . . ."

"No one will ever find it," Crystal said.

"Good," Capo said, although he was not feeling especially good, especially since they had killed Søren only because Capo had ordered them to. He supposed that it was necessary to kill the person who had come to kill the person under his protection, even if that assassin would never be able to bring himself to be anything but a would-be assassin. But still, the whole episode seemed miserable and brutish and excessive and totally lacking in nuance and gamesmanship. Not at all like it used to be. "Denmark!" he said. "Copenhagen, of course, is a wonderful city. But there are so many others. Vejle, for instance, with its fjord, its gentle river, its Munkebjerg! An unlovely name, but such a lovely mountain! And its people! Such amazingly generous people! Carsten, for instance, the old mapmaker whom I befriended in the old city and who took me into his home!" But then Capo remembered that before Carsten had been an old mapmaker, he'd been a young Nazi collaborator. So Capo stopped midreverie. Not that Doc and Crystal seemed to be listening to him anyway. Perhaps they had heard this sort of thing too often from him. Or perhaps they were distracted by Joseph's loud retching. Capo picked up his fork and began eating. Doc's scrambled eggs and corned beef hash! But the first bite tasted vile and the second bite worse. Even the English muffin tasted like soap. Everything is ruined, Capo thought, including my favorite meal, and also my brother's marriage.

"It's time to move Henry," Doc said.

"I hardly think that's necessary," Capo said.

"It's necessary." When Capo didn't respond, Doc said, "He's in danger here." Capo didn't say anything to that, but he did make a face that said, Too bad. "You don't like him very much, do you?" *Still,* Capo didn't respond. "Why?" Doc asked. "Because of his cartoon?"

"Well, it did reveal an impressive lack of cultural sensitivity," Capo said. "But, no."

"Because it made it harder to do our jobs?"

"Our jobs are supposed to be difficult," Capo said.

"Then why?" Doc asked.

"Because Henry can't keep it in his pants," Crystal said.

"Must you be so vulgar?" Capo asked.

"And when he can't keep it in his pants, he shares it with Capo's brother's wife. His brother's *ex*-wife."

"One does feel a certain loyalty to one's brother."

"Because your brother is a saint."

"My brother is the reason Locs will come back," Lawrence said. "And we'll be waiting for her this time."

"Oh really?" Crystal said. "And how are we going to get her to come back, exactly?"

I don't know, Capo thought but did not say. I don't know, but when she comes back, I'm going to stab her in her face with this fork until she's dead! But where did that thought come from? It seemed to have come not from Capo's mind but from the miserable, brutish world's. A horrifying thought, thought Capo, and even more horrifying to have thought it. Capo dropped the fork, picked up Søren's phone, and began idly opening and closing it, and then suddenly he had another thought, a thought that Capo thought was much less the world's, much more his own.

"How was Mr. Korkmaz to contact Locs to let her know that he'd killed Henry?" Capo said, just as Joseph returned from the bathroom and sat next to him at the counter. He looked more pitiful and wrung out than ever, and Capo patted him on the shoulder in an attempt to reassure him that everything was going to be just fine.

"And that's the third thing," Crystal said. She handed a piece of paper to Capo. On it was an e-mail address. "He was supposed to use the phone to e-mail her."

"I see," Capo said. "It might be amusing . . . ," he said, and then he explained to them his plan. When he was done, Crystal said, "You know, I like it."

"Me, too," Doc said.

"I guess it might work," Joseph said. His head was bowed, his back hunched. Even his hair, as short as it was, seemed lank. It seemed as though his whole self was weeping. Capo might have paid more attention to this if he weren't so enamored with his plan.

"It *will* work," Capo said. "And it will also be *fun*." He typed the first of his four e-mails, hit Send, and then added, "We so rarely get to have any fun anymore."

47
...

Locs was sitting in her house, drinking coffee, listening to the sand scratch and brush on the roof, when she got the latest e-mail from Søren.

Thursday, October 7, 2011, 12:05 a.m.
From: undisclosed sender
To: undisclosed recipient
Subject: Re: Broomeville

You write, "I hope you know what you're doing." I do not know what I'm doing. But then again, neither do you.

Fuck, fuck, fuck, Locs thought and then typed, and then after that she typed several other words and then tried to send the e-mail. But the Internet was down again. It didn't work more often than it did. Why is this happening to me? she wondered. But that was a rhetorical question.

She turned off her laptop computer, then turned it on again. Locs thought of it as her computer, but in fact she had stolen it from a café in Roskilde. She thought of this house in Skagen as hers, too, even though she was just squatting in it. Her Internet connection: she was poaching from one of the other houses nestled in one of the other dunes. Her Toyota: she had not stolen it, and she had not stolen the credit card she'd used to pay for it, but she'd acquired the credit card using a fake passport and a bank account that didn't exist but looked real enough on the application. This was the credit card with the PIN Locs had been told she didn't need; Locs had never had to deal with PINs when she was a secret agent. This was what they didn't tell you about the fantastic life of a secret agent: that it rendered you surprisingly feeble for ordinary life when you were no longer a secret agent. Or as ordinary as a life could be when lived in secrecy and in constant fear of being discovered and assassinated by your former fellow secret agents. Anyway, after Søren agreed to do what Locs wanted him to do, and after she gave him instructions about how he should do it, she drove him to Copenhagen, where she then used her PIN to get a cash advance, used some of the cash to get Søren a fake passport, used her credit card to buy Søren a plane ticket to New York, and then gave him the rest of the cash before leaving him at the airport. Then she got back into her car, feeling very good about herself, very accomplished. That's done, she thought; now I can go anywhere. And yet she was surprised to find herself heading north, back to Skagen, and surprised again to find herself thinking of Skagen as home. I'm going home, she thought. It felt good to think that.

But then Locs tried to use her credit card to get over the toll bridge at Vejle. She put the credit card into the slot, and it shot back out at her in what seemed like an especially emphatic way. A word popped up on the screen. It was amazing how the word *rejected* was so similar in so many different languages. There was a line of cars behind her now, and people were beeping at her. You know you're in a bad way when you make even Danes impatient. It was probably the first time many of them had used their horns. She'd turned the credit card over and blew on the strip, the last desperate act of someone who doesn't want to believe her credit card has been canceled. Rejected again. Locs had ended up digging around in her pockets for kroner and then dropping the coins into the basket just like all the other sad people whose lives hadn't worked out the way they'd wanted and who asked themselves pathetic rhetorical questions like, Why is this happening to me?

But at least she had a home to squat in, a home that someone had abandoned, true enough, but clearly it had been abandoned by a rich person, or a formerly rich person, and in any case it was a definite improvement over the places she'd lived in over the past two years, two years of living in secret and squalor after seven years of living in secret and comfort. At least she had this house. At least she'd gotten Søren to Broomeville. At least he would kill the cartoonist and then she would never have to think of him, or Broomeville, or anyone in it, ever again. She'd been feeling good, and clean, and new, at home in her skin and in Skagen, and in the world, and in fact, she had started typing a letter to Matty telling him these things before she'd started getting all these screwy e-mails from Søren. The computer was fully booted up now, but the Internet still wasn't up, so Locs opened the letter and continued working on it.

Dear Matty,

Your brother Lawrence is a CIA agent. You don't know that because you're too stupid to know that. Although not necessarily more stupid than your stupid brother, who goes by the stupid nickname Capo. He insists he was given the nickname during his time infiltrating the Cosa Nostra in Calabria, but probably he just gave the nickname to himself. Anyway, he's a CIA agent. Doc and Crystal are CIA agents, too. They all used to be active spies. Now they recruit future active spies. Meaning, they recruit your students—not the smartest ones, just the ones most in need of being recruited, the ones most in need of a home. Like me.

You'll notice I addressed this letter to Matty, not Matthew. Because you'll never be a Matthew. I know that now. I'll never be a Locs, either. I'm a Lorraine. Lorraine is not a lovelorn spy. Lorraine lives in a rich person's house on the North Sea. Lorraine does not miss Locs at all. Because if Locs were in this house, she'd be thinking ridiculous thoughts. She'd be thinking not of how happy she was in this house, in between these dunes, next to this blue-black sea. No, she'd be thinking of you and of how much happier she'd be if only you were in this house with her, and since she, Locs, would know that you'd be happier if Kurt were with you, too, then she'd be thinking of Kurt, also, in his room, with his posters on the wall, his dirty socks all over the place. Socks? Posters? Locs was too stupid to live; Lorraine is glad she's dead. Lorraine is better off without her, and without you, too, and once Søren has killed that cartoonist, she'll be absolutely perfect. Although maybe it's possible that Søren won't kill that cartoonist, and that's another reason that Lorraine doesn't miss Locs: because deep down, Locs knew that Søren would fail, and if he failed, which she knew he would, then she would have to go back to Broomeville and take care of it herself. But Lorraine is not going to do that. For one thing, Lorraine is suffering from a little credit card problem, a little cash flow issue, and if she wanted to come back to Broomeville, then she would have to steal a credit card to pay for the plane ticket, etc. And she does not want to do that. Locs was the one who stole credit cards. Lorraine is going to be the one who is going to stay in Denmark, the home of the happiest people in the world, and be happy, and that is basically why I'm writing you, to tell you that I'm never coming back to Broomeville, not to be with you, not to kill the cartoonist, not for any reason, because it's beautiful here, and I have a home, and I'm happy, even if the Internet connection is pretty spotty.

Just then her computer beeped. The Internet was back on, and she had another message from Søren.

One more thing. Why did you not tell me that Mr. Larsen is about to marry the school principal's former wife? Is it possible you didn't know that, either? Is it possible that you were too stupid to know that?

Marry? Former wife? Lorraine thought. Oh, Matthew! Locs thought. And because she was once again Locs, and once again in love, she did not think, You idiot, it's a trap! and she would not think this until it was way too late. Anyway, Locs was just about to start trolling the Web for its large supply of illegal available credit in order to buy herself a plane ticket from Copenhagen to New York when there was a knock on her door. Locs actually went to answer it. Because she was not thinking like a spy, a spy on the run squatting in someone else's house in someone else's country, a human being who never, ever should answer a knocked-on door. No, Locs was thinking, Oh, someone is at the door! She was thinking, Matthew, oh, Matthew! And then she went ahead and opened the door like it was her door to her house in her country, and like Matthew would be on the other side of it. She even greeted Matthew in that musical way she'd heard Danes greet each other: "Hi, hi," she said. And only then did she notice who was standing in the doorway. It was not Matthew, of course, of course, although it was a man, a hollowed-out, clean-shaven, light-dark-skinned old man, a man who was wearing Western clothes—jeans, sneakers, a waterproof blue jacket with the collar up—and who was pointing a gun at Locs. When Locs saw the gun, and when she saw who was pointing it, she felt her eyes go wide. The man probably recognized the look. It had very little to do with the gun. The look was the look white Danes sometimes had when strange nonwhite Danes who were also probably Muslims knocked on their door. But Locs was not a Dane, and this man was not a stranger. Locs knew exactly who he was.

"Your son burned down the cartoonist's house," Locs blurted out, and to her surprise, Faruk Korkmaz responded, "I know. And yet he did not have sufficient faith in my confidence to share with me that information." He looked at Locs to see whether she'd understood—his English was the kind of very formal, somewhat mush-mouthed, contractionless English spoken in novels by characters who are not speaking English even though their novels are written in English—and when she nodded that she had understood, Mr. Korkmaz added, "How do you think that makes a father feel?"

"WHERE DID YOU GET your gun?" Locs asked him. This wasn't merely a time-buying technique. She was genuinely, professionally curious. In her two weeks in Denmark, she'd tried—tried and failed—to buy a gun, by either legal or illegal means. Never before in any other country had she been unable to acquire a firearm. It was the most frustrating thing ever.

"How is that of your concern?" Søren's father asked. Locs was now sitting on a kitchen chair; he was standing in the middle of the kitchen, gun still pointed at her. Locs didn't recognize the handgun model, but it didn't look especially heavy. But even so, Søren's father was holding it with both hands and struggling to do even that. Locs knew from reading Søren's file that his father was in his early sixties; a decade earlier he'd had heart surgery. Then, he'd been way overweight; now, he looked underweight and hunched over, like someone had carved out some important part of the middle of him. When he breathed, his nose whistled. Locs doubted that he'd ever held a gun before, let alone fired one. Which is not to say he would not fire this one now.

"Professionally curious," Locs said. "That's all."

"Where is Søren?"

"Well, it's complicated."

"Where is my son?"

"Søren has gotten himself in some bad trouble."

"And so have you."

"Fair enough," Locs said, and then she thought, If this old man kills me, then I will never hear Matthew say those stupid words again. Meanwhile, Mr. Korkmaz was looking at Locs, obviously in need of some translation.

"What is fair enough?"

"It's an expression." Locs saw Mr. Korkmaz lower his gun a little. Nothing is more fatiguing than not knowing what someone else is talking about. Keep talking, she told herself. "It's Matthew's expression," she said, and she watched the gun lower a little bit more, and then she knew, or thought, that everything was going to be just fine after all. "Matthew is the man in America who hired the cartoonist."

"The cartoonist remains alive?" Søren's father said.

"Not if Søren has anything to do with it," Locs said, and then she watched as Mr. Korkmaz's mind caught up with her meaning.

"Oh no," Søren's father said. He lowered his gun almost all the way to his waist and then quickly raised it again. "How do you know everything of this?"

"I just do," Locs said, and Mr. Korkmaz took a step forward, his gun raised and pointed at her again. "I was a spy. But then I stopped being one. I came here to tell Søren that he didn't kill the cartoonist after all. He must have felt such guilt," Locs said, trying to make her face sympathetic, wondering how one does that, what that looks like, not really knowing, trying anyway. "I just didn't want him to feel guilty anymore."

"That terrible man," Mr. Korkmaz said, and at first Locs thought he was talking about his son. "That awful drawing." He was quiet for a minute, possibly picturing Jens Baedrup's cartoon. Then he said, "And what became Søren's response?"

"He didn't believe me."

"Of course. Because you had already lied to him."

"Well, not me personally," Locs said, and then she watched Mr. Korkmaz's hands go fidgety on the gun. "But yes. And so to prove that I was telling the truth, I told him, 'Jens Baedrup is now calling himself Henry Larsen. He's a guidance counselor in Broomeville, New York.'"

"A guidance counselor?"

"Exactly," Locs said. "I thought that would be the end of it."

"The end of it?" Mr. Korkmaz said.

"I tried to stop him," said Locs. "But your son is . . ." And here she tried to find just the right word to counter any correct sense Mr. Korkmaz might have that she was lying.

". . . Quite stubborn," Mr. Korkmaz said, world-wearily, as though he was all too familiar with his son's stubbornness. Locs wondered whether Søren had inherited the stubbornness from his father. She could see Mr. Korkmaz wondering that, too. His face went slack and sad. It is a terrible thing to have a son, to worry that you are the source of all his worst qualities, to have to scramble to find other plausible sources. "Søren's mother died when he was young," Søren's father said. "Such a death does very terrible things to a boy, as it did to Søren."

"I'm sorry."

"You will tell me where I can locate Broomeville, New York."

"I'll do better than that," Locs said. "I will take you there."

Mr. Korkmaz seemed to consider this. He studied Locs's face. How can I trust you? he seemed to be asking. But that, they both knew, was a rhetorical question.

"You don't know these people," Locs said. "They'll eat you alive."

Mr. Korkmaz thought about that for another moment. Then he did something interesting. He handed his gun to Locs. Once she was holding it, she knew it was a fake. A fake gun! She hadn't held one of those since she was a child. It almost made her nostalgic. The almost nostalgia made her not mad but amazed. This old man had menaced her with a fake gun! She looked up at him and could tell Mr. Korkmaz was trying not to smile. "Fine," he said. "You will take me."

"Great," Locs said, trying not to smile back. She pointed the gun at him and said, "Bang!" And then they both laughed. And when they were done laughing, Locs said, "Although you might have to float me a loan for the airplane tickets."

48
• • •

Ronald. Monday night, eleven o'clock. Ronald had a computer at home; he also had Internet access. So why was he in Matty's office, on Matty's computer? For no good reason except that he had the vague sense that he might end up causing even more trouble this way.

"Jens Baedrup," he said and then also typed. Up came the news. It was pretty much as that sack-of-shit guidance counselor had said: Danes, Muslims, cartoons, fires, murder. Supposedly murder. That was the interesting part. Trouble, trouble, thought Ronald. He looked at the pictures of Jens Baedrup. Ronald had seen only the back of the stranger's head. The stranger had had short dark hair. The Jens Baedrup on the computer also had dark hair, but it was long in the back. In the front, there wasn't that much of it. His face was round, which was a polite way of saying pretty fat. It looked vaguely familiar. Of course it did. He had just seen the guy yesterday. Except he'd not seen his face. God, this guy looked like a clown, with his fat face and his gruesome beard and his red glasses. His huge, huge smile, too. It looked like he was trying out for the part of the

Happiest Person in the World. What a jerk. He was married, too. Who would marry this guy anyway?

Ilsa Baedrup, originally and now currently of Aarhus, that's who. He found a phone listing for her, no trouble. Trouble, trouble, Ronald thought again. But for whom? Henry, he hoped. And Matty, he also hoped. But who else? Then again, did it matter? Ronald was like most people who get hurt: they think they have immunity for every hurt they cause while seeking full reimbursement for their own original hurt. And by hurt, he wasn't thinking about his hand. He wasn't even really thinking about his sister, Sheilah, either. It was just everything. By this point, Ronald thought of life as one large hurt-giving enterprise, and he was just going to keep giving and giving until . . .

Ronald looked up the country code for Denmark, then dialed the number. After two rings a woman answered. "Hi, hi," she mumbled. She'd clearly been asleep.

"Is this Ilsa?" Ronald said, in English obviously.

"Yes," Isla said in the same language. She'd said the word at normal volume, too. Not like she was in bed with someone and trying not to wake them up. Ronald could picture her: lonely woman, middle of the night, wondering about her long-lost husband.

"I know where your husband is," he said.

"Is he safe?"

"Yup," Ronald said. "Just saw him a few hours ago."

"Oh, thank you," Ilsa said, sounding like she really meant it. "I've been worried about him. I've missed him."

"Really?" Ronald asked, not really caring about the answer, just thinking out loud. "You have?"

Ilsa laughed. "I know," she said. "That surprises me, too."

"I'm glad I called, then," Ronald said. "I just thought you'd like to know that he's thinking about you, too." And then it was Ilsa's turn to say, "Really?" "Yes, really," Ronald said. "He asked me to call you and tell you so."

"Why didn't he call me himself?"

"Safety reasons," Ronald said.

"He's still not safe?"

"Anywhere else, maybe not," Ronald said. "But here, yes. More or less."

"Where is here?"

"Broomeville, New York," Ronald said.

"*Where?*"

Ronald laughed at that, and then told her.

PART SIX

· · ·

49
· · ·

Thursday morning. Henry, up by six and without the help of the alarm, as usual, spotting a piece of paper on the floor by the door, not as usual. Henry got out of bed, quietly, quietly, so as not to wake Ellen. He remembered the last time he'd found paper on the floor by the door. It'd been his first night in Broomeville, his first night with Ellen, his first night as Henry Larsen. On those pieces of paper had been the Danish and English words for "counter," and also the cartoon he'd drawn of himself, with a big black X scratched through it. He'd thought Kurt was responsible for the X. I'll have to keep my eye on Kurt, he'd thought back then. And he had. And what Henry had learned from two years of watching was that he loved Kurt, like a son, but also that he didn't totally trust him, also like a son.

He bent over, picked up the piece of paper. On it, the name JENS BAEDRUP had been written in large, uneven black block letters, with a big black X scratched through the name. Whoever had written the name and the X had pushed down so hard that in places the pen had poked right through the paper.

"Kurt?" Henry thought and must have actually said, because Ellen repeated, still mostly asleep, "Kurt, honey? Are you OK?"

"He's fine," Henry said.

"He?" Ellen said. "Kurt?"

"I'm fine," Henry whispered. "Go back to sleep." Luckily, Ellen did that, and Henry crumpled the note, stuffed it into his satchel, and then went into the bathroom to get ready for work.

50
. . .

Arson! Now *that,* they all agreed, was the way to protest something. Not the way so many other people did it. For instance, that kid who had graduated from the high school a few years earlier. This was during the graduation ceremony. The kid had apparently had some long-standing beef with the school about something. Or maybe he just didn't like to sit. Or maybe that was his beef with the school: that it had made him sit. In any case, when it was his turn to walk onstage and accept his diploma and shake Kurt's dad's hand, he brought his folding chair with him, in protest of whatever. Everyone laughed at him except for Kurt's dad, who, to his credit, just shook the kid's hand that wasn't holding the chair and then stuck the diploma into it. The kid seemed oblivious to how pathetic the whole thing was: after he received his piece of paper, he turned to the crowd and raised both the diploma and the chair in triumph, as if to say, See! I did it! Now the kid worked down at the pharmacy, where he was allowed to wear a pharmacist's smock even though he wasn't really a pharmacist. He was one of those people who dress like someone they will never actually be. This was what happened when you chose such a piss-poor form of protest. But arson!

"But what's he *doing* here?" said Tyler. He was sitting next to his twin, Kevin, on the ratty, burn-marked tan corduroy couch. Across the steamer trunk from them was *Dr.* Vernon, sitting on a kitchen chair. Next to him, semisubmerged in a black beanbag chair, was Kurt. This was in *Dr.* Vernon's office. Not his school office, which as a permanent substitute teacher he did not even have, but his home office, which only he called his office, which only he found hilarious when he called it his office. His office was the second story of his detached garage. In it, he dealt and did drugs. Mostly pot, which he dealt to and smoked with students, mostly. Mostly before school. It was the only way *Dr.* Vernon could face the day. "Sticky bud courage!" he called it. "Wake and bake!" he said. "Breakfast of champions!" he said. All of this spoken at top volume. Sometimes, Kurt had to smoke pot before going to *Dr.* Vernon's office just to endure the pot smoking in *Dr.* Vernon's office before then going to school.

"Who doing where?" *Dr.* Vernon said. He'd just finished telling them about what he'd heard the night before in the Lumber Lodge about the stranger who'd come to see and then fled from Mr. L. and who, if he really was who Mr. L. said he was, was involved in this crazy situation involving cartoons and Muslims and murder that was apparently not murder and Scandinavia and also arson.

"The new guy," Kevin said.

"Yeah, the arsonist," Tyler said.

"What?" *Dr.* Vernon said. "No?" He paused seemingly to consider the steamer trunk, on which was a Habitrail of marijuana buds, stems, and seeds; rolling papers and one-hitters; Baggies and twist ties; a scale and a bong and the bong bowl, which *Dr.* Vernon himself had just emptied. On the floor, next to the trunk, was one of those shower caddies, if that was the term for it, and in his current state Kurt was not at all sure that it was, but anyway, it was a white plastic contraption with a handle that contained several bottles of Visine, a tin of breath mints, a bottle of mouthwash, and some kind of vaporizer or deodorizer spray bottle thingy that made you smell like a just-cleaned public restroom but at least stopped you from smelling like you'd just smoked a lot of pot. But deodorizer? Vaporizer? Was either of those correct? No. More like a bug bomb. Or not a bomb. A fogger. That's right. A bug fogger. Jeez, Kurt was feeling pretty fogged himself. Although not nearly as fogged as *Dr.* Vernon. "Right," *Dr.* Vernon finally said, and he started whacking the cartridge against the trunk, trying to empty it. "Not sure *why* the arsonist is here."

"Come on," Kurt said. "The stranger isn't the arsonist."

"That's what I said," *Dr.* Vernon said. "The arsonist is the other guy."

"What other guy?" Tyler said.

"The *other* guy," Kevin said, and he socked his twin in the right thigh and then socked him again. "*Not* the stranger."

"Stop calling him 'the stranger,'" *Dr.* Vernon said. "The man has a *name*." And here he stopped, clearly trying to remember the man's name, clearly failing. As for Kurt, he had no idea what the stranger's name was, either. During his telling of the story, *Dr.* Vernon had referred to him only as "the stranger." "But, anyway, yes," *Dr.* Vernon finally said.

"Yes what?" Tyler asked, but *Dr.* Vernon didn't answer. He repacked and reinserted the bowl and passed the bong to Kevin, who stuck his face into the bong's cylinder and sucked. Then he handed it to Tyler, who did the same. Tyler passed the bong to Kurt, but Kurt had had enough. He knew he'd had enough because before he started smoking pot he'd intended to ask *Dr.* Vernon whether he thought Mr. L. might be a spy. But now after smoking pot for an hour, the idea seemed unforgivably stupid. Some people knew they'd smoked enough pot when the most stupid ideas started making a lot of sense; Kurt, on the other hand, knew he'd smoked enough pot when ideas that had earlier seemed quite reasonable now seemed unforgivably stupid. "I'm good," Kurt said, and then he passed the bong on to *Dr.* Vernon.

"Come on, just one more," *Dr.* Vernon said in an accent—British, supposedly—that let Kurt know that what *Dr.* Vernon was saying came from a movie *Dr.* Vernon would say he couldn't believe Kurt hadn't watched after Kurt told him once again that he hadn't watched it. "It's only a wafer thin."

"No, thanks," Kurt said. *Dr.* Vernon then smoked Kurt's share, then his own, and then he put the lid on the bong, put the remaining pot in an ornate wooden box, wrapped the one-hitters in a piece of velvety blue cloth and placed them in another ornate wooden box, sprayed himself and the room with his fogger, put several breath mints on his tongue, and in general conducted all the various rites of his particular priesthood. The boys were mesmerized by this display, even though they'd witnessed it many times before. When he was done, *Dr.* Vernon said, "You know, I think the stranger might be a narc."

This was entirely predictable: *Dr.* Vernon tended to think pretty much everyone might be a narc. The only person who he seemed to think was not a narc was his wife, mostly because she treated him so fondly, like he was a somewhat mischievous child she couldn't help but love. Speaking of which, Grace Vernon yelled up from the garage below: "Don't come to school reeking of pot, you old fool!"

"I won't!" he yelled back, his voice bright with love. They listened as the automatic garage door went up, the car started and pulled out of the garage, the door closed. Then *Dr.* Vernon turned back to the boys, his face and voice dark with treachery again. "A narc," he repeated. "That's why I'm being so careful these days." This struck Kurt as the most ridiculous thing he'd heard that morning—*Dr.* Vernon was possibly the least careful human being he had ever met—but then *Dr.* Vernon reached inside his billowing orange-and-blue riot of a shirt and pulled out a handgun.

"Is that a gun?" Kevin asked, and then it was his twin's turn to punch him in the thigh.

"You can't be too careful, can you?" *Dr.* Vernon said. This was clearly a rhetorical question, and so Kurt didn't respond to it. He tried to climb out of the beanbag chair, but the chair resisted, and Kurt ended up having to kind of wrestle the chair into submission before getting out of it. By the time he did so, he felt like something had changed for him. He did not want to smoke pot in that chair in this office with these human beings ever again. It was *Dr.* Vernon whipping out that gun that had changed everything. It wasn't that the gun had scared him. It was that it made him feel deeply ashamed. He had an image of his father walking into this stupid room and seeing Kurt stuck in that stupid chair after smoking stupid pot with these stupid people, one of whom was waving around his stupid gun. And how would that make his father feel? He had never thought or cared to ask that question before. But he was asking it now, possibly because his father had asked him to keep his eyes open and had given him that important task, and here he was, getting high with these idiots, his eyes barely open, his lids so heavy, not keeping his eyes open for Mr. L. or the stranger or anyone. And how *would* this make his father feel? He was asking the question, but he did not want it answered. If you had to ask the question, How would that make your father feel? then you already knew that you didn't want to know the answer.

Kurt's skateboard was leaning against the wall next to the door. He walked toward it. "Hey, where you going?" one of the twins said, but Kurt didn't turn to see which one, and he didn't answer the question, either. Good-bye, he thought, good-bye, good-bye, good-bye.

"I think his buddy might be a narc, too," *Dr.* Vernon said.

"His buddy?" Kurt said. He turned around. *Dr.* Vernon was pulling a blue linen blazer over his garish shirt, which presumably was once again hosting the handgun. In any case, it wasn't in *Dr.* Vernon's hand anymore. He grabbed the lapels of the blazer and stretched it, then buttoned it.

"Yeah," Tyler said. "Mr. L."

"That's what I was saying," Kevin said. "The *other guy.*"

"Mr. L. is the arsonist?" Kurt said.

"What?" *Dr.* Vernon said. He sat back in his chair, clearly thinking about what he was supposed to be saying. His stomach bulged, testing the moorings of his blazer's buttons. "No," he finally said.

No? Kurt thought but did not say. There was something important about Mr. L. that was floating in the outer atmosphere of his memory. But in between him and the memory were all sorts of other memories, plus the pot he'd smoked, and also all the people in this room, talking, talking. He'd never get to the memory if he stayed where he was. So he grabbed his skateboard, told everyone he'd see them at school, and left the office.

51

. . .

enry walked to work. He had a car, but he preferred
to walk because it was not far and because in doing
so he often walked by people who liked him. For instance, now: Lee Truesdell, whom everyone called Lugnut. He
had just emerged from his car, parked in the lot outside Ham-
mond Lumber, where he worked. Lugnut was a large man with
large feet made even more enormous by his tan work boots
with their steel toes and foot-long laces. Lugnut's son, Dana,
was a sophomore at the high school, and Henry had just talked
Dana through an especially difficult time during which Dana
did not feel like doing any homework. Basically, Henry had
asked Dana why he didn't feel like doing any homework and
then said nothing, just frowned, arms folded, and listened to
Dana figuring out for himself that his reasons for not feeling
like doing any homework made some sense and were shared
at one time or another by every other student who had ever
gone to school at Broomeville Junior-Senior High or for that
matter any other school on the planet and so did not make him
anointed or rebellious in any way, and by the time he was done
talking, Dana felt like doing some homework again.

"Mr. L.," Lugnut said.

"Lugnut," Henry said.

"You know, my name is Lee," Lugnut said. Like a lot of big men, Lugnut's voice was soft and gentle, and in fact his whole bearing was completely pacific, which had the strange effect of making him seem constantly on the verge of committing some terrible violence. "But everyone calls me Lugnut."

Henry nodded to indicate that he, too, had been guilty of calling Lugnut by that name.

"People have called me Lugnut since I was fourteen. Do you know why?"

"Because you're so big?" Henry guessed.

"That's my theory, too," Lugnut said. "Except, have you ever *seen* a lug nut?"

Henry said he never had. "You're saying they're small."

"They're big," Lugnut said. "But only compared to other nuts."

"Have you asked people to call you Lee?" Henry asked, but he didn't even require an answer: of course Lugnut had, and of course people had not done what he'd asked. You could not just ask people to call you what you wanted to be called if they'd already been calling you something else. He and Ellen had tried this with Kurt. Kurt had always called him Mr. L. But it seemed strange to Ellen that Kurt would call his stepfather by this name.

"What about 'Dad'?" Ellen had asked, and Kurt had made retching noises.

"Henry?" Ellen had suggested.

"But that's what *you* call him," Kurt had said, as though Henry were not right there, in the room, listening to this conversation.

"Call me Mr. L.," he'd finally suggested, back then, to Kurt, and he said to Lugnut, now, "Call me Lugnut."

"Lugnut," Lugnut said.

"Attach other words to the name, as in a greeting," Henry said, turning his back to Lugnut. "Pretend you're greeting me in the morning, afternoon, evening. Ask me if you could borrow my lawn mower."

"Good morning, Lugnut," Lugnut said. "Good afternoon, Lugnut. Hey, Lugnut, my grass is getting kind of long, Lugnut," etc. Each time, Henry made no response. When Lugnut seemed to have had enough of the exercise, he said, "OK, Mr. L," and Henry turned around and said, "See?"

"But your name isn't Lugnut," Lugnut said. "Oh, I get it."

Then Lee shook Henry's hand, told him that would probably never work but thanks for trying anyway, and disappeared into the lumberyard. This was why Henry liked walking to work. This was why Henry liked living in Broomeville. Because people here trusted him. But would they trust him once this man he'd said was Jens Baedrup was through with him? The stranger would probably try to kill him, especially once he discovered that Henry had given him the name of the man he was probably going to try to kill. That was bad enough. But what else would he try to do before he tried to do that?

Henry resumed walking. Past the Nice n' Easy. Past the fairgrounds. Just ahead was Bonny Courts, a subdivision between the fairgrounds and the school. At the entrance of the subdivision was a wooden sign carved into the shape of a castle, and behind the sign was a fiberglass statue of, for some reason, a brown bear, eight feet high on its hind legs, its front paws held

palms-out. The effect was probably intended to be menacing—
Don't enter here unless you live here! the bear probably wanted
to be saying with its paws—but to Henry, the gesture seemed
full of joy, like the bear was on the top deck of a cruiseship,
saying, Good-bye! Good-bye! to the nice people on the pier
below. Anyway, Henry was ten feet from the bear when he
saw a boy on a skateboard careen out of the subdivision and
onto the sidewalk. It was Kurt. Henry knew this because Kurt
was the only person who rode a skateboard in Broomeville.
The skateboard was a large wooden thing, so wide that you
wouldn't think anyone could fall off it. But once on the sidewalk, Kurt attempted some sort of hopping maneuver and in
doing so lost his balance and struck his head on the castle, and
his skateboard shot forward at an incredible speed, hopped off
the sidewalk, and sailed across the road and into a ditch. Kurt
rolled around on the ground for a few seconds, then made a
loud animal sound, then pulled himself into a sitting position,
head between his knees. "Fuck!" he yelled, three times, and
then suddenly he got to his feet, sprinted to his skateboard,
picked it up, and then sprinted back toward the sign, with the
obvious intent of beating the castle with his board, but before
he got close enough to the castle to beat it, he slipped and fell,
striking the back of his head on the sidewalk. He was still lying
there when Henry reached him.

"Ouch," Henry said. Kurt opened one eye, saw who it was
standing over him, closed the eye again.

"Where's my skateboard?" Kurt said, even though it was
still in his right hand.

"You might be hurt," Henry said.

"Or I might be . . . ," Kurt said, but he didn't finish the sentence. Instead he sat up, and Henry got a good whiff of what Kurt might be. Oh, buddy, he thought but did not say. ". . . High," Kurt said, finishing the sentence.

"You do smell high," Henry said.

"Please don't tell my father," Kurt said.

"Does that mean I can tell your mother?" Henry said. Although he had no intention of telling anyone anything. He was not a psychiatrist or a doctor, and even less a lawyer or a priest, and in any case he had taken no oath of patient-counselor confidentiality. But that was one of his policies, unwritten and unspoken but by now well known: if a student told him something and did not want Henry to pass the information on to the student's parents or teachers or whomever, then Henry would not. Usually, if a student felt bad enough about something that he confessed to it and then asked Henry to keep the information secret, then the student would end up either spilling the beans himself or he would just stop doing it.

"I guess not," Kurt said, and then he started crying. Crying and crying. The kind of crying where you didn't care who sees or hears. Lots of people were seeing and hearing, too: buses, cars, pedestrians, passed by and gawked, and still Kurt wept. The public weeping produced a great feeling of residual Scandinavian embarrassment in Henry, and at first he began hugging Kurt in an attempt to just get him to stop crying in the presence of all these other people. But Kurt did not stop, he kept weeping, and suddenly Henry had an image of the near future. In two days, Ellen and Henry would be married. They had transformed the four apartments above the Lumber Lodge into a home: a television room, a kitchen, a bathroom in the hall, a master bedroom for Henry and Ellen, and a bedroom for Kurt. Kurt had not yet moved into the bedroom: Ellen had felt very strongly that he not do so until she and Henry were legally wed. But anyway, Henry had a vision of the room in the near future, and in it there were posters on the wall, dirty socks everywhere, and also, of course, a bed, and on the bed Kurt was weeping, and Henry was hugging him and telling him that everything was going to be just fine, just like a real father would tell his real son, except if that were true, then why in the middle of the night was the real son sliding a piece of paper under the real father's door with the real father's real name on it, crossed out with a big black X?

Henry went to break their embrace, but Kurt had already done so. He wasn't crying anymore. Instead he was looking at Henry the way Henry had been planning to look at him, eyes wide open. I think I know what you did, the look said. I think I know who you are.

Please don't tell your mother, Henry thought but did not say, because he was afraid to say anything, and also because Kurt had already remounted his skateboard. "I wonder if the stranger will show up again today," he said, and then he skateboarded off.

52

. . .

Three thirty, Thursday afternoon. Matty was in his office. The school buses had left; the stranger had not arrived. Matty had been thinking about him all day. Matty felt that his reappearance was somehow key to stopping Ellen from marrying Henry in two days. Two days, two days. Then, two knocks on the door. "Come in," Matty said, but his secretary, Gina, was already coming in. Gina was a small woman, always armed with small yellow sticky notes. She was holding one now.

"I just got a call from accounting," she said.

"Huh," Matty said. They were always getting calls from the state education board's accounting office. Usually they wanted to know why the school had bought the second-cheapest kind of volleyball instead of the cheapest, why they'd purchased two sacks of rock salt instead of just one, etc. Matty extended his hand, and Gina gave him the note. On it was a bunch of numbers.

"And this is . . ."

"A telephone number," Gina said. "In Denmark."

"OK."

"You called it from your office phone."

"I did not," Matty said, but his mind was already at work, asking who, why, and of course when. "When?"

"Last night," Gina said. "A little after eleven."

Eleven o'clock the night before. Matty had been home, in the kitchen, next to the woodstove, watching TV. Kurt had been there, too, if Matty was looking for an alibi. But he wasn't, necessarily, and he wasn't necessarily worried about accounting, either. All accounting wanted was for you to be aware that they knew what you were doing, and to not do it again.

"Huh," Matty said. "And what else did accounting say?"

"They said don't do it again."

"Don't do what again?" Ellen said. She was behind Gina, and as soon as Gina heard her voice, she exited the scene, the way you do when the boss's ex-wife enters. Ellen entered. It felt illicit to have Ellen in his office, alone. Matty had to stop himself from saying something ridiculous, something like, I want to start our life together again, right now. Instead, Matty gestured for her to sit in the empty red plastic chair to the left of the door. Ellen shook her head, then leaned against the wall, left eyebrow raised (which she'd always done), arms crossed, frowning (which she had never done). She must have picked it up from Henry. Ellen was close enough for Matty to smell her cigarette-smoke smell if she'd smelled of smoke, which she didn't. Henry had probably made her quit. No, Henry never made anyone do anything. But he'd probably *helped* her quit. Henry, Henry. Two days, two days. In two days, Ellen would be married to Henry, but only if Matty couldn't help it.

"Don't do what again?" Ellen asked a second time.

"Call Denmark on my office phone," Matty said.

"Denmark," Ellen repeated, arms uncrossed now, but still frowning. She sat in the chair. "Why'd you do that?"

"I didn't."

"Huh." Ellen said. "Then who did?"

"That's what I'd like to know," Matty said. He leaned back in his chair, being quiet, trying to let Ellen come to her own conclusion, which Matty wanted to be identical to his own conclusion. This, of course, was also known as the Socratic method. At Cornell, Matty had been taught that the Socratic method was intellectually bankrupt. Which is not to say that it wasn't effective.

"It has to be Jens Baedrup," Ellen said. "The Danish stranger who came to Henry's office."

Matty nodded. "That was my first thought, too. And I guess it *could* be him." He paused to think, or pretend to. "But the school was locked. He'd have to have gotten a key from someone."

"Who has keys?"

"Everyone who works here has keys to the front doors," Matty said. Then, again, he stopped talking, long enough to allow Ellen to think, Well, then, it could have been lots of people, and then to counterthink, But who among those lots of people would want to call Denmark?

"Why would he have used your phone?" Ellen said, and Matty did not miss the pronoun. He, Matty thought but did not say. Because Matty wanted to appear in all ways principalic: fair minded, objective, an indisputably good guy.

"Maybe because there are only two outside lines in the whole school: mine and Gina's. And Gina locks her office door at night."

"You don't lock yours?"

"Nope," Matty said, and he shrugged, as though to say, I know, stupid, huh, but hey, my office door is always unlocked, that's the kind of good guy I am and always have been. And anyway, everything Matty had said so far was absolutely true, were Ellen inclined to check. She didn't seem inclined. Ellen pulled her blond hair off her forehead, held it, then let it fall back. Her hair, her hair. Matty had always found it incredibly soft, less like hair and more like white-blond feathers, with slightly darker blond roots.

"What time?" Ellen said.

"What time," Matty repeated, trying to buy himself some. Gina had said, "A little after eleven." Henry had probably been with Ellen then, in the bar, or upstairs, waiting for her to close the bar. Henry couldn't have made the phone call then. A few hours before that, Henry was in the bar, telling everyone the stranger's name. A few hours before that everyone had been wondering about the stranger, and Ellen had been wondering about Henry. "I wonder where Henry is," Matty had heard Ellen wonder several times in the three hours between when Henry had left the baseball game and when he'd shown up at the bar. As for Matty himself, he'd gotten to the bar a little before five o'clock.

"A little after five o'clock," Matty said. It was the only lie he'd told over the past couple of minutes, and in the end he would have cause to regret it. Also, by this point, Matty had stopped wondering who had actually made the phone call, and had dedicated himself to suggesting that most likely it was Henry. He would later have cause to regret that, too. "Five seventeen, to be exact," he said.

"Huh." Ellen again. She was biting her lip, eyes pinched, remembering who had been where and when yesterday, doing the math. Matty let her do it. Then, when she'd done it for long enough, he reminded her, "Hey, tomorrow's Kurt's band concert."

"Right," she said, and even as distracted as she was, she made a face. Kurt played trumpet in the school band's annual October concert, which was always a somewhat painful experience. The band director, Mr. Ferraro, had never quite gotten over the rock music of his youth, the greatness of which he was convinced was a product of the era's spontaneity, which led him to forsake regular rehearsals, and which also led him to have the kids perform wildly inappropriate material. Last year, for instance, their finale was the Rolling Stones' "Let's Spend the Night Together," and when some parents complained, Mr. Ferraro pointed out that the kids did not actually sing the lyrics (which was true, although Mr. Ferraro did mouth the words during the enthusiastic prosecution of his conducting) and that, besides, the kids' version was "much more brass than ass," which did not necessarily help Mr. Ferraro's cause with the parents but was nonetheless also true.

Anyway, the concert was to begin at 2:55 tomorrow. Matty and Ellen always went to Kurt's public events—in addition to

band, he was on the track team—together. It was important
to Kurt, Ellen said. Of course, Kurt had never said so himself. Nevertheless, it was a good thing, Ellen said. Matty supposed that was right. He also supposed it was a good thing that
Henry sat apart from them during these performances. "*We're*
Kurt's parents," Ellen had said before last year's concert. "It's
important that Kurt sees us together. Henry would probably
just be a distraction."

"That's true!" Matty had said, maybe a little too enthusias-
tically, because Ellen had raised an eyebrow and said, "Yeah,
it was Henry's idea."

"Henry!" Ellen was saying now. Because there he was,
standing in the doorway, looking at Ellen, a huge, toothy, very
un-Henry-like smile on his face. Love, love, Matty thought,
it made you into something you were not. Wow, I hate you,
Matty thought but did not say to Henry. But then he noticed
that Ellen wasn't exactly smiling at Henry the way he was smiling at her. "Where . . . ," she started to ask. Then she glanced
at Matty and said, "Where *were* you?"

Then Henry began looking more like Henry. He frowned.
Crossed his arms. Ellen turned to Matty to explain. "We're *supposed* to go to Walmart to buy wedding stuff, and then back to
the Lodge to decorate." Then she turned back to Henry. "You
were *supposed* to meet me at three thirty!" she said. Henry
glanced at his watch, and Matty at his. It was only 3:32. When
he looked up again, Henry and Ellen were walking out of his
office. Without even saying good-bye. Although Matty wasn't
thinking too much about that. He was instead thinking about

Ellen. "Where *were* you?" Ellen had asked Henry. But Matty knew what she'd wanted to ask. She'd wanted to ask, Where were you at five seventeen last night?" When, Matty wondered, would she ask that question? And how would Henry answer when she did?

53

. . .

How many times had Ellen been about to ask the question? Once, when they'd stood in the PARTY aisle at Walmart, trying to decide how much yardage of streamers they would need and in what colors; twice, at Comstock's Food and Beverage Wholesale Distributors, listening to Bill Comstock Sr. congratulate himself on what a great deal he was giving them on kegs of Michelob because, hey, she was a longtime, valued customer, and hey, she was getting married, but hey, don't expect the same great deal if she got married again, that is, if they even made Michelob at that future date and time, because as it was, pretty much no one drank it anymore, even though it used to be one of their biggest sellers, but anyway, you're welcome; thrice, at the gas station, looking back out the passenger's side-view mirror as Henry filled up the tank in her truck with regular unleaded. Now, for the fourth time—was there another way to say "the fourth time"?—at the Lumber Lodge. It was six o'clock; the place was pretty much empty, except for two old guys whom Ellen remembered from back when she was a girl and her mother ran the bar and who always only drank their beer out of juice glasses, and Ellen herself, and Henry, who was sitting at the bar, addressing a basket of chicken wings. Until very recently, Henry had watched in disbelief as the drunks at the Lumber Lodge ate those grotesque bird parts by the dozens. How can you eat that stuff? his pinched face had always seemed to want to know. But now apparently he knew; now he couldn't stop eating the things. Although he also couldn't seem to quite make himself believe that they really were chicken wings.

"They're so small," he said to Ellen, who was standing behind the bar. "Are these really the wings of a chicken?"

"Yes," Ellen said. Although really she had no idea. Now that he mentioned it, they didn't look like the wings of any chicken she'd ever seen. Some of them were drumsticks, not wings at all. But they did come in an enormous bag that said CHICKEN WINGS. "That's what it says on the bag," Ellen said. But it didn't seem to matter to him what they were: Henry kept eating them. If he didn't stop, eventually he'd get fat, like everyone else. But for now, here he was, the slimmest, most handsome chicken-wing-eating Swede Ellen had ever seen. A Swede, not a Dane, right? She wondered that, because why would a *Swede* be calling *Denmark* at 5:17 at night from Matty's phone? Did you call Denmark from Matty's office phone last night at five seventeen? Ellen almost asked him, for the fourth time. But she didn't. There is a kind of IOU embedded in the psyche of the about-to-be-wed, the postponement of the paying of the bet that is the marriage itself. I'll forgive, or ignore, this latest thing, the engaged thinks. But if there's one more thing . . . Although maybe this wasn't limited to people who were preparing to be married. After all, Ellen had made similar promises to herself about Matty when she was still married to him, until finally there was the one more thing, which was Henry.

"Did I ever tell you," Ellen said, "the name of the woman Matty cheated on me with?" When Ellen said that, she thought of Matty—not of him cheating on her, but of how he, in their distant past life together, had gently teased her about ending sentences with prepositions. Later on, in their more recent past life together, the teasing had been so ungentle that it couldn't be called teasing. But back further, when Kurt was a baby, a toddler, the teasing was gentle, full of love. Those were good times, Ellen thought, and then thought, *Why am I thinking about this now?* Meanwhile, Henry was still working on his wings. She'd never talked about this before with Henry. In some ridiculous but definite way, she thought talking about it would diminish her in Henry's eyes. And if it did that now, if she told him about Locs and Matty, and Henry looked or acted or talked about it as though her talking about it made her a lesser person, then that would be the one more thing. "Her name was Locs." Henry didn't react; he was busy stripping the *meat* from the *bones* with his *teeth*. Had he always eaten this loudly? Maybe he hadn't even heard her over the deafening crunching of his disgusting wing eating. Ellen said, louder this time, "Locs!" This time Henry flinched.

"Yes, I heard you," Henry said. He placed the last gnawed bone in the basket, wiped his hands on a napkin, crumpled it, threw it in the basket also. "Locs," he repeated. "Was that her first or last name?"

"Neither."

Henry nodded as though this made sense. He stood up and walked behind the bar until he was standing in front of her. He put his hands on her shoulders, gently. "I knew about this," he said.

"This what?"

"This Locs."

"How?"

He shrugged. "People talking," he said. And there, he'd done it! He'd made her feel diminished! But now he was looking at her like she wasn't diminished in the slightest. "I am going to marry you in two days," he said. And then he kissed her, and then she didn't feel diminished anymore. She did almost ask him, for the fifth time, Did you call Denmark from Matty's office phone last night at five seventeen? But then she didn't because they were kissing. But one more thing, she thought. And then she stopped kissing him and refilled the old guys' juice glasses, and then she and Henry started putting up streamers in preparation for their wedding, day after next. They worked in silence—hammer, nail, streamer, repeat—until Ellen said, "Kurt's band concert is tomorrow." Henry nodded. He looked at her as if wanting more information. "You don't have to go, you know." Because unlike the baseball game, faculty and staff attendance at the concert wasn't required. Henry got down off his ladder, and Ellen hers. They moved both several feet to the right and then climbed their ladders again, holding another streamer between them.

"Kurt is going to be my stepson," Henry finally said. It was just another declarative sentence; Henry was locally famous for them—famous for approving or disapproving of them, famous for speaking them. But this one felt more important—for Ellen, and maybe for Henry, too. "I want to go," he said.

"I want you to go," Ellen said.

"Then I will go," Henry said.

54

. . .

Downstairs, Matty and Lawrence were drinking their drinks, sitting next to the woodstove. Upstairs, Kurt was messing around with his trumpet. You could not call it practicing, although a few minutes earlier Matty had reminded Kurt that he needed to go practice his trumpet for the concert tomorrow. Now, intermittent aggrieved noises drifted downstairs; it sounded, to Matty, like a lamb who every now and then remembered that it was supposed to bleat. Meanwhile, Lawrence was looking thoughtfully at the woodstove, bobbing his head as though in actual appreciation of the sounds coming from upstairs.

"Vienna!" he started to say, but Matty interrupted.

"Yesterday," he said, "Kurt thought Henry was a spy." Lawrence listened—to Matty, to Kurt and his trumpet—nodding, nodding. "Today, he's not so sure."

"No?" Lawrence stopped nodding. He looked at his brother. "What do you think?"

"I think he's the guy who stole my wife," Matty said, and Lawrence started nodding again. "I think he's also the person who called Denmark on my office phone last night." And then

he told Lawrence the story: Of how Gina had told him about
the phone call. Of how Ellen had come into the office. Of how
Matty was pretty sure she and he were reaching the same conclusion about the phone call. Of how . . . and wow, Matty
really wanted to tell Lawrence the truth. Ever since Ellen had
left him, ever since Locs had disappeared, Matty had really
wanted to be able to confide in someone; he had really wanted
someone to trust. He had always loved Lawrence, but he had
never exactly trusted him. Things were different now. Besides,
if you can't trust your brother . . . But that was a rhetorical question and not worth finishing. Matty told his brother
the truth anyway. "According the phone records, the call was
made just after eleven. But I told Ellen that it was made at five
seventeen."

Lawrence stopped nodding again. He looked at his brother
with wide eyes, as if seeing him for the very first time. "Which
was when our Henry was out perambulating."

"I guess."

"By himself."

"I miss Ellen."

"Do you miss Locs?" Lawrence said. Matty had never
mentioned Locs to Lawrence. But he'd assumed he knew; he
assumed everyone in Broomeville knew. Now he knew they
knew; he knew his brother knew. Matty felt it again: shame,
regret, defiance, loss, shame. But Lawrence was nodding in an
encouraging way. You can tell me anything, the nod seemed
to say.

"That doesn't matter anymore," Matty finally said.

"Probably not."

"I shouldn't have lied to Ellen about that phone call."

"Probably not." But Lawrence was smiling when he said it. That made Matty feel very good. For the first time in a long time, maybe ever, Matty felt what a lucky thing it was to have a brother. "The great game!" Lawrence shouted.

"What does that mean?" Matty asked, and then he was sorry he had, because all the joy drained out of Lawrence's face. Lawrence sipped a little raki in a transparent attempt to try to compose himself and then tried to explain his meaning.

"East versus West!" Lawrence shouted. "Old World versus the New! Democracy versus communism! Ex-husband versus future husband! The great game!" Matty didn't say anything. He knew that no matter what he said, it would sound to his brother like Matty was saying, God, you're weird. Why have you always been so weird? Meanwhile, Lawrence was looking at Matty, clearly waiting for some sort of response.

"Right, sure," Matty said. "I get it now."

And his brother really did seem to want that: he really did seem to want Matty to understand. Lawrence finished the rest of his raki in one gulp and then leaned toward Matty as though preparing to tell his brother an important secret.

But just then, Kurt came bounding down the stairs. His face was red and his lips were white, in the way of trumpet players. "I *practiced*," he said, and he hurled himself onto the couch, next to his uncle. His uncle leaned back, too, his empty glass resting on his chest. Matty got up to pour Lawrence some more, but Lawrence shook him off. Whatever he'd been about to tell Matty was gone. They were back to being the kind of brothers who'll never quite get each other. Lawrence turned his head to look at Kurt. "I hear," Lawrence said, "that you have an interesting theory about your future stepfather."

"I thought he was a spy, but he's not."

"Well, what is he, then?" Lawrence said thoughtfully.

"I don't know," Kurt said. "I feel like it's right *here*." He then started pounding the side of his head, the way you do when there's water in your ear. After a few moments of this, Lawrence stopped his nephew's hand and gently placed it on the couch between them.

"My Civics Club has its weekly congress tomorrow afternoon," Lawrence said. "Perhaps you'd like to join us."

Kurt laughed at that. Matty didn't blame him. The boys in the Civics Club were all freaks, dressed in their jackets and ties like they were perpetually trying out for the part of Little Nixon. But then Kurt seemed to get that his uncle was serious, and stopped laughing. And then Matty was proud of his son. If it were Matty, he would have kept laughing and laughing until his brother wanted to punch him in the face. But Kurt wasn't like that. Kurt would end up different from his old man, maybe; he would end up better than his old man, maybe. "Maybe," Kurt said to his uncle, and then he went back upstairs to practice his trumpet some more. And only once they began to hear the bleating sounds of Kurt's trumpet again did Lawrence wonder, out loud, "Who *did* call Denmark from your office phone?"

PART SEVEN
• • •

55

. . .

Friday. The plane was in the air. They were well on their way to New York.

"If you want to ask any questions," Locs said, but then she stopped. She couldn't believe how loudly she was talking. Nor could she bring herself to stop. Wow, she hated to fly. And Locs hadn't been able to score any of her usual calming narcotics before she'd gotten on the plane. Now, every hum, every rattle, every acceleration and deceleration, seemed to surge through her, through her bones, her lungs and heart, and up through her throat and into her mouth. Even with the drugs, she'd probably talked this loudly, but the drugs didn't let her hear that. That's what they were good for. "If you want to ask any questions," she said again, shouted actually, "now would be the time."

Mr. Korkmaz didn't hesitate. "Why do you hate us so much?"

"Us," Locs repeated, not really listening, fingers drumming on her armrest, looking around the airplane—not for anyone or anything in particular, just hoping that the sight of someone much calmer than she might make her much calmer. No

one. Everyone else looked nervous, too. Fuck! Locs looked at
Mr. Korkmaz. Now, *he* looked calm. He was drinking orange
soda through a straw, and his shirtsleeves were rolled up, like
a businessman's on vacation, although now that she was paying attention, Locs knew what he was asking her. "You mean
Muslims."

"Yes," Mr. Korkmaz said. He pushed the straw aside with
his nose and sipped directly from the cup.

"We don't hate Muslims," Locs said with a sigh. Capo, that
asshole, had been adamant on this subject during her training.
Muslims are good people, he insisted; Islam is a noble, peace-
ful religion with a long, rich history of intellectual inquiry and
scholarship, he taught them; Muslims are not our enemies. He
made them say that out loud, like they were kids in school.
Locs had not liked that.

"They're our friends except for the terrorist murderers who
hate us and who you're training us to kill," Locs had said once
and possibly more than once. Capo had not liked that.

"Why are you like that?" Capo had said.

"Like what?" Locs had said, although she knew what he'd
meant, sort of, and sort of also knew the reason: she'd always
been like that. Contrary. So unhappy. So angry. Matthew
wasn't the reason; Matthew, she'd felt, was her chance for not
being like that, and that made it twice as bad when she'd twice
lost that chance. But now . . . "I don't hate Muslims," she said.

"You hate my son."

"We knew who your son was. We knew what he'd done.
And we still didn't arrest him."

"That doesn't mean you didn't hate him."

This was true enough. But Locs decided to argue some more; maybe pointless arguing would calm her the way the drugs did.

"Your son was a terrorist-arsonist," Locs said. "But actually, I kind of liked him."

Mr. Korkmaz looked alarmed when Locs said this. She wondered why, until he said, "You said 'was.' You said 'liked.' As though Søren . . ." He didn't need to finish the sentence. Locs had actually already been wondering whether Søren was dead. She'd not gotten any more e-mails since the initial four. She closed her eyes and saw all four of them—Capo, London, Crystal, Doc—and also Søren, who was in a chair, probably tied to the chair, probably with a hood over his head, and then that vision made her want to open her eyes, and when she did she saw herself on a plane from Copenhagen to JFK, just as a week earlier Søren had been on a plane from Copenhagen to JFK. And Locs had paid for Søren's ticket; Locs had more or less made him get on that plane. Yes, she thought, Søren probably was dead.

"He's not dead," Locs said. "And I still do kind of like him. Even if he did try to kill that cartoonist."

"And of course the cartoonist is certainly blameless."

"The cartoonist is a fucking idiot," Locs said, more loudly yet. She unbuckled her seat belt, stood up slightly, and looked around to see whether anyone was paying attention to her. No one was. Across the aisle from her was a thin blond woman wearing yoga pants, and in fact somehow her legs were crossed in a yoga position, even though the seats were so small. A pair of clogs was on the floor. She was wearing clunky black-framed eyeglasses and was flipping through a magazine that focused on modern design. There were at least a half dozen other women on the plane who looked more or less exactly like her. The woman might as well have a sign around her neck that said DANE. Locs sat back down and turned to Mr. Korkmaz. "A fucking idiot who drew a fucking cartoon. Which was bad enough."

"The cartoon was very bad."

"But not as bad as, say, burning a person's house down."

"I have known this argument," Mr. Korkmaz said. He was smiling with his eyes. "This argument is at the time when you defend free speech."

"It is."

"This is when I must talk about the importance of you having the proper respect for our religion. And in response, you must talk about the importance of free speech."

"You know," Locs said, "I don't really care too much about either of those things."

Mr. Korkmaz nodded. He raised the cup and shook some of the ice into his mouth. He crunched on it. Then he shook the rest of the ice into his mouth and crunched on that, too. "I have not been making the argument that the cartoonist deserved to die," he said.

"Oh, he deserves to die all right," Locs said. She'd pictured it many times over the years. She was picturing it now, too. Maybe Søren wasn't dead. Maybe he really had managed to kill the cartoonist. Wouldn't that be great? But wait: would that be great? If the cartoonist were dead, then Ellen couldn't marry him. And if she couldn't marry him, would she go back to Matthew? Would Matthew go back to her? Locs hadn't thought of this. How had Locs managed to not think of any of this?

"I really hope Søren doesn't kill that cartoonist," she said to herself, but of course Mr. Korkmaz heard her. He placed his now empty cup on the tray and turned to her as fully as the tray and seat belt would permit.

"Do you have any children?" he asked.

"Yes," she said. She said it so quickly that it felt like it really was true.

"A son?"

"His name is Kurt," Locs said. "He's sixteen years old." And then she just kept talking: About how Kurt lived with his father in Broomeville, New York. The father's name was Matthew. He and Locs had never gotten married. They'd had their share of troubles. They'd had their share of other people's troubles. But all that was past them. She and Kurt and Matthew were all going to be together now. It was time. Mr. Korkmaz listened to this, nodding, nodding, as though he understood perfectly. When she was done, he said, "When was the last time you saw him?"

"Way too long."

"You must have missed him."

"I can't even say," Locs said. This was true. She felt that if she were to say more, she would start to cry. Matthew, I've missed you so much, Matthew. Although of course Mr. Korkmaz thought they were talking about Kurt, not Matthew.

"What would you do if someone tried to hurt him?"

"I would kill that person."

Mr. Korkmaz nodded. "So you and I feel very much exactly

the same way." Just then the plane banked; the engine made some ominous shifting sounds. A *ding* sounded overhead, and the attendants began fast-walking their carts down the aisle, and Locs was absolutely certain that this was the first moment in what would be a series of moments that would conclude in each and every person on this airplane dying in a terrible crash. Locs turned to Mr. Korkmaz, and he was smiling. "I have been an imam," he said.

"What's that?"

"I have been an imam, but only to Søren." And then Mr. Korkmaz told her how he'd pretended to be an Internet imam, how every Saturday night he'd gone to the Internet café and contacted Søren in that disguise, using that medium, just so that Søren would know that he wasn't alone, just so Søren would have someone to talk to.

Why didn't you just talk to him as yourself? Locs thought but did not say. Because she knew. Because everyone knows that there's nothing more antagonizing to a son than a father who tries. "Did it work?" Locs asked.

"Not as of this moment," Mr. Korkmaz said. He did not sound sad; he did not even sound resigned. There had even been a note of hope somewhere in his sentence. Locs thought she understood why. Sometimes the most difficult problems called for the most ridiculous solutions. And even then you weren't sure they would work. But that did not mean you stopped trying. On the other hand, it might be that to stop trying would end up being the solution. And it also might be that Locs herself was the problem. But it was ridiculous for her to be thinking that. Why was she thinking that? Maybe it was the plane, which was now bouncing around as though some enormous being, some large meteorological presence with hands, was actually shaking it. She closed her eyes and the shaking got worse. She opened them and looked to Mr. Korkmaz for some more of his wonderful, calming influence. But he was putting up his tray and stuffing his cup in the seat-back pouch and straightening his seat and basically doing all the things that people who are worried on an airplane do when they're trying not to act worried.

"Perhaps you'd better fasten your seat belt," Mr. Korkmaz said to Locs. And those were his last words to her before they landed at JFK.

56

. . .

It was 2:55. Ellen and Matty were seated next to each other in the auditorium, third row, off to the right. Ellen was nervously drumming her fingers on the armrest; Matty had to resist the urge to cover her hand with his. Meanwhile the musicians were making their rude warming-up sounds. Kurt was with the rest of the trumpeters, in the second row, behind the flautists. Mr. Ferraro, that round-faced, black-Converse-All-Star-and-tuxedo-wearing ham, bowed low to the audience —students, parents, faculty, and staff—and then turned back to his musicians. Nobody really knows *what* conductors do, if anything, but it was still sweet to see how closely the kids paid attention to their leader. Kurt, too, was looking intently at the band director: Just tell me what to do, Kurt's eyes said. Ferraro raised his baton, Kurt put his trumpet to his lips; Ferraro started moving his baton, Kurt and the other kids started blowing. In concerts past, Matty oftentimes did not recognize a song unless Ferraro said, after the song had been played, "That was . . ." etc. But Matty recognized this one right away: it was The Who's "My Generation," that famous adolescent call to suicidal arms. Hey, Matty realized, the band was actually pretty good this year. And Kurt seemed particularly great. It is a truism that every father in the audience at a school band concert thinks he can distinguish his child's trumpeting from the other children's lesser trumpeting. But Matty really could tell. Kurt somehow had gotten really good. Matty looked at Ellen to see whether she was hearing what he was hearing. But she wasn't looking at the band. She was scanning the audience, looking for someone, wondering where he was, why he wasn't there. Matty knew who, of course; he didn't see him, either. Good, he thought. Forget Henry. I'm here. Kurt is here. And he's really good. Did you know he was really good? "When did Kurt get to be such a good trumpet player?" he whispered to her. When Matty whispered that, Ellen sort of snapped to, smiled at Matty, and then started looking toward the stage.

57
...

All day, all day, all day. For the second straight day, Henry had waited all day for something to happen: for the stranger to show up again; for Kurt to slip another menacing note under Henry's door; for Ronald, Matty, Ellen, *everyone,* to figure out who he really was. None of that had happened. Now, 2:55. Time to go to Kurt's band concert. A certain kind of insanity overtakes a person who makes it through what has promised to be a difficult day. He thinks, I knew something bad was going to happen to me. But nothing bad has happened to me yet. Maybe nothing bad will happen to me at all. Wouldn't it be incredible if Kurt's band concert was the worst thing that happened to me?

Henry got up from his chair, walked around his desk, and opened the door, and standing there was that odd security guard. Joseph, that was his first name. Henry didn't know his last. They had barely spoken. Every time Henry happened to walk toward Joseph in the hall, Joseph ducked his head or bent down to tie his shoe or veered off in an entirely different direction, usually the one from which he'd just come. Odd. Henry thought Joseph looked familiar, too, but maybe that's because we always think we recognize people who are trying to avoid us.

"Did you get my note?" Joseph said.

"Your note," Henry repeated. He'd received probably a dozen notes that day—from students, teachers, secretaries—and each time the note sender had followed up with a personal visit. And why did Americans, or at least Broomevillians, always do that? They would send Henry a note or an e-mail, or leave him a phone message, and then come to him in person and ask whether he'd gotten their note, e-mail, or phone message.

"My note," Joseph said, whispered actually. The words seemed to cause him some discomfort: he wiped the sweat away from his hairline and bent over at the waist, either in an attempt to get closer to Henry or in reaction to a stomach pain— Henry honestly couldn't tell which. "Under your door at the Lumber Lodge," Joseph whispered.

"Your note," Henry said, finally remembering the note he'd woken up to yesterday morning. He took a step back; Joseph took a step forward and then closed the door behind him. He was wearing a blue uniform onto which were stitched many badges onto which were stitched many initials. He was also wearing a thick belt with many holsters: in one was a radio of some kind; in another, a black stick or club; in yet another, what looked to Henry like an actual gun, although it was probably fake. In thinking this, Henry was still properly Danish: to citizens of countries where gun ownership is looked down on and in any case pretty much impossible, all guns looked like they were probably fake guns. Even though Henry was fully aware that lots of people in Broomeville owned and carried real guns, and he wasn't aware of a single person who owned and carried a fake one. And then Henry put up his hands, even though Joseph's gun was still in its holster, and blurted out the thing he'd been trying not to say but also had been really desperate to say ever since he'd first arrived in Broomeville two years earlier: "I'm Jens Baedrup."

"Well, yeah," Joseph said.

"Don't kill me," Henry said, and when Henry said that, Joseph doubled over, in genuine agony now, no fooling. He cradled his stomach with his right arm while he groped around with his left until he found a chair. And into the chair he fell, hunched over, moaning.

"I'm not going to kill you," Joseph said. "Why would you even *say* that?"

Henry was sitting behind his desk now. He'd placed his satchel on the desk. Inside the satchel was Joseph's note, now crumpled. Henry extracted it, placed it on the desk, smoothed it. "I understood this as a death threat," Henry said.

"What?" Joseph said. He leaned forward to get a better look at the note, the name, the big black X. "Well, you know what, I can kind of see where you're coming from," Joseph said. "It's that X, isn't it?"

"Yes," Henry said. "Did you not mean it to be menacing?"

"No," Joseph said. He looked at the note, thinking. "Kind of," he said. Henry sat back in his chair, arms across his chest now. He was used to this kind of stammering as students haltingly made their way toward their true meaning. "It actually has a double meaning," Joseph said. Now he looked more proud than pained. It was that look that students get when they realize they've grasped what heretofore had seemed like a forbiddingly foreign concept. Henry knew that when Joseph had said "double meaning," what he'd really wanted to say was "double entendre." But he hadn't. Who knew why. He'd probably been uncertain about how thickly he was supposed to apply the French pronunciation. "The first meaning is, don't mention the name Jens Baedrup again."

"OK."

"And whatever you do, stop telling people that the stranger's name is Jens Baedrup."

"Is this the second meaning?"

"No, this is still the first," Joseph said. "Do not mention the name Jens Baedrup. Do not say you are Jens Baedrup. And definitely do not say that Søren Korkmaz's real name is Jens Baedrup."

"Søren Korkmaz," Henry said.

"Søren Korkmaz is the man who burned your house down, and when he found out you were still alive, he came here to kill you. And now he's dead."

That was the second meaning. Henry understood that, without Joseph having to tell him so. Henry also understood that Joseph had killed him. He knew this because Joseph was starting to sweat and moan again, but also because this was the way students, and perhaps all people everywhere, confessed: they told you one thing that seemed big enough but that was only in preparation for the truly large confession to come. Henry kept his arms crossed, kept frowning, waited.

"I killed him," Joseph said.

"I'm sorry," Henry said. Although that wasn't quite right.

"Thank you," Henry said. Although that wasn't quite right, either. What do you say when, after four years of running and wondering and hiding, you learn the name of the person who'd tried to kill you and also that that person is dead? Henry tried to picture a cartoon that would do justice to the feeling. But he couldn't. The part of him that could think of cartoons that would do justice to anything was gone. Perhaps it had never existed. Certainly, Ilsa had thought so. He was sure Locs had thought so, too.

"Are you working for Locs?" Henry asked. And when he did so, Joseph straightened up somewhat. "Well . . . ," he said, and then he scooted forward in his chair, and that's when Henry recognized him. The scooting, the headphones, the sweatshirt, the air guitar, the Stevie who was not Stevie Wonder. Joseph had been the man on the bus that had brought Henry to Broomeville. Although Joseph's hair had been much longer back then.

"You got a haircut," Henry said, and Joseph nodded, ruefully ruffled the back of his head.

"He doesn't feel like me."

"Who?"

"The guy with this haircut."

"Why did you get it cut?"

"Capo made me," Joseph said.

"Capo?" Henry said, and then he thought Joseph was actually going to put his hands over his mouth, but he didn't. "Listen," Joseph said, "about Locs . . ." But then he stopped, head cocked, as though he'd heard something. Joseph got up, opened the office door, stuck his head out into the hallway, looked one way, then the other. Then he stuck his head back in, turned to Henry. He looked different now. His eyes were big. "Someone was out there," he said.

"Who?"

"Jenny."

"Jenny Tallent?"

"Yes," Joseph said. He looked down, thinking, thinking. "Now, Jenny's a good girl," he said, more to himself than to Henry. In any case, that uttered sentence seemed to decide something for Joseph: he took his gun out of his holster, put it on Henry's desk, pushed it toward Henry. Henry didn't touch it. Just a few weeks ago, Henry and Ellen had watched a movie in which a police detective had placed his gun on a table, pushed it toward the criminal sitting across the table. "Go ahead, take it," the detective had told the criminal, and when the criminal had tried to go ahead and take it, the detective had shot him with his other gun.

"Go ahead, take it," Joseph said.

"But it's your gun," Henry said.

"I don't even *want* it anymore," Joseph said. Quickly, quickly, Joseph picked up the gun he'd just given Henry and showed him how to use it. Then he put it back on the desk. "Got that?" Joseph said. Henry nodded. It wasn't hard. Any idiot could do it. Not that he was going to.

"I'm not going to use that gun."

"But you might have to."

"Why?"

"Oh, I can think of lots of reasons," Joseph said. And with that, he got up and left the room, and also left the door open. Henry was suddenly highly conscious of a gun sitting on his desk where anyone could see it. He was also conscious of really not wanting to touch the gun. He picked up the note, then used it to pick up the gun, then deposited both in his coat pocket. Henry closed his office door behind him and walked toward the auditorium. It was three thirty when he arrived. The band concert was almost over. The band was playing its last song. Henry recognized it right away. It was that famously plaintive rock-and-roll song about swimming in a bowl with fish and wishing people were there. Henry looked for and then spotted Ellen, sitting next to Matty near the front of the auditorium. I'm here, he wanted to shout but didn't. Ellen didn't seem to be looking for him anyway. She was looking at the stage. Henry looked, too, and saw Kurt stand up and begin playing a mournful solo on his trumpet. It really was beautiful, and suddenly Henry was trying hard not to cry. Schoolchildren's band concerts do strange things to the adults in the audience. Don't cry, Henry told himself. And then, to Søren: I'm sorry you're dead, but I'm glad I'm not. I'm glad that's all over. And to Ellen: I'm going to marry you tomorrow. And then to Kurt: I'm sorry I thought you were the person who wrote the note. I'm sorry I didn't trust you. And then came the chorus, and all of a sudden, many people in the audience were singing it. Henry could see that Ellen and Matty were singing it, and he started singing it, too: "How I wish, how I wish you were here," he sang, and then he really did start crying. Harder than he'd ever cried before. But why? Everyone that mattered to Henry was here. There wasn't anyone to miss. Was there? Who was here? Who was not here?

58

· · ·

Out in the country north of Broomeville there was a winding two-lane road that, briefly, when it crossed the Otanga River, turned into a one-lane wooden bridge. There were older wooden bridges in the state of New York, but this was the oldest one that still allowed automobiles to cross. Schoolchildren were often bused to the site to appreciate the bridge's historical significance and also its sturdy architectural features.

And on the other side of that bridge was an ice cream stand. It, like so many of its kind, had picnic tables overlooking the river, encouraging people to enjoy watery nature while eating their soft-serve. Ellen and Kurt were doing that. They'd come straight there after the band concert, to celebrate. But it was a muted celebration. This was the last week of the ice cream stand; on Sunday it would close and not reopen again until Memorial Day. There is a melancholy known only to the owners and patrons of seasonal businesses. Still, Ellen was doing her best.

"When did you learn to play the trumpet like that?"

Kurt smiled, shrugged. Ellen had chosen vanilla; Kurt, a twist.

He twirled and addressed the dark side of his cone. They were sitting on the same bench, their backs against the table, watching the river, which was full to the point of possible flooding. Ellen liked the river when it was this way. It was fun to watch fallen tree trunks roar down the river and then get hung up on the other big logs jammed together under the bridge. Suddenly a guy wearing a wetsuit and a cap with many lures attached and holding a fishing pole came bobbing by in an inner tube. He waved to them with his feet as he drifted past, going under the bridge and out the other side, not getting stuck on the logs. Ellen had never seen any such kind of person on this river before. The sight of him made her even more uneasy than she'd already been. Where did he come from? she wondered. And where is he going?

"Well, you really were great," she said.

"I didn't see Mr. L. there."

"He was late," Ellen said.

"How late?" Kurt asked, and now it was Ellen's turn to shrug. In truth, she didn't know. After the last song, Ellen had gotten out of her seat, and there Henry was, standing toward the back of the auditorium. He'd smiled at her. But there was something *wrong* with his face. It looked red, wet. Had he been crying? Why the hell had he been crying? Why the hell had he called Denmark from Matty's office? Before Ellen had seen him standing there, she'd thought, Just one more thing, and she was thinking it now, too.

"Køkkenbord!" Kurt said, suddenly, loudly, startling Ellen into dropping her ice cream.

"Jeez, Kurt."

"Sorry."

"What was *that*?" she said. He repeated the word, and she asked, "What does that mean?"

"Counter," he said. He had a kind of secret smile on his face. "*Køkkenbord* equals counter."

"In what language?"

"Swedish, I guess." He told her about the day that Henry had come to town, two years ago. How Henry had dropped two pieces of paper on his way out of Doc's. One was a cartoon of Henry sitting at the counter in Doc's with Kurt watching him from outside. On the other piece of paper, Henry had written the words KØKKENBORD=COUNTER. Kurt told Ellen that he and his cronies were trying to figure out how to pronounce the word when this strange woman started hassling them. And then they couldn't find the piece of paper. And then Kurt couldn't remember the word, until now. It'd been driving him crazy. "Weird, huh?" Kurt said.

Yes, Ellen thought but did not say. Cartoon? Strange woman? *Køkkenbord*? Suddenly she remembered that cartoon, that word, although not the strange woman. The pieces of paper on which they'd been written and drawn had been on Henry's floor the first night she'd slept with him. He'd said he'd drawn the cartoon; he'd said the word was Swedish. The explanation seemed reasonable, so reasonable that she'd forgotten about the whole thing. "Not that weird," she said. Still, Ellen took her phone out of her pocket. "Spell it," she said. Kurt did; Ellen typed the letters. *Køkkenbord,* her phone said, was the Danish word for "kitchen counter." Then she translated *kitchen counter* into Swedish; a word came up, but it was not *køkkenbord.* Her first thought was, Deny! But Kurt was already looking over her shoulder at the phone.

"Huh," Kurt said.

"Huh," Ellen said, putting the phone back in her pocket. "I'll have to ask Henry."

"Yeah," Kurt said. He was almost done with his cone. Meanwhile, Ellen looked at hers, lying on the grass, which was dead. The cone was ruined, she thought, the grass was ruined, everything was ruined. These were her thoughts. And then to counter those thoughts she thought, Don't be ridiculous. And then she thought, Counter. She thought, Cartoon. She thought, Denmark. She thought, Strange woman. She thought, This is that one more thing.

"Where do you think that guy in the inner tube went?" Kurt said. And when his mother didn't answer, he said, "I really want to go somewhere."

"Where?"

"Anywhere," Kurt said. "Another country."

"You've been to Canada," Ellen said. She and he and Matty had taken a trip to Niagara Falls four years ago. They'd walked across the bridge and said, "We're in Canada!" and then walked back. That was her only time out of the country, too.

"Canada doesn't count as another country," Kurt said, finishing off his ice cream and wiping his hands on his jeans. "Come on, Mom. Everyone knows that."

"I don't know that," Ellen said. Because she and Henry had been planning to go to Canada—to Montreal—for their honeymoon. They were to leave on Saturday, after the wedding. She got up and then Kurt did, too, and they walked to the truck, got in. Kurt drove. He drove in a way engineered to make his mother crazy: casually, one hand out the window, the other at the bottom of the steering wheel. But just now, Ellen barely noticed. The truck made loud thumping noises as it crossed the wooden slats of the wooden bridge. But the rest of the ride was smooth to the point of unconsciousness. It was as though Ellen had fallen asleep and twenty minutes later woke up in front of the old stone house. I'm home, she thought, and then she thought, What a weird thought to have. This hadn't been her home for two years. Meanwhile, Kurt was already out of the car and leaning in through the driver's side window, looking at her worriedly.

"You OK?" he asked. Kurt seemed genuinely worried about her. God, she loved him. There was always that, right? No matter what happened, she would have Kurt, and Kurt her. That would be enough, right?

"Just taking a little nap."

"Your eyes were open."

"Yup," Ellen said. And then she scooted along the length of the bench seat, put the truck in gear, and drove in the direction of the Lumber Lodge.

59
. . .

Ronald's plan, if you could call it that, was to get this Ilsa to Broomeville and reunite her with this Jens Baedrup and see what trouble that might cause. It seemed simple enough. But now there were all these problems. Starting with Ilsa's bus, which was late.

"You're taking a bus?" he'd asked her on the phone. Buses, thought Ronald, were for poor people; Ilsa did not strike him as poor, maybe because Ronald was poor and she spoke better English than he did, even though it wasn't her language. "You're taking a *bus*?"

"Is there a train or a bus that will take me to Broomeville?"

"There's a bus," he said. "You could also rent a car."

"A car," she said, as though the word itself were extremely distasteful. "For just one person? So wasteful."

"Fine," Ronald had said. "Take the bus."

"Will Jens be there to meet me?"

"Sure," Ronald said. "Why not?"

Except now the bus was late. At least an hour late, they said at the drugstore that was also the bus station. Meanwhile no one had seen this Jens Baedrup character since that first time,

two days earlier. Ronald had not counted on the guy just disappearing like that. And he had really disappeared, too. Ronald
had looked for him everywhere. He'd even taken the day off
from work today to search for Baedrup. But he didn't see him.
No one had seen him. The last person to see him was Ronald
himself, as far as Ronald knew. And the last person before that
was Henry.

Well, *that* was interesting, thought Ronald, and then he
further pursued the interesting thought. Baedrup had gone to
see Henry. That was a fact. It was also a fact that four years
ago someone had killed Baedrup. Except that Baedrup wasn't
dead, apparently. He shows up and visits Henry, and then no
one has seen him since.

Henry Larsen had killed Jens Baedrup—this was the place to
which Ronald's interesting thought was leading him. To keep
it interesting, Ronald allowed the thought to briefly turn upon
himself. Ronald, after all, was the last person to see Baedrup; if
anyone had killed him, it could well have been Ronald. Except
that Ronald had gone directly to see Ellen at the bar, to tell her
about seeing this Baedrup with Henry.

Meanwhile, where had Henry been during that time?

He'd been walking around. This was what he'd said, three
hours later, when he got to the Lumber Lodge: "I took a walk."

"With your friend?" Ronald had asked him, and Henry had
made that face. Henry's mouth had said, "What friend?" But
his face had said he knew exactly what friend. And no one had
seen the friend since.

Henry Larsen killed Jens Baedrup. Ronald returned to the
place where his interesting thought had brought him. Henry

Larsen killed Jens Baedrup, just like Henry Larsen killed my
sister, and I know he killed my sister because he killed Jens Baedrup. But why would Henry have wanted to kill either of those
people? This was the next place to which Ronald's interesting
thought led him, or would have, if it hadn't already led him to
drive home to get his gun.

Five minutes later, Ronald returned to the square, got out
of his car, holding the gun, as he was allowed by law to do.
Ronald's gun was one of those hunting rifles that you could
swear was really an assault rifle, but if you swore that, then the
hunter who carried the assault rifle would swear that it was really a hunting rifle because he hunted with it. Anyway, Ronald
was holding the gun. His intention was to charge into the Lumber Lodge and shoot Henry to death. If Henry wasn't in the
Lumber Lodge, then Ronald was prepared to shoot Henry to
death in another place, too. But before he could shoot anyone, the bus pulled into the station. It was more or less on
time after all. The door opened. Ronald heard the driver call
out, "Broomeville! Who's getting off at *Broomeville*!" Ronald
could see a woman walk down the aisle, then down the stairs,
stopping at the last step when she saw Ronald standing there
with his gun. She was a pretty woman with white-blond hair
and sharp cheekbones and black-rimmed glasses. She was
wearing dark brown wool leggings and green clogs and on her
back was a pack with many pouches for water bottles and two
thick shoulder straps, of course, but also a thinner strap that
crossed the chest, just in case, and all in all she appeared to
be one of those forty-five-year-old women who looked about

twenty years younger than they were, but who acted, and also felt, about forty years older than they looked.

"Are you Ilsa?" Ronald asked.

"That is certainly a fake gun," she said, and when Ronald said that it certainly was not, Ilsa nodded. Her clogs made clomping horse-hoof noises as she walked backward up the stairs and into the bus. The door closed. The bus drove away.

60
· · ·

The end comes only after you think it's already come. Henry was behind the bar, feeling good, as though the past were finally and truly behind him. Tomorrow, this time, he would be married to Ellen. He was already practicing for their life together. He'd even made the executive decision to open the Lumber Lodge earlier than its usual five o'clock opening time. Across the bar from him was *Dr.* Vernon, drinking a Saranac. My wife and I own this bar, Henry was thinking. Together, we run the bar. Together, we live above the bar with Kurt, her son, my stepson. *Dr.* Vernon's glass was empty. Henry reached across, grabbed it, refilled it, pushed it back toward his colleague, who nodded his thanks, red eyes flashing off the red palm trees on his yellow shirt.

"I know you sell drugs to Kurt," Henry said. *Dr.* Vernon stopped midsip. He looked at Henry over his glass.

"Drugs?"

"I want you to stop," Henry said. "And if you don't, I will tell Matty and Ellen. And I'm sure they will tell you to stop, too, if they don't tell the police first." The deep fryer hissed. Henry walked over to it, put on a mitt, grabbed the metal basket handle, removed the basket from the bubbling fat, dumped the twelve wings into a plastic basket lined with wax paper. He arranged six celery stalks around the perimeter of the basket, squeezed blue cheese out of a large bottle into a small cup, placed the cup between two celery stalks, picked up the basket, and placed it in front of *Dr.* Vernon.

"I knew you were a narc," he said.

Narc? Henry didn't know that word. But surely Ellen did. She was walking into the bar right now. She walked underneath the streamers, past the table on which the DJ would set up his turntable and play his wedding tunes, and then moved behind the bar, toward Henry. She leaned forward, as though to kiss him, and Henry leaned forward also, but she did not kiss him. Instead she whispered, "*Køkkenbord* equals 'counter' in Danish." Then Ellen stood back. Her eyes were flashing many things, but love and marriage were not among them.

"Ellen," Henry started to say, but Ellen held up her hand to stop him.

"I don't want to hear it," Ellen said. "I told myself just one more thing."

"My real name is Jens Baedrup," Henry started to say, but Ellen stopped him again.

"Well, yeah," she said. "But it doesn't matter. You *lied* to me. Now go away forever."

Go away forever? To where? He had only ever lived in two places. Here was one of them. The other place was Skagen; he was told he could never go back there again. Meanwhile, *Dr.* Vernon was watching and listening with the keen, undisguised interest of a man who suddenly is less pathetic than the man who is about to be seated on the barstool next to him. "But there's nowhere else for me to go."

"You can start," Ellen said, "by getting the hell out from behind my *køkkenbord*." Henry did that. He moved to the other side of the bar and sat next to *Dr.* Vernon, who pushed the basket of wings in front of Henry. Henry picked one up and ate it, almost without thinking, already in that loser's living afterlife of a loser, where you take consolation from wherever you can find it, even while insisting that you're not giving up, you're not going anywhere, until somebody *listens* to what you have to say. When he was done eating the wing, Henry dropped it into the basket, and he was about to say to Ellen that he was not going to go anywhere until she listened to what he had to say, when he noticed that her eyes had gone big and were staring at something behind him.

61

. . .

Capo was in Doc's, sitting at a table, surrounded by his students. "Have I ever told you," he asked them, "about my turn as Don Pedro in that very interesting production of *Much Ado* in Sarajevo?" The students shook their heads to indicate that he had not. In attendance were four boys who looked like younger versions of Mr. Klock in their knit ties and corduroy blazers and trimmed blond beards and who had been regular participants in Mr. Klock's after-school club for some time now. "I was there, of course, because of the so-called Butcher of the Balkans. He was playing Don John to my Don Pedro. And do you know that the Butcher said something very interesting to me." Capo paused, as though trying to remember the Butcher's exact words. "The Butcher said, 'I pretend to be Don John. But you, you *are* Don Pedro. You do not pretend.'" Capo paused to let his students consider the point. "My point is this: when you are in our funny little business, you must not 'act,' even when you are 'acting.'"

The students nodded. They sipped their coffee, legs crossed, trying not to seem awed by the Butcher or the Bard or Sarajevo or the funny little business or anything. They were following Capo's suggestion: they were being adults by acting like adults. Meanwhile, Capo had grown thoughtful. Doc and Crystal were watching him from behind the counter. Crystal whispered to Doc, "He's talked about acting; now he'll talk about the Mass Grave." "Sadly," Capo said, "the Butcher was right about his performance, which was lacking. Perhaps he would still be alive if he'd dedicated himself a bit more to the Stage, and a bit less to the Mass Grave."

The door opened, its bell tingling; everyone turned in that direction and watched Jenny enter. The students asked Capo, with their alarmed looks, What's *she* doing here? He ignored them. "Jennifer, you're late," he said, and Jenny stood in the doorway, nervously fingering her neck stud. He beckoned with his hand and she walked toward him. When she was close enough, Jenny leaned over, placed something in Capo's hand, and then whispered several things in Capo's ear. "But sometimes tardiness is unavoidable," he said when she'd finished whispering. "You've more than redeemed yourself, Jennifer." He gestured toward an empty seat and Jenny took it. Then Capo turned and said in the direction of Doc and Crystal: "Quickly, quickly, find"—and here he glanced at the boy students, then back at Doc and Crystal—"*London.*"

"What about his car?" Crystal said. Because this was the procedure: when you do not want someone to flee, you first take away his preferred method of flight. But Capo shook his head, held up several greasy plugs with wires growing out of them. "Perhaps I erred after all," he said to the boys, "in forbidding you to take Automotive Shop. It seems that Jennifer, at least, has learned something useful there." He swung the plugs in lazy circles as he thought about Joseph, not Joseph now but Joseph ten years earlier, when he was just sixteen years old, and like all sixteen-year-olds was wondering, wondering, wondering what kind of adult he wanted to be, listening to Capo's stories, thinking this was the kind of adult he wanted to be. It turned out that this was the worst kind of adult for him to want to be. And now, Capo thought, he would never have the chance to be another kind. But that was an imprecise thought. Capo would never let him have the chance to be another kind. That was a more accurate thought, although of course Capo did not like to think it.

"Please just find him," Capo said. But Doc and Crystal were already at the door. They looked out it, and Crystal said, "Found him." Capo stood up and then walked over to the window. Through it he saw the bus pulling away from the square, and Joseph running after it, waving his hands and shouting wildly in the "why is this happening to me?" manner of people who have just missed their bus. Then Joseph stopped running, looked in the direction of Doc's, and saw the three of them looking at him. Then he started running in the other direction, back toward them at first, and then he cut into the alley between the post office and the Lumber Lodge. But before disappearing into the alley, Joseph had passed Ronald, who was holding an automatic weapon and walking with great purpose toward and then into the Lumber Lodge. Capo had been waiting, waiting for Locs to arrive in Broomeville; in fact, he'd pictured her holding a gun, walking with great purpose toward the Lumber Lodge. But once Capo saw Ronald, he forgot all about Locs, the lesson being that the person you see with a gun trumps the expectation of the person you might see with a gun.

"Children," Capo said to the students. "Go home."

"But we are home," one of the boy students said. Capo, of course, had taught them to talk like that, to think like that. But sometimes it really broke his heart to see how fully they'd learned their lesson. Even Jenny, whom he hadn't really even begun to teach, was looking at him in a pathetic way, fingers furiously messing around with her piercing. "Jennifer," he said, his meaning clear enough. Jenny moved her hand away from her neck and put both hands in her jeans pockets as a failsafe. "Go to your other homes," he said to the students. "I will see you all at school tomorrow." The students did what their Capo told them to. Then he turned back to Crystal and Doc. He could tell what they were thinking: they were thinking that they were going to have to shoot a lot of people. But that was not the way Capo liked to think. He told Doc to get Joseph. "He ran down a dead-end alley," he said. Capo, thinking, thinking. He asked Doc if he had his badge, his cuffs. Doc patted his jacket pocket to indicate that he did. Not many people knew that Broomeville County even had a coroner, let alone that Doc was that coroner, let alone that that's why Doc was called Doc, let alone that Doc, as the coroner, was automatically deputized, which meant that he had a badge and cuffs and had the right to arrest people.

"Bring poor Joseph in cuffs into the Lumber Lodge," he said

to Doc. Doc nodded, ran out the door. "Come," Capo said to Crystal.

"You know we're going to have to shoot a lot of people," she said.

"That's not the way I like to think," Capo said. But she was already running toward the Lumber Lodge.

62

...

They had not taken the bus, because Locs hated taking the bus, and so she lied to Mr. Korkmaz about there not being a bus to Broomeville. Instead they rented a car. Who knew what kind it was. Locs wasn't paying attention to that. She drove, following the snaking highways and bridges through New York City, then up the Hudson to Albany, then west, along the canal as far as Utica, then north. She registered the changes in scenery without really paying any attention to them. The entire way she was thinking nothing but, Matthew, Matthew, love, love, until thirty minutes from her destination, when she remembered to think: Broomeville. Five minutes later they came to the house of the guy who was well known for selling illegal fireworks and much less well known for selling illegal firearms. But Locs knew: two years earlier, on the run from Broomeville to Denmark, she'd sold her many guns to the guy for traveling money. Now she was back. "You're back," the guy said. Everyone called him Buddy, but Locs refused to call him by that name or to refer to him, even in her head, as anything but "the guy." Locs was hoping the guy would sell her something high caliber. But all he had were handguns. With Mr. Korkmaz's money, Locs bought two handguns.

"Who's the fucking old man?" the guy said, easily loud enough for Mr. Korkmaz to hear. The guy himself was probably forty, but he had an enormous white beard, big enough to hide things in, and dressed in denim overalls and dusty brogans and a faded floppy hat, as though at any second he expected to be whisked back to the Dust Bowl, and in all respects he looked like an old man himself, which presumably, in his mind, gave him the right to refer to actual old men as fucking old men, rather than with the respect they deserved. Locs didn't know why she was getting so worked up about this. Maybe because she was preparing to get worked up about other things. Quickly she loaded the gun and handed it to Mr. Korkmaz. "Go ahead and shoot him," she said.

Then she walked back to the car. "Hey!" the guy said, but then she didn't hear Mr. Korkmaz shoot him, which was too bad. Locs got into the driver's side, and a second later Mr. Korkmaz got into the passenger's. They drove onward. Locs turned on the heat. It had gotten cold; snow was starting to fly. That was the right way to describe it, too: the snow was not falling; it looked, as with an airplane, like it was proceeding horizontally from one place to the next. Broomeville, Broomeville. Then a sign saying it: BROOMEVILLE: 7 MILES.

"I would not shoot that hairy man," Mr. Korkmaz said.

Locs almost drove off the road. Not because of the sentence, but because Mr. Korkmaz had spoken: Was it possible that he'd really not spoken for over four hours? What had he been thinking? It occurred to Locs to ask him something. Locs knew *her* plan: She would somehow evade Capo et al. and go to Matthew's house, where he would be, and then they would figure things out from there. Love. Barring that, she would shoot people until she found Matthew, and then they would figure things out from there.

"What's your plan?" Locs asked Mr. Korkmaz. She didn't see the gun. He was wearing a heavy waxed coat with many pockets. Locs assumed the gun was in one of them. She'd bought both guns for herself; she had not intended to give one to Mr. Korkmaz. But she didn't ask for it back. Old, frail Mr. Korkmaz would not look, to anyone who didn't know him, as though he was likely to have a gun, let alone be able to use one. It might end up being good to have someone who didn't look like he'd have a gun, have a gun.

"My plan?"

"We get to Broomeville . . .," she said, turning to look at Mr. Korkmaz, who was looking out the window at a billboard that said NIRVANA: THERE'S ONLY ONE! She had no idea what the billboard was advertising or whom it was quoting.

"You assist me to find Søren. I prevent him from murdering the cartoonist. We return to Skagen." He shrugged, rubbed the dashboard as though for good luck. "Or we stay here."

"In Broomeville?"

"In America," Mr. Korkmaz said. "PT Cruiser."

"What?"

"What does it mean, PT Cruiser?"

Locs realized that he was talking about the rental car. It was a PT Cruiser, the most ridiculous of all the ridiculous American

cars with their ridiculous names: it was humpbacked and
clunky and was supposed to remind you of American gang-
sters standing on the running boards with tommy guns in the
movies and no one actually getting hurt except for the one or
two guys who absolutely deserved it and the one or two guys
who were totally expendable.

"It doesn't mean anything," Locs said. "It's supposed to remind you of America."

"Well, it succeeds," Mr. Korkmaz said. "I like it."

"You do?" Normally, Locs would have thought the person
who would say such a thing too stupid to live. But Mr. Korkmaz
had already lived such a long time. Plus, she really did like him,
or would have, had she not been manipulating him and had
there been more time. They were almost in Broomeville now:
one mile to go. "Listen," she said. "Suppose Søren has already
killed the cartoonist?"

Mr. Korkmaz shrugged again, still looking out the window.
It was starting to gust: the trees were bending and bowing;
the ground was still bare, but the air was getting thicker with
snow, and little tornadoes of it were touching down here and
there on the road. It got even colder in the car, even with the
heater on high. It felt, atmospherically, like something big was
about to happen.

"Søren could not kill anyone with intention," Mr. Korkmaz
finally said. Locs thought he was probably right. On the other
hand, she knew of several people who could definitely inten-
tionally kill Søren. But she didn't say that. The sign told Locs
to turn left to get to downtown Broomeville. She did, driving
through the narrow chute of trees and tenements and railroad

tracks and railroad cars. The snow was now pouring through the narrow opening above; it was as though they were at the bottom of a mailbox and someone was dumping snow in the slot. But through the snow, Locs could see the town square up ahead. "I would shoot that hairy man if he had previously killed Søren," Mr. Korkmaz said. "That would be the only reason." And before Locs could respond to that, she saw Matthew and Kurt pull up outside the Lumber Lodge. Matty—wearing his Cornell hat, of course—got out of the passenger's side; Kurt got out of the driver's side. Kurt is old enough to drive, thought Locs. Oh, Matthew, we've wasted so much time. And while she was wasting time thinking this thought, Matty and Kurt walked into the Lumber Lodge.

63

. . .

As soon as Kurt had told Matty what he'd remembered about Henry, what he'd told his mother, Matty had insisted they go down to the Lumber Lodge immediately. He barely knew why himself. Matty just had some vague sense that if Ellen dumped Henry for lying to her, which Matty was sure she would do, then Matty needed to be around, the way Henry had been around when Ellen had dumped Matty. And Matty also had the vague sense that it'd be better if Kurt were there, too, so that Ellen could see the whole family to which she could be returning, not the broken Dane (Dane?) she should be leaving behind. But Matty didn't know how to explain all this to Kurt, so instead he said, "We need to go to the Lumber Lodge." And then, before Kurt could ask why, Matty added, "You can drive."

Kurt had, adequately. Now they were walking into the Lumber Lodge. The first thing Matty saw was the streamers. Some of them were sagging low, and Matty had to resist the mighty urge to tear them down. The next thing Matty saw was Ronald standing in the middle of the bar holding an enormous gun. *Holding* was perhaps the wrong verb. His left hand was on the trigger—if that's what you called the firing mechanism on a gun that was as big and menacing as the one Ronald was holding, and Matty wasn't at all sure that it was—and his right hand, his crippled hand, was kind of supporting the barrel. When Ronald noticed Matty and Kurt, the barrel slipped a little bit, but he caught it with his claw and raised it again. And only then did Matty look at where Ronald was pointing the gun. To the left of the bar, standing up against the wall, one hand in the air, the other in his coat pocket, was *Dr.* Vernon. Behind the bar was Ellen. Sitting on the other side of the bar was Henry. His back was to Ronald; he was sitting there, apparently eating chicken wings, like there was nothing else in the world to do.

"Kurt!" Matty said. Because Kurt was walking across the room now. Past Ronald, at whom he nodded, and who nodded back, gun still trained, it was obvious, on Henry. Kurt walked past Henry, whom he smacked on the shoulder, as you'd do with anyone you knew who was eating wings at the bar. To his mother. He put his left arm over her shoulder and left it there. Had he ever done that before? Ellen wondered. Was this what stupid people meant when they said stupid things about all the good that came out of the bad? Meanwhile, Matty was standing across the room. He should have been over there, with her, with their son. But no, Matty was standing there on the far side of the room, paralyzed. I can't believe I was ever married to him, Ellen thought, and then she thought, But then again, I kind of can't believe that I'm still not.

"I really am going to kill you now," Ronald said. It was clear that Ronald was talking to Henry. But Henry didn't turn around. "Guidance counselor!" Ronald shouted. And still, Henry just sat there, eating! Ellen started to itch all over. What is wrong with you? Ellen thought. Who *are* you? Don't you know how much trouble you're in? Is there anything more infuriating than someone who doesn't seem to know he should be terrified? But then Ellen saw Henry's barely raised eyes looking at the huge mirror behind the bar. Eating, eating, calmly, unimpressed, in his very Henry way, but also looking in the mirror, seemingly aware of everything going on behind him, and next to him, too. He glanced at her, raised the chicken wing to his mouth, smiled with his eyes, then returned them to the mirror. And wow, Ellen realized how much she loved him and always would. She loved him so much that she couldn't believe that she wasn't going to take him back, that she wasn't going to forgive him for lying to her. It would be, she thought, something she would probably always regret. But. Ellen put her arm around Kurt, and together they walked across the room, toward Matty, whom Kurt was trying to command with his eyes.

Go! Kurt was trying to tell his father as they walked toward him. Back up slowly, slowy, out the door, and go get help! But just then, through that door, came Kurt's uncle Lawrence and Crystal, Crystal looking as though she'd really like to hurt someone, maybe his uncle Lawrence, who was going on in his usual way, not paying attention to the scene into which he was walking, talking about some other place, some other time, some other person—Kurt couldn't really concentrate on the particulars, it was very difficult to concentrate when there was a gun in the room. Anyway, his uncle Lawrence, talking,

talking, until he and Crystal reached the center of the barroom. And only then did he seem to notice Ronald and Ronald's gun.

"Well," Lawrence said. Smile, he told himself, and then he did that—at Ronald, and then at Crystal, who had moved to the far left side of the room and whose right hand was in her coat pocket, and then back at Ronald, who was kind of turned, half his face toward Lawrence, but the rest of his face, and his whole body and gun, still trained on Henry. Relax, Lawrence was trying to say with his smile. Everything is going to be just fine. Thinking, I should have stayed in Beirut, Palermo, anywhere else. Looking at all these miserable, scared faces. Thinking, The world is full of happy people. Wondering, Why are all of you so, so unhappy? Thinking, But that's a rhetorical question. Saying, "Ronald."

"I *am* going to kill him."

"Because he killed your sister," Lawrence said. And only then did Henry swivel on his stool to face the rest of the room. He had his hand in his jacket pocket, too. Ronald looked to Henry's left. That garish *Dr.* Vernon was standing there, *his* hand in *his* pocket. That made five armed people in the room. Out of them, one was a Dane, one was no doubt on narcotics, one had a crippled hand, and one was a borderline psychotic, although a borderline psychotic in Lawrence's employ. And all he could think was, They are so lucky the other person with a gun is me. Everyone in this room is so lucky to have me. The world is so lucky to have me.

"No," Henry said, looking at Ronald, at Ellen, at everyone, everywhere.

"He murdered the stranger as well."

"No!" Henry said.

"Yes," Ronald said, his gun still somewhat pointed at Henry, but his face somewhat pointed at Lawrence.

"It's a compelling theory," Lawrence said. Just then, Doc came in the door, and in front of him Joseph in handcuffs. Joseph's head was down, as though in preparation for its being lopped off. Doc steered him into the middle of the room, between where Lawrence and Crystal were standing. "Compelling, but incorrect." Doc patted Joseph on the back, and Joseph said, with his head still down, "It was me. I killed both of them."

Ronald dropped his gun to his side, holding it with his good hand. He was looking at Joseph, thinking, Who the hell are you? Aren't you the school cop or something? Do you even have a *name*? To Ronald, this was the saddest thing yet: that his sister had been killed by a nameless nobody, a person so unimportant that Ronald hadn't even considered him a suspect. It left him almost speechless. "You're a coroner and also a cop," Ronald finally said to Doc.

"Deputized," Doc said.

Ronald raised his gun again, pointing it at Joseph now. "Why?" he said. "Why would you kill my sister? Why would you kill the stranger?"

These were good questions. Lawrence hadn't gotten so far as to come up with an answer that would explain Joseph's guilt while not incriminating Lawrence himself. But before he could come up with an answer, he saw movement to his right.

"Oh my," he said. Because Locs had walked into the room, and next to her was an elderly gentleman of Middle Eastern descent. Turkish, Lawrence guessed, by the color of his skin, the secularity of his dress. Istanbul! he thought. "Locs," he said. But Locs wasn't looking at Lawrence. She was looking at Matty, who was standing with Ellen and Kurt. The happy family. Overhead, there were streamers. Oh God, it was a party. Probably a party for the happy family. Oh God, she was stupid. Matty was looking at her with a sick look on his face. It might have been love. But it was probably only apology. I'm sorry you're so stupid, he was probably trying to tell her. I'm sorry you're so stupid that you're still wearing my stupid hat. She took it off her head and flung it toward him, but Ellen caught it and then immediately dropped it. Kurt bent over and picked it up, remembering now, from two years ago, the woman in the hat who had almost run over him and his cronies while they were looking at Henry's cartoon, at the Danish word that meant "counter." Here you are again, Kurt thought. But who are you? Whoever she was, he felt like an idiot holding her hat. He walked across the room, gave the woman her hat back, and then returned to where he'd been standing. Meanwhile, Ellen had sort of wandered into the middle of the room, moving in the general direction of the cartoonist. They both had dazed looks on their faces. He reached his hand out to Ellen; she seemed to be strongly considering taking it. Good: that gave Locs some hope. But then Matty opened his mouth to speak. Locs could almost see the words coming out of them: Ellen, he would say. I'm sorry for whatever. Please forgive me. And Ellen would. The idiot. Married forever to *Matty,* the idiot. Was everyone in this room (the fat guy in the ridiculous shirt, for instance, and the guy with the crippled hand and the big gun, and certainly Joseph, who looked like he was going to take the fall for something because he was too stupid not to take the fall for something, not to mention Capo, fucking Capo, and his Crystal and his Doc) too stupid to live? Was everyone in this town, this *world,* too stupid to live? Locs was sure they were. Might as well kill them all. Except . . . Matty didn't say anything. He just looked at Locs, smiling sheepishly, as though to say, I think we're really going to do this thing. And suddenly Locs could see the future: In it, Ellen really would marry Henry. Matty would marry Locs. Kurt would split his time between them. Capo would not kill her, would not have her killed. Because you did not kill your sister-in-law. Because you did not kill someone in love. Love, love: it does not make you stupid, it makes you invincible. Finally, Locs thought, I'm going to be happy; finally, everyone is going to be happy; finally, everything is going to be just fine.

"Who is meant by 'the stranger'?" Mr. Korkmaz asked. But he knew. Everyone knew. "Oh, Søren," he said.

"Oh no," Locs said. But it was too late. Mr. Korkmaz took the gun out of his pocket. He pointed it at Joseph and then seemed to change his mind and pointed it at Henry, and when he did that, Ellen stepped in front of Henry, but by that point Henry had already taken out his gun and fired it at Mr. Korkmaz. The sound was so loud that it sort of scrambled everything, for everyone. It took a second for everyone's normal way of seeing and thinking to return. When it did, Henry saw Ellen lying on the floor, Kurt kneeling down next to her, Matty standing, paralyzed, over both of them. Henry dropped his gun, put his face in his hands. "Please just kill me," he thought and then also said, through his hands. Mr. Korkmaz once again trained his weapon on Henry. And then he and everyone else in the room who had a gun just started shooting.

64

. . .

Two days later. Henry had disappeared. Kurt had been shot, but just barely, and had already been released from the hospital in Utica. He'd be OK. Kurt's father was still in the hospital. He would probably be OK. Uncle Lawrence was still in the hospital, too. He would definitely not be OK. He would die. Everyone else who'd been in the Lumber Lodge, including Kurt's mother, was already dead. Now, Kurt was back in the hospital, in his uncle's room, trying to find out why.

"Why is this happening?" he asked his uncle Lawrence, and Uncle Lawrence told him. Uncle Lawrence told him every last thing he knew, which was a lot. It was a long story. By the end, Uncle Lawrence was gasping more than actually speaking. "What's going to happen next?" Kurt asked him, and Uncle Lawrence told him that, too. "It is illegal for private citizens to buy, sell, or own firearms in Denmark, unless for the purposes of hunting or sport shooting, and only then on rare occasions, and with a hard-to-procure permit," Uncle Lawrence said. It was like he was making a presentation in social studies or something. If there was anything more pathetic than an adult making a school presentation on his deathbed, then Kurt didn't know what it was. "But just because it's illegal to buy a gun doesn't mean it's impossible."

Soon after that, Uncle Lawrence died. Several weeks after that, Kurt's father was well enough to go home. By now, it was the second Sunday in November. Kurt got the woodstove going. He sat his father in the chair right by the stove, with a blanket over his lap. Kurt made his father a drink. They watched the late football game, mostly in silence. When it was over, Kurt turned off the TV and told his father that they were going to go find Henry. Jens. It didn't really matter to Kurt what his real name was, as long as they found him and killed him for killing Kurt's mom. Matty didn't argue. The shooting had changed their relationship. Matty was forty-eight, and Kurt was sixteen, but they were already at the point in their lives where the son had become more capable than the father. "But where do you think he is?" Matty asked. "If you were him, where would you run?"

Here, Kurt thought. "Home," he said. And a week later they were on a plane from JFK to Copenhagen.

PART EIGHT

• • •

65
· · ·

Upon exiting the Copenhagen Airport, the first thing Matty asked Kurt was, "So where can we get a gun?" Matty had never owned, held, or fired a gun, let alone bought one, let alone bought one in another country. Except for Canada, which everyone knew didn't count, Matty had never even *been* to another country before now. Neither had Kurt. But Matty knew that Kurt had done his homework, meaning that he'd probably just looked it up on the Internet before they'd left home.

"It is illegal for private citizens to buy, sell, or own firearms in Denmark, unless for the purposes of hunting or sport shooting, and only then on rare occasions, and with a hard-to-procure permit," Kurt began. It was like he was making a presentation in social studies or something. Oh, buddy, I love you so much, Matty thought. If there was something more guaranteed to make a parent love their child than watching that child make a presentation at school, then Matty didn't know what it was. "But just because it's illegal to buy a gun doesn't mean it's impossible. According to my research, the best place to buy a gun in Copenhagen is Nørrebro." They took the train to Nørreport Station, then walked across one of the bridges that spanned one of the five lakes, about which Matty wanted to say, Wow, look at all the pretty lakes. Except that the lakes were really ponds and most of them were so choked with algae and who knows what else that even the swans were swimming with care, trying not to drink, eat, or even touch anything that might make them throw up later on.

Anyway, Matty and Kurt walked across Dronning Louises Bro and onto Nørrebrogade. Kurt knew where they were supposed to be going, so Kurt was in charge of the map, so Matty was able to look around. As far as he could see, Copenhagen was gloomy and beautiful. It was a very northern kind of beauty. Once in a while a shaft of sunlight would break free of the black clouds, and when it did, you could really appreciate how dark and gloomy everything was. They were walking through a neighborhood of churches. The churches looked prosperous but sooty. This is not to say they were dirty. Matty was pretty sure they'd been made to look that way. Even the stained-glass windows were black in the sun. If you didn't find that kind of thing beautiful, then you might as well get out of Copenhagen. Matty thought it was the most beautiful place he'd ever been to. But then again, he'd only been to a few places, and regardless, he and Kurt were getting out of Copenhagen, just as soon as they managed to buy a gun.

"Dad," Kurt said, yelled actually. He was a block ahead. He flapped and then folded the map, then gave his father a look that said, Come on, old man, this gun isn't going to buy itself. Matty had two questions: Who is responsible for turning my sixteen-year-old son from Broomeville, New York, into someone who knows how, and can't wait, to buy a gun in Copenhagen? And, Are we really going to do this? But the first was only a rhetorical question. And it was too late to ask the second. He ran to catch up to his son, and then they continued north, north, toward Nørrebro.

66

. . .

W ho do you buy your pot from?" Matty asked. They were in the heart of Nørrebro now. Or what Matty assumed was the heart. It was crowded, at least. On their right was an endless stretch of somewhat shabby three-story apartment buildings that at some point had been painted pink and yellow but now had gone mostly to grime. The buildings' first floors were storefronts that still had their metal curtains pulled down. On Matty and Kurt's left were card table after card table loaded with cassette tapes, CDs, books that had probably been lifted from a library, pipes you could smoke tobacco and drugs out of, pipes that were intended to make water flow in and out of your kitchen sink, kitchen appliances and utensils of all kinds. There was one table that featured only ceiling fans, a half-dozen ceiling fans, all of them with the wires sticking out. But mostly the tables were laden with blue jeans. Piles and piles of blue jeans, piles so tall that you wouldn't be able to riffle through them to find your size without causing a huge mess. Where did all these blue jeans come from? Matty wondered. And who bought them? None of the people selling them were wearing jeans; they were wearing dashikis. That's

what Matty thought they were called, at least. And very few
of the potential customers were wearing the jeans, either; they
were mostly wearing dashikis, too. The only people wearing
jeans were Matty and Kurt and most of the people riding their
bikes and ringing their little bells as they streamed past in the
bike lane. The bikers never yelled. If someone even looked like
they might cross their path, the bikers just gently went *ding,
ding*. And people actually got out of their way! It was incredible. The bike lane separated the tables and the street proper.
Behind the tables was a ten-foot-high yellow wall, and the wall
was periodically interrupted by enormous wrought-iron gates.
Matty could see through the gates that on the other side of the
wall was a cemetery. Matty wondered aloud what is was called
and whether it was known for anything.

"Assistens," Kurt said. "Søren Kierkegaard and Hans Chris-
tian Andersen are buried there." But mostly Matty and Kurt
didn't talk. Mostly they just walked slowly by the tables. To
Matty it felt like they were window-shopping for a gun, which
Matty guessed would not be on display, and in any case there
were no windows. Kurt was saying the same word over and over
again, under his breath, so that only the vendors, or whatever
you called them, could hear. The vendors all looked, more or
less, from Matty's point of view, like the stranger who'd ended
up not being Jens Baedrup—most of them had dark beards,
some of them were sleepy-eyed, all of them had dark skin,
or at least skin that was darker than Matty's or Kurt's—and
so far none of them had responded to the word Kurt was
saying, although several of them raised their eyebrows and
screwed up their faces, the universal sign for, Sorry, what?

Matty couldn't quite understand the word; it was probably some Danish buyer's code for guns. Kurt had probably learned that from the Internet, too. Or maybe he learned it when he'd learned the American buyer's code for pot. "Who do you buy your pot from?"

"Who," Kurt repeated. "From." This was Matty's own tactic, and the tactic of all educators and parents everywhere. Anytime one of his students or his son made a grammatical error, Matty repeated the error, out loud, just so the poor kid could hear how incredibly *wrong* it sounded. But you know, sometimes it didn't sound all that bad. Better, at least, than the grammatically correct alternative. Matty could tell by the tone of Kurt's voice as he said the word in Danish that he was starting to get impatient. But even so, Kurt was obviously having a hard time not smiling now; Matty knew Kurt was looking forward to hearing his dad say, *From whom* did you buy your pot?

"Who do you buy your pot from?" Matty repeated.

"*Dr.* Vernon," Kurt said.

"No." This genuinely shocked Matty. He'd always considered Vernon a friend, or at least not an enemy. At the very least he didn't think the guy dealt drugs to students. Matty should have been furious with him. But all he could think was, Poor guy. Although it did explain some things. Although mostly he still couldn't believe it. "*Dr.* Vernon sold you pot?"

"Sometimes," Kurt said. "But mostly I just smoked his."

"Well, that *is* a relief," Matty said, and Kurt looked at him. The look was strange. With it, Kurt seemed to be trying to say, I don't want to hurt you anymore. It was basically the opposite of every look Kurt had ever given Matty since Matty could remember. It made Matty want to take back all the things he'd ever said that had caused Kurt to look at him that way in the first place.

"Don't worry, I'm done with that," Kurt said. Then Kurt started muttering that word again. Muttering it and muttering it until they were almost at the end of the block. Matty could see the cemetery wall turn left. Straight, across the intersection, were more tables, more blue jeans, more dark-skinned men in dashikis. But right before the intersection, there was a man standing alone behind one of the tables. On the table were two enormous towers of blue jeans. Kurt leaned over and said that word, and the man smiled, scratched his beard, and in English told Kurt, "Your friend needs new dungarees."

Dungarees! Matty thought but did not say. "No, thank you," Matty said.

"Dad," Kurt said. And then to the man, he said, "How much?"

"I don't need new jeans," Matty said.

"I think you do," Kurt said.

"Two thousand kroner," the man said.

"*Two thousand kroner?*" Matty repeated. He tried to do the math in his head. "How much *is* that?"

"How much is two thousand kroner?" the man asked. He seemed honestly baffled by the question. He scrunched his face in Kurt's direction, and Kurt scrunched his in Matty's.

"Dad, please," he said.

"But isn't that way too much for a pair of jeans?" Matty said. Denmark was expensive, but he knew it wasn't that expensive. Plus, there was nothing special about these jeans. They seemed to be Wranglers, but not really: There was something wrong with the stitching on the back pockets. The W's were all wobbly, as though they'd been sewn by a passenger on a small boat sailing in a big sea.

Kurt leaned away from the man, toward his father, and whispered, "I don't think we're really paying for the jeans." And then Matty finally got it. He reached into his front pocket—he could not be made to say "fanny pack," let alone wear one—pulled out his wallet, and handed the man the cash. The man took it and counted it. He then folded the jeans carefully and slid them across the table. Kurt held the jeans to his chest, and he and Matty went back the way they'd come, past all the tables, back on the train, back to the airport, to the rental car counter, where Matty got the car, because Kurt was too young to get the car. Kurt did drive it, though, out of Copenhagen and onto the highway, as though he'd been doing this all his life. At one point, just outside the city, after the traffic had thinned, Matty turned and noticed that the dungarees they'd bought were flung across the backseat. Clearly there was no gun in them. Kurt must have put the gun in his jacket pocket. And only then did Matty ask his son, "What was the word you kept saying in Nørrebro?" Even Matty heard himself mangling the pronunciation. He was like a lot of Americans: he pronounced foreign words with a dramatic French accent, even though he didn't speak French, either.

"Nørrebro," Kurt said, getting it right, Matty assumed. "Capo."

"What?"

"Capo," Kurt said. "That's the word I was saying."

"Capo," Matty repeated. The word didn't sound Danish. Matty was pretty sure it was Italian—he'd probably heard it in a gangster movie—and that it meant "boss," or something. "Isn't that Italian for 'boss'?"

"No," Kurt said. "It's a made-up word. It doesn't mean anything." Matty recognized Kurt's tone. It's the tone you take with your kid when you want him to stop asking you annoying questions and go to sleep already. Matty did that. When he woke up, they were going over a bridge. The bridge was enormous. So were the fjords. The cliffs. The yawning open water. How was it possible, Matty had wondered, for such a small country to be made up of such big things?

And then they reached the other side, and the landscape had changed, dramatically, away from the dramatic.

"Is that wheat?" Matty asked. He pointed out the passenger's side window at the fields, where something stumpy and brown was growing, or dying, in neat rows that stretched from the road to the sea. Kurt told him that they were just over an hour from Skagen. The rain was falling, dark was falling, the temperature was falling: the dashboard said it was 2°C, whatever that meant. They were driving a white BMW sedan; it had been the cheapest rental car available at the Hertz in the Copenhagen Airport. Which is not to say it was cheap. I am in Denmark, Matty thought. I am in Denmark with my son, who is driving a luxury automobile. Then Matty pointed out the window again. "I wonder if that's wheat," he said, and when he did, he could hear Ellen laughing. Matty liked to think that he was the most cosmopolitan man in Broomeville. And other than his brother, that might have actually been true. But one second in any place outside upstate New York, and Matty had always started to act like the rube he'd always tried very hard not to be. On his and Ellen's honeymoon in New York City, for instance, Matty hadn't been able to get over how expensive everything was. When they went out to dinner, he took one look at the menu and said, unbelievably loudly, as though he were addressing not just Ellen but the entire restaurant, "Jeez, I hope the water's free!" Ellen had laughed at him then, and he wondered whether she would have laughed at him now, too.

"Do you think that's wheat?" he asked, and then he started laughing.

"What's so funny?"

"I was just thinking about your mom," Matty said, and then Kurt's face went stony. This had been happening lately. Kurt would not talk about his mother. He would not talk about her at all. The subject made Kurt mute. For instance, a week after the shooting, when Matty was still in the hospital, Kurt had come to visit him and caught his father crying.

"Hey," Kurt had said. He'd leaned over Matty's hospital bed and hugged him.

"I was just thinking about your mom," Matty had said into Kurt's shoulder, and immediately Kurt had stopped hugging him. He'd plopped down into the chair next to the bed and started watching the soap opera on the television set, not looking at his father, not saying a word. He wasn't saying a word now, either. They passed a sign that read SKAGEN 90 km. Matty had run a 10K once, and so he knew that ninety kilometers was fifty-five miles, more or less. He could imagine his son not speaking for the rest of the trip, and maybe not ever, if Matty kept talking about Ellen. "I'll shut up," Matty said.

"That might be a good idea," Kurt said. His voice was strangled. It's the way your voice sounds when you're mad at someone for almost making you cry.

"Fair enough," Matty said. But he was surprised when, a minute later, Kurt said, "Anything you want to tell me?"

Matty turned and saw that Kurt was looking at him with cold, tired eyes. He was like the cop in the movies who says to the criminal, I know about everything you've done, so you might as well just tell me about everything you've done.

And wow, Matty almost told Kurt. He almost said, I cheated on your mother with a woman named Locs. He almost went on through every terrible thing, every lie, every bit of deception and duplicitousness and doubt. And Matty actually might have done it, too. He might have told that story, if it had ended with, And that's why your mother died. That's why every single person in that room except for me and you and Henry died, and I'm sorry, because really, if you look at it a certain way, if you look at it a lot of certain ways, if you look at how it began and who it started with, then it started with me, and it's my fault that your mother was killed, and I would do anything to change that, but I can't, it's my fault, I'm sorry, please forgive me. Matty might have actually told that story, if it had ended there. But it would not have ended there. It would have gone on, into the hospital room, when Kurt had caught Matty crying and Matty had said he'd been thinking about Ellen, which was not true. He'd thought and cried plenty about Ellen, just as he'd thought and cried about his brother, his poor, weird brother, whom he'd never loved well enough. And he'd thought and cried plenty about Kurt himself, Kurt, whom he'd turned into a half orphan, Kurt, who clearly would have been better off if Matty had been killed and Ellen had lived. But in the hospital room that day, Matty had not been thinking of any of those things, nor of any of those people. No, he'd been thinking about Locs, about the first time he'd kissed her; he'd been thinking about how he really did love her; he'd been thinking about how all of this could have been avoided if he'd just gone ahead and done what he'd promised Locs he would do, and that if he'd done that, everything and everybody would have ended up just fine. That's what he'd been crying and thinking about in the hospital room that day. That's where the story would have ended. And Matty just couldn't tell Kurt that story. He looked away from Kurt and out the window.

"That's gotta be wheat," Matty finally said, and neither he nor Kurt said another word until they reached Skagen.

67

...

When they got to Skagen, Matty wondered aloud, "Well, what now?"

Kurt shrugged. It was his first moment of indecision this entire trip, if you could call what they were on a trip. They were sitting in the car, at a red light. Off to their right was the harbor, which was also, apparently, known as a *havn*. There were no boats in it. It was too late in the season. The little waves washed over the slips. Somewhere a bell made its lonely clanging sound. The rain had turned to snow. "I hear," Kurt finally said, "that they have good hot dogs on the pedestrian mall."

So they parked their car and walked to the outdoor pedestrian mall. In the middle of it was the hot dog stand. It served a dozen different kinds of hot dogs. The descriptions of the dogs were in Danish, but the names of the dogs were in English. There were French hot dogs and German hot dogs and also Chicago hot dogs and New York hot dogs and, of course, Danish hot dogs. Matty and Kurt each had two of those. Basically they were hot dogs. But they were very good. Matty and Kurt ate them while sitting on the bench and watching the pedestrians: there were more people in the mall than boats in the *havn,* but not many more. When they finished their dogs, Matty got up to get them two more. And that's when he saw Henry. He turned to see whether Kurt had seen him, too. Kurt had: he was already on his feet. Henry was walking in the direction of their car. They followed him, keeping twenty, thirty feet back. The wind was up and with a *clang* it knocked over a metal sandwich-board sign. Henry wheeled around and Matty and Kurt ducked into a doorway. Too late, Matty thought. Matty thought that Henry must have seen them, but maybe not: he kept walking in the same direction, at the same speed, until he reached a car that was parked a couple of blocks away from theirs. Henry got in and drove off. Matty and Kurt ran to their car, jumped in, tried to follow. It seemed as though they had lost Henry, but Kurt kept on the main road, which was called Oddevej. The water was still off to the right, but Matty couldn't see it until they went around the traffic circle, following the sign pointing toward Grenen. Suddenly there was ocean; suddenly there was sand. It was not even four o'clock, but the sun was almost gone. Soon the road was gone, too. It ended in a parking lot. Out of the parking lot was a path that led, it seemed, through the dunes. They parked their car right next to the car Henry had been driving. He was not in it. But he'd stuck a parking pass on the dashboard. The parking pass had come from a machine near the mouth of the path. Jesus, the man is being chased and he stops to make sure he isn't parked illegally. What a . . . , Matty started to think, until he noticed that Kurt was doing the same thing. Oh, buddy, he thought, and he smiled at his good son, and then his son caught him smiling and said, "What?" not smiling.

"Nothing," Matty said. Kurt stuck the pass on the windshield of their car, and then they walked toward and down the path, which led to the beach, which then led to a long, long spit of land. Matty could barely see the end of it in the light. But he could see a human being between the end and them. Matty and Kurt walked toward the human being, who was looking out at the waves, the dying sun, the tankers way, way off in the distance. "Henry!" Matty called out when they got a little closer. Henry turned to face him. Matty kept walking, and as he did, he keenly felt his bullet scars: one on the right side of his rib cage, one in his right calf. No one had seemed to know whether Henry had been shot. Even if he had, the wounds couldn't have been so bad. He'd gotten away, after all, out of Broomeville and all the way here. But now Matty was near enough to see Henry's face. God, he'd lost a lot of weight. It looked as though his cheekbones were the only things preventing his face from pouring into his neck. He smiled sadly at Matty. The last thing Matty had heard Henry say was, "Please just kill me." Matty knew Kurt had dreamed of doing just that. Matty had dreamed of it a few times himself. But now he wondered, Are we really going to do this? Is there a point in killing someone who is worse off than you? Because Henry was clearly worse off than Matty. Henry was all alone and Matty was not; Henry had lost everything, but Matty still had Kurt. So Matty was going to say to Kurt, Let's just go home. And because Matty was Kurt's father, Kurt would listen to him. He would give Matty the gun, and Matty would throw it into the water, and then they would go home. But before they did, they would look at the pretty scenery. "It's really beautiful," Matty said to Henry, and Henry smiled a little less sadly and turned, and they watched the waves from two different seas crash into each other over and over and over again. It was difficult to watch something that beautiful and eternal without thinking that everything really was going to be just fine after all.

"Turn around," Kurt said. "Both of you." Matty could tell from Kurt's voice that he was pointing his gun at them. Matty looked at Henry, and Henry nodded, and then they did what Kurt had told them to do. Kurt was standing not five feet away from them. Both of his hands were on the gun, his right index finger curled around the trigger. Even in the darkness, Matty could see that his son did not look scared or angry. He looked like a man who was totally prepared to shoot two men who deserved it. "Kurt," Matty said, but Kurt wagged the gun as though to say, Don't. That was fine. Matty didn't know what he'd been about to say anyway. He tried to think of something fatherly and authoritative. Put the gun down, Kurt, we've all suffered enough, he wanted to say, but Kurt would probably think that wasn't even close to being true. Is that thing even loaded? Matty thought to ask, except that he was leery of the way Kurt might try to answer that question. Come on, buddy, he thought of saying, let's just go home. That sounded better. He almost said it, too. But then Matty thought of home, where every little thing would remind him of all the lives he'd ruined or ended, where everything—the school, the bar, the diner, the woods, the woodstove—would make him think of his brother, of Locs, of Ellen, and now of Kurt, who hated his father so much that he'd wanted to shoot him to death on a beach in Denmark, because his father deserved it and would always deserve it.

"Oh, buddy," Matty said. He closed his eyes and took a step toward his son. "Please just kill me," he said. Then Matty took another step. He felt something on his right, close by, and realized that Henry had taken those steps, too. Matty wasn't sure how to feel about that. Would it be better or worse to die standing next to someone who also deserved it? Anyway, he and Henry stood there, waiting. Matty knew, even through his closed lids, that it was dark outside. He felt dark inside, too. The waves crashed into one another, so loudly that Henry couldn't hear anyone breathing—not Kurt, not Henry, not even himself. For a second he wondered whether he was dead, whether Kurt had already shot him and Matty had somehow missed it, when he heard Kurt yell, "Fuck!" three times. Then Matty heard sprinting noises. He opened his eyes. Kurt wasn't standing in front of him anymore. He glanced to his right, and Henry was standing there, looking at Matty with big eyes. Matty then turned to his left and squinted into the dusk and saw his son, his beautiful boy, run into the sea, up to his knees, and then hurl the gun as far as he could. It landed with a *plunk*. Then Kurt turned and walked back toward them, jeans wet, looking sheepish, the way you do when you make a big, dramatic gesture and then have to go hang out with the people who saw you make it.

"Don't say anything," Kurt said when he got back to where Matty and Henry were standing. They didn't. They turned away from the sea into which Kurt had thrown the gun and stared at the other sea for a while, until finally Kurt said, "I don't want to go home."

"Me, neither," Matty said.

"But where . . . ," Henry began to say. His voice sounded scratchy, as though he hadn't spoken to anyone in a very long time. He cleared his throat and tried again. "But where will you go?" Henry asked. And frankly, Matty had no idea. He thought of all the places they could go, all the places he'd never been. There were too many of them, and he was afraid that in all of them, there would still be his brother, there would still be Locs, there would still be Ellen. No, Kurt would have to decide. Kurt had decided not to kill him, and now Kurt was going to have to keep deciding until he decided otherwise.

"Tell us about Denmark," Kurt said. "Tell us about Skagen." When Henry heard that, his head jerked back toward the other sea, where Kurt's gun was. It seemed, for a second, like he was going to run toward it. But instead he stood there for a long while, armed crossed, frowning, seemingly in the process of making his own decision. His lips were moving, as though he were talking to someone, even though neither Matty nor Kurt could hear any words. Finally, Henry nodded and said, "It is said that the Danes are the happiest people in the world, and if that's true, then the people from Skagen are happier even than that."

"That sounds nice," Kurt said. He'd meant for that to be sarcastic but was in fact startled by how much he wanted it to be true. Henry smiled at him and said, "It does." The three of them then walked away from the water, toward their cars.

When they reached the dunes overlooking the parking lot, Henry said, "I think everything is going to be just fine. I really think you're going to like it here." He didn't sound as though he totally believed it himself. But they got into their cars and drove back toward Skagen anyway. They had to. There was absolutely nowhere else for them to go.

ACKNOWLEDGMENTS

Thanks, once again, to Keith Lee Morris, Trenton Lee Stewart, and Michael Lee Griffith.

Thanks to all the people who, over the last four years, listened to me talk about this book, or distracted me from talking about this book, especially: Sarah Beth Estes, David Stradling, Jodie Zultowski, Nicola Mason, Leah Stewart, Pete Coviello, Mike Paterniti, Sara Corbett, Mark Wethli, Cassie Jones, Aaron Kitch, Allison Cooper, Ann Kibbie, Kevin Wertheim, Jon and Naomi Mermin, Justin Tussing, Sarah Maloney, Barb and Michael Stoddard, Marilyn Reizbaum, Nicole Lamy, Josh Bodwell, the Longfellow Books crew, Rupert and Kiki Chisholm, Dorn and Jan Ulrich, Tara and Trent Ulrich, Anne Maclean and Colin Clarke, Alonzo Clarke and Carla Romano Clarke, and E. G. and Peter Clarke.

Thanks to the writers who allowed their kind words to be printed on this book's back cover.

Thanks to my friends, colleagues, and students at Bowdoin College, University of Cincinnati, and University of Tampa.

Thanks to Bowdoin College for its financial support.

Thanks to the editors at *Five Points,* who published an excerpt from this novel.

Thanks to my agent, Elizabeth Sheinkman.

Thanks to Chuck Adams, and to everyone at Algonquin Books.

And thanks especially to Lane, Quinn, and Ambrose, for traveling with me to Denmark, and for everything else.